PRAISE F

"Endearingly quirky . . . Emotional yet funny . . . Confronting grief, change, and a new way of being, Nyhan's lovely story captures the rejuvenating power of hard work that can start right in the backyard."

—*Publishers Weekly*

"Charming . . . Nyhan has fun with a bubbly satire of business culture."

—*Kirkus Reviews*

"On the surface, this is a sweet novel about aging, grief, and redemption. But Nyhan (*All the Good Parts*, 2016), who has experienced loss herself, shares very insightful observations. She reminds readers that comfort and hope can come in the most unexpected encounters if the heart is open."

—*Booklist*

"For the two years since her husband's death, Paige has been concentrating on putting one foot in front of the other . . . Nyhan uses details from her own personal tragedy to harness the pain, tenderness, and empowerment of Paige's transformation in *Digging In*."

—Associated Press

"This is a vision of love, hope, and pressing onward even when it doesn't seem possible . . . Highly recommended."

—*USA Today*'s *Happy Ever After*

PRAISE FOR *ALL THE GOOD PARTS*

"Quirky and laugh-out-loud funny, we loved *All the Good Parts*! Nyhan had us at page 1 with this unique yet relatable story of the deep bonds between sisters and family and the yearning for motherhood. Readers who want to be swept up and taken on an emotional roller coaster will love *All the Good Parts*!"

—Liz Fenton and Lisa Steinke, authors of *The Year We Turned Forty* and *The Status of All Things*

"*All the Good Parts* is wildly original and features a mixture of heartfelt and laugh-out-loud moments. The main character's quest for motherhood is poignant and relatable . . . [but] it's the ensuing complexities that arise as the main character tries to find a suitable daddy donor from a varied potential list that make this story hard to put down."

—RT Book Reviews (4 stars)

"[Nyhan] creates an original and endearing contemporary heroine in Leona Accorsi . . . [Her] novel tells a surprising, sweet, and unconventional story about family and friendship."

—*Booklist*

The Other Family

ALSO BY LORETTA NYHAN

Digging In
All the Good Parts
Empire Girls
Home Front Girls

The
Other
Family

LORETTA NYHAN

Text copyright © 2020 by Loretta Nyhan
All rights reserved.

Published by Lake Union Publishing, Seattle

www.apub.com

Amazon, the Amazon logo, and Lake Union Publishing are trademarks of Amazon.com, Inc., or its affiliates.

ISBN-13: 9781542006439
ISBN-10: 1542006430

Cover design and illustration by David Drummond

Printed in the United States of America

To all those fighting an autoimmune battle, especially my favorite warriors, Hannah, Alex, and Andrew— three of the bravest kids I know.

CHAPTER 1

Which type of person are you?

Personality Test results for ALLY!

ALLY, you are 97% FRUSTRATED EXPLORER!

Feeling lost? Directionless? Like your ship has no captain? ALLY, you are a FRUSTRATED EXPLORER, Personality Type 6! You take action but get no results. You find yourself rushing headlong into life's dead ends. You often feel as though you are running down a dark, endless tunnel with no light to guide your way. But don't worry! Click the link below to receive a detailed Type 6 report, which lists five easy ways you can take charge of your life and make impactful change!

I clicked the link. Cost of the report? Twenty-nine dollars and ninety-five cents. Starbucks equivalent? Four to five drinks, depending on how fancy I was feeling. Hmmm . . .

ALLY, would you like to share your results with your friends?

Okay, that was a hard no. I would *not* like my 337 Facebook friends to know that I am personality type six, the woman without a GPS system for living. But apparently, I didn't mind sharing this vital information with my daughter. She sat in the passenger seat of my parked VW bug, staring at her own phone.

"Get this," I said, dangling my results in front of her face before tossing my phone in my bag. "Ugh. Why do these things matter?"

"Because they're always a little true," Kylie said, sounding much older than her ten and a half years. She returned her gaze to a YouTube celebrity sticking slime up her nose. "Take the test again. You might get something better."

"Or something worse," I said before realizing I shouldn't be spewing negativity. Especially not now. "But you might be right. Maybe next time I'll get fearless warrior."

"Maybe," Kylie said, but she sounded unconvinced.

"So . . . are you ready to go in?"

"Nope."

We'd parked directly in front of the Integrative Spiritual, Health, and Wellness Center of Chicago. Housed in a stately greystone, it proved my theory that the most successful doctors were the ones who understood that elegant, expensive surroundings could have a definite placebo effect.

"I guess we can stay here for a while," I said. "Spend a few minutes enjoying our rock star parking spot." I reached over and unclicked her seatbelt. Then I caught her stricken expression. "That's just to make you comfortable, sweetie. We can even go home, if you want." I turned the car back on to show her I meant it.

"Waste of gas," Kylie muttered.

"It's only ten thirty. I can get you back to school for lunch period."

She shrugged. "It's Fifth Grade Fun Lunch today. That means pizza. I can't eat it, so why bother?"

"We can pick up something on the way."

"Really not a big deal, Mom."

White coat syndrome was a big deal, though. And my daughter, after being dragged to medical professional after medical professional, had a clear case of it.

I turned off the car and stared out the window, hoping the late-September morning—clear and bright and sunny—would offer some answers. After a moment, it did. "Want to do some yoga breathing? The oooh-jai thing?"

Kylie laughed. "It's called *ujjayi*."

"I think that's Sanskrit for 'Darth Vader breath.' At least that's what it sounds like."

"Okay," Kylie said, "let's make it loud." She exaggerated her inhale and exhale. "We're supposed to sound fierce, like warriors."

"See, maybe I can learn to be a warrior instead of a wanderer!"

"You have to practice a lot. Like, *a lot*."

"Well, then I'd better get started."

We spent a moment trying to breathe directly into the back of our throats without hocking up something vile, and a longer moment giggling at how ridiculous we sounded.

"Want to go in, little warrior?" I said softly when we wound down. "Up to you."

She went silent. I knew why. I wasn't just asking her to go inside. I was asking her to risk, to hope, to open herself to the scrutiny of strangers, however well meaning.

Kylie sighed. "Do you think they'll have bubbly water? I kind of want some."

"If the inside of this place looks anything like the outside, then yeah. Pretty fancy-pants. I bet they'll have water brought over in glass goblets from the French Alps."

Kylie opened her door. "That's good enough for me," she said. "Fun Lunch is totally overrated anyway."

~

I signed us in at the glossy front desk, and an intimidatingly beautiful woman in a well-cut black suit asked us to follow her down a maze of a hallway. We passed tastefully decorated office after tastefully decorated office, all curiously empty. When we reached the end of the hallway, the receptionist opened a door to a not-so-elegant exterior wooden staircase, Chicago tenement–style.

"Up one level," she said. "The door sticks, so you might have to kick it."

I couldn't tell if she was joking. "Really?"

"Really. The doctor's waiting for you." She turned on one perilously high heel and was gone.

"This is weird," Kylie whispered.

"It's an adventure."

"Uh-huh."

When we got to the top of the stairs, the door did stick, and I had to kick it twice before it opened.

We stood in another hallway, but this one smelled like fried onions and burnt coffee.

"Go in and have a seat," ordered a modulated, professorial voice. We craned our necks, wondering where it was coming from, but couldn't spot a single human being. Shrugging, Kylie and I stepped into the only open door we saw.

It was obviously the "spiritual" office of the wellness center, more suitable to an ashram in California than a tony practice just off the Magnificent Mile.

I chose to sit in a leather chair worn smooth by countless enlightened butts, immediately regretting it because the spider plant dangling above my head tickled my forehead. Patchouli essential oil wafted noiselessly from a phallic-shaped diffuser. Though the scent was not entirely unpleasant, I could feel it nestling into my pores, certain it would sweat out on the long drive home. Kylie perched next to me on a Turkish-style ottoman, trying not to crinkle her nose. She laced her fingers together, probably to keep from scratching the rash that had appeared on her inner arm after breakfast.

Kylie, at ten years and eight months, was sweet as the local honey displayed on the office desk, but sick. Sometimes very, very sick. Her immune system was acting like a mean girl, poking at her weak spots, taunting her cells, inflaming the whole of her. Doctors didn't quite know how to put a stop to this bullying. We'd heard a lot of *maybe it's this* and *possibly it's that*, which meant no one really knew how to treat her. I'd known for years that my little girl was severely allergic to peanuts and a host of other things, but these new developments, mysterious and threatening, had us running through an HMO-approved maze of doctors and specialists and hospitals all over Chicagoland.

We'd come through the maze, weary and disoriented and still seeking answers. Desperate, I shifted our focus to the surprisingly expensive practitioners of alternative medicine. They had inconsistent Yelp reviews and strange addresses, and we couldn't afford any of them. I'd borrowed the fee for today's visit from my mother, a retiree on social security. "Kylie needs it," Mom said. "Don't think twice."

Which brought us here, to be . . . ignored? I debated taking Kylie's hand and making a run for it. Maybe she could squeeze a little bit of fun out of Fifth Grade Fun Lunch. She definitely deserved a little fun.

Before I could make up my mind, a woman entered the room. She wore a green and mustard-yellow striped maxi dress and a gold nameplate bearing her eye-roller of an alliterative hippie moniker, *Dr. Indigo, integrative allergist and immunotherapist.*

Dr. Lucinda Indigo had a Yelp average of two and a half stars and thirteen reviews. *Weird. Condescending. Expensive. Hippie Bullshit.*

And then, the one word that had me on the phone making an appointment: *Effective.*

Only a few people had heard of her on the Facebook group for allergy families. The ones I could find who'd actually sought her treatment were happy with their outcomes but vague about the process. *She's a character!* one said when I'd private-messaged her. I hoped that meant Dr. Indigo actually *had* character.

The doctor smiled tightly in our general direction. "Kylie?" she said, searching for something on her overcluttered desk. "How are you today?"

"Fine," Kylie muttered.

Dr. Indigo gave Kylie her full attention. Her eyes were so dark I couldn't see her pupils. "Are you?"

"Fine" was how the chronically ill answered when they were too tired, too scared, or too hopeless to answer with the truth. I hated "fine." But Kylie needed it—"fine" was one of her few defenses. The problem was, we had to come in to any new doctor completely defenseless if we wanted her to truly help us.

"It's okay, baby," I said. "Tell her about this morning."

Kylie glanced at me and said, "After I ate a banana this morning, I got a rash." She stuck out her skinny arm. "Like, inside my elbow. It itches. I get them a lot. My throat doesn't hurt today, though, and I don't have a fever. At least I don't think so."

"Hmmm," Dr. Indigo said. She snatched a green file from a haphazard pile and started flipping through some papers. I'd dutifully filled out a mountain of forms and questionnaires in preparation for this meeting and sent them in weeks ago. Had she even glanced at them?

"Hmmm," the doctor said again.

I knew that probably meant she had no clue where to start, but still I looked at her as I'd looked at all the others—potential holders of the magic key to healing. I carried hope around with me for the same reason I kept my passport in my purse—it hadn't done anything for me in years, but I knew that someday it could take us to someplace completely new. In the beginning, each doctor we'd visited held the stamp that could set us off on a journey toward normal. I longed for normal. I worried that Kylie had forgotten what it felt like.

The doctor was frowning, her unadorned-by-lipstick mouth turning down, down, down. *Well, okay then.* I took a deep patchouli-tainted breath. *Maybe she didn't hold any healing keys right now, but . . . after some research? Some tests?*

Dr. Indigo fiddled with my daughter's file.

Oh, please, my heart begged. *Please.*

She sighed.

A bad feeling settled in my gut—the fear that this woman wouldn't be the last doctor who failed to explain why my girl suffered. Which meant my sweet girl was going to continue suffering.

"Your daughter is allergic to peanuts?"

"Yes. She's had two severe reactions, one in which her throat started to close up. We're really careful about reading labels, and she always brings her own food to events. We wash our hands a lot and carry an EpiPen everywhere we go. Our house is nut-free."

She glanced at the file again. "Her peanut numbers are high."

"But not almonds," I said defensively. "And hazelnuts aren't bad."

Dr. Indigo accepted that information without a flicker of emotion. I wasn't expecting an impromptu parade, but surely she had learned in doctor school to accentuate the positive?

"So," she continued, "have you truly gone gluten-free as well? Dairy-free? Sugar-free?"

"Yes, yes, and yes," I responded. I couldn't keep the attitude from my voice. Our life was free of everything and nothing at all. "We've green-juiced and probioticked, tried all kinds of herbs, Chinese and—er—American, and I've been super strict with the elimination diet. At this point, I don't think she could recognize a slice of bread if she was in a bakery."

"And the headaches remain unchanged?"

"She gets them frequently. And the hives. Dry mouth and eyes. Random low-grade fevers. Swollen joints. The symptom list keeps growing."

What I didn't mention was the psychological toll. The quiet. Kylie turned inward to deal with pain. She'd become a Zen master, going into an altered, meditative state. I detested what this illness had done to my daughter, but I so admired her reaction to it. She was strong. She was resilient. I lifted a hand and patted her soft brown hair. "Will you do blood work?"

"I'd like to," the doc said. She glanced at Kylie. "That's okay with you, right, sweetie?"

"It's okay," Kylie said automatically. They all wanted blood. I was amazed she wasn't anemic on top of everything else.

"Is there anything I can do now that I'm not already doing?" I pointed to the file that listed so many failed attempts. "There's got to be something, right?"

If I wasn't so worried about Kylie, I would have enjoyed watching the doctor wrack her brain to come up with something substantive to say. "In addition to her allergies, there is a slight possibility that Kylie is suffering from a hereditary illness. You detailed your husband's family's health history, and I see you suffer from some food sensitivities, but you left your family history section blank. Why is that?"

"I was adopted." I hated the way my voice sounded vaguely apologetic, like I was admitting to some past criminal behavior.

Dr. Indigo tapped her bottom lip with her index finger. "Oh. I . . . see."

My defenses rose up faster than Kylie's hives. "A lot of people are, you know."

She caught herself, and nodded. "Of course! I didn't mean to imply otherwise. It just makes sussing things out more difficult."

"Uh-huh," Kylie said.

"Do you know anything about your family history?" the doc asked, slightly hopeful.

"No," I said. "Nothing at all." I hoped she didn't press the issue. My reasons for never searching out my biological history were a little fuzzy, even to me, so not something I was ready to explain.

Dr. Indigo didn't pursue the topic further and merely nodded once, though clearly frustrated by the lack of information.

"I'm currently in pretty good health," I said, "if that means anything."

It didn't seem to. The doctor grabbed a legal pad and scribbled something on it. "DNA tests are relatively inexpensive, and the data you'll get will go well beyond the basic ethnic breakdown."

"More blood?" Kylie asked. "I guess that's okay."

"No blood," Dr. Indigo said. "Just saliva. I can give you a link where you can plug in the data from the file you'll receive and get some really detailed medical information regarding susceptibility to a number of genetic diseases." She tore off the page and presented it to me with a flourish. "It's a start," she said brightly.

I wasn't there to start; I was there to finish. Would I drag Kylie back to this office, which smelled like a Dead show but charged enough to feed us for a week? Was it worth it?

"Depending on how quickly you get the results," Dr. Indigo continued, "we can add them to the discussion about Kylie's blood work next time you come. Some people hear back in a few weeks." She shook Kylie's hand, and then grasped mine. "I don't believe in throwing pills at people to temporarily mask their symptoms. I want to help your daughter, but it's going to take time. I promise you that I'll try my best to heal her, and I won't easily give up. I've been doing this a long time, and I'm good at what I do."

I'd trusted before and been sorely, devastatingly disappointed. With the amount of probiotics I'd been ingesting, my gut should have been sending clearer messages, but nothing came. I studied the doctor more closely. Her face was finely etched with lines that came from squinting and frowning and pursing her lips—lines very similar to my own. Her part revealed a stripe of gray. The bags under her eyes could hold everything I owned. The physical evidence said Dr. Indigo worked very, very hard.

Could I swing this? I let go of the doctor's hand, my mind going immediately to my bank statement, credit card debt, and accrued medical bills. I couldn't afford to integrate anyone's spirituality and wellness. But then, when your kid needs help, money becomes less a tangible thing and more something that could materialize by sheer willpower. "We're paying out of pocket," I said, figuring it would be better to be direct. "Do you offer discounts for those who can't use insurance?"

"Discounts?" The doctor looked truly confused. "I'm sorry, but I don't think so."

"Why not?" Kylie asked. Her tone was quizzical but not disrespectful. "Our last doctor had a Groupon."

Dr. Indigo smiled in a way that seemed more genuine, less blandly professional. "Maybe I'll come up with a Groupon just for you," she said, bending to help Kylie with her jacket.

"Then it wouldn't be a *group*-on," Kylie said, grinning back at her.

"Smart girl," the doctor said, and then addressed me. "These things have a way of working out. Don't let the cost add stress to an already stressful situation."

"Thanks," I said, the word sticking in my throat, as if I'd developed an anaphylactic reaction to hope.

~

"Another quack?"

My mother stood at her stove, whisking eggs for veggie omelets. Breakfast for dinner. We started the tradition when Kylie got sick. In the beginning, she sometimes slept until the afternoon, so we ate breakfast when she finally dragged herself out of bed.

"Why do you always ask that?" Kylie said, laughing. "It makes me think of ducks." Mom offered her a spear of red pepper, which she accepted. Kylie nibbled her food, taking teeny-tiny rabbity bites.

"It might be too early to tell," I said. "But she seemed all right. Smart. Competent. Definitely expensive."

"They all are. Think she's worth it?"

"I think so. We didn't really talk specifics yet, but she's definitely committed to helping us."

"Then we'll figure it out," Mom said.

"I'll talk to Matt tonight."

She snorted. "Good luck with that."

"*Mom.*" I tilted my head toward Kylie.

Mom nodded, abashed, and flipped a nut-free, gluten-free, dairy-free pancake. "Just write down everything you want to say before you get on the phone. Get it all on paper. Make a shopping list."

My mom had spent her entire working life behind the bar of Stef's Tavern, a narrow, dimly lit neighborhood joint wedged between a dry cleaner's and an insurance office on the main stretch of one of the tiny blue-collar suburbs ringing the city. Her parents had bought it when the local men did mostly shift work, and the bar was open for business from 6 a.m. to 2 a.m. during its heyday, the early morning bartender sleeping on a cot in the storeroom during the split in his shift. When my grandparents retired, my mother took over managing the bar, which she felt was most effectively done by standing behind it, mixing drinks, and playing psychologist to the (mostly) men who spent hours knocking back beers and telling stories. She knew the inventory like the back of her calloused hands—every bottle running low, the maraschino cherry count, the number of lemons and limes and how many slices she could get from each, the frozen hamburger patties, the rolls of toilet paper—the hundreds of items it took to run even a very basic, old-school establishment. Every morning, Mom flipped to a clean page on a legal pad and jotted down everything the bar needed for the day. Toward the bottom of the page, she jotted down what *she* needed. *Don't back down when you ask Jim to finally settle his tab. Remember to be kind to Raymond—he lost his job again. Don't be afraid to fire the accountant.* Sometimes I'd steal a look at her list and just see phrases scrawled at the bottom—*calm down, stop being chickenshit, consider the other side*—it took a certain kind of woman to run a bar solo, and Mom knew *she* was the most qualified person to keep herself focused and in control.

They say adopted kids eventually end up looking like their adoptive parents. I spent considerable time hoping this was true, and that it also meant I'd eventually inherit mom's personality traits. As much as I wished, it didn't happen—my hair stayed dark instead of dirty blonde, my eyes never morphed from chocolate brown into my mother's crystal blue, and I tended to act impulsively instead of steadily mapping out possible consequences, a leaper not much interested in looking more than a foot in front of me. But . . . dealing with my soon-to-be ex-husband meant I needed to channel my mom as best I could and gather my scattered thoughts and emotions into some kind of order. *Shopping list, it is.* I grabbed a legal pad and pencil, and sat down on the corner bench Mom installed when I was eight. It offered comfort then, it offered comfort now.

On top of the page I wrote, *Dr. Indigo.*

And then, I didn't write anything else.

I had to think.

Matt and I were estranged. Though it was an appropriate description, the word was not exactly accurate. It implied we'd become strangers to each other, but what actually happened, as we negotiated the particulars of Kylie's health care, was we got to know each other even better.

Matt was surprisingly more rigid than I thought, more conservative in his thinking, and had less trust in my judgment.

I was gullible when I thought I'd been pretty savvy, bull-headed when I thought I'd been pretty open, and much, much angrier.

Neither of us meant any harm. Both of us wanted to help Kylie.

But I'd read countless articles about how previously solid marriages began to fray at the seams when a child gets sick. It was a sad reality, but a reality all the same. Our bickering got to the point where the only thing we could agree on was that we loved Kylie and wanted to seek out the best care for her. That should have been enough to keep us together.

It wasn't.

This shamed us, but still didn't change the fact that for the last year, we'd slept in different beds, in different houses, and lived different, sadder lives. And so did our daughter.

I called Matt without writing a shopping list.

"I really think this doctor is going to help," I said. "She seems smart and committed."

"They're all smart," he said, "but never smart enough. Why are you putting her through this again? Think this through, Ally. And I thought we agreed to give it a rest for a while. How many more days of school does she need to miss before they hold her back a grade?"

"She's ahead of the other kids. They won't do that."

Matt sighed. "This doctor wants to do tests, right? Tests are expensive. There's no need to test for things that have already been tested. Can she take a look at the old files and come to some conclusions?"

"She wants to do her own blood work." I waited, knowing what would come next.

"Out of pocket, right?"

"Yes. But I think I can work a discount."

"Ally—" Matt paused. He'd become increasingly careful with finances, which made me think what he was going to say next required some finessing. It scared me.

"We need to start saving our money for the future," he said, voice low, as though Kylie were in the room. "We haven't got any answers, so we can't plan. What if she needs some kind of long-term therapy or a hospital stay? Our insurance is not good. Our savings account is nearly dry. I don't think we need to take yet another risk with another doctor."

He was absolutely right and oh-so-wrong at the same time. It was my turn to pause. Was I reacting because I wanted to win this one, or because I thought Dr. Indigo could help Kylie? I thought about the lines on the doctor's face, about the way she held my hand, that firm grip. "I think it's worth it. I want to give this doctor a chance."

"Well, then you're going to need to take the money from your tip jar," Matt countered, voice tight.

He hung up before I could respond.

I wished I could say Matt was a bad guy. He wasn't. That was the problem with this scenario—the only thing we could blame with any fairness was the illness. And we didn't even know what that was exactly.

It was enough to make anyone inflammatory.

CHAPTER 2

"It requires spit. So much spit. When I did it, I seriously dehydrated myself."

Jenn with two *n*'s was talking DNA tests while I cut her hair. Every hairdresser has a client who works her every last nerve, and Jenn was mine. But she was loyal, and my appreciation for that valuable trait overrode my irritation at her constant need to complain. Jenn had sat in my chair every six weeks for the past eight years, and that formed a relationship of sorts, tenuous as it was.

Today Jenn requested an asymmetrical bob because she was hosting an '80s party. *She'll hate it*, I thought to myself, but Jenn with two *n*'s could rarely be dissuaded.

"I think Kylie will be okay," I said, though it did worry me a little, given her persistent dry mouth. "The vial looks pretty small. I'll give her a lot of water before and after."

Jenn's shrug was almost violent. She didn't like to be wrong. "I guess. It's your daughter's well-being we're talking about. I just think you should give it more thought."

I *had* given a lot of thought to the DNA test since visiting Dr. Indigo's office. On the ride home, after I explained what the test could uncover, Kylie pressed me to do it, saying she thought it was cool that something as gross as spit could tell us stories about our ancestors. When we got home, I'd ordered the kit immediately, my thoughts racing when I imagined plugging all that info about genomes and whatnot into a formula that could potentially give us some clues for helping Kylie.

As soon as I logged out of PayPal, guilt settled over me like Kylie's weighted blanket. Though my mother and I had never spoken about it, there was a tacit agreement that who I was biologically had nothing to do with who we were as mother and daughter. My origins were barely ever mentioned, as though Mom had conjured me out of thin air. And from what I understood, it was as if she had—my birth mother had never tracked me down, and my adoption was as closed as a locked door. Those DNA results might tell Kylie exactly who she was, but they'd only remind me who I wasn't. I could handle that. But, they'd also remind my mother of the one fundamental thing we didn't share. How much would that hurt her? I wasn't sure, but I knew that it would.

I forced myself to refocus on Jenn with two *n*'s. "Anything surprise you about your results?"

"They were exactly what I expected. My results were almost pure—ninety-eight percent Northern European. I suppose that's why my hair is so blonde."

Though she liked to pretend otherwise, her hair was so blonde because I made it that way. With bleach. I smiled at her in the mirror. "I'm not so concerned with the ethnic breakdown. I want to see what kinds of genetic diseases are lurking in my family tree."

Jenn made a face. I guessed her disease profile was 98 percent pure as well. The other 2 percent was a propensity for self-absorption.

"I found out I have a third cousin who lives just outside of San Diego," she said. "Never knew it. Can you imagine? I contacted her, and we are like, the same person. Seriously. We both prefer lasering instead of waxing, and she's really into CrossFit, just like me. Truly unbelievable."

I didn't want to go into the stats on how many thirtyish suburban women liked body hair maintenance and keeping fit. Again, I smiled into the mirror and said, "Wow. What are the chances?"

Jenn nodded vehemently. "I know, right? I have a ton of distant cousins, apparently, but I only contacted her so far, because she posted a photo. So many of them are anonymous—who knows what kind of person you're dealing with? You're practically putting your life in someone else's hands when you go online these days. You know Tina, right? The one who works at the coffee shop near the library? Well, she decided to try Tinder, and you are not going to believe . . ."

I zoned out. I knew it wasn't nice. But I kept replaying the conversation I'd had with Matt the night before, and regretting the conversation I failed to have with my mom. I didn't want Mom paying for Kylie's services. She simply couldn't swing it financially. She'd sold the tavern three years ago when it sadly became clear her long-time customers were sucking down prune juice instead of Budweiser—it was currently a craft cocktail bar that catered to people like Jenn. After paying her bills and settling up her tax bill, Mom had very little left. I couldn't ask her to squeeze the last dollars from her savings account. If I cut three or four more heads every week, I might be able to cover the fees, but the long hours meant more time away from my daughter. Matt was always happy to spend time with Kylie, but I felt like our schedules should be somewhat regimented and equal. The phrase "custody agreement" had not been uttered by either of us, but it hovered ominously over our heads, like a low-hanging rain cloud.

I finished snipping and started blow-drying. Jenn kept telling me about Tina's dating life, and I tried my hardest to follow what she was saying, but I still couldn't focus. That morning, Kylie woke with a sore, scratchy throat and a low-level headache. I sent her to school anyway. Was that the right decision?

Parenting requires constant questioning of yourself. Parenting a sick child requires self-interrogation worthy of CIA operatives at Guantanamo Bay. And in the end, you've tortured yourself so much mentally that you aren't sure what you believe.

"It's lopsided," Jenn with two *n*'s said, breaking into my thoughts.

Jenn always complained. I knew this. But today my patience was thinner than her overly lasered eyebrows. It took everything I had, but I forced a benign expression. "Didn't you ask for asymmetrical? That means the two sides won't match." I ran my hand along the bottom. It was a good cut, not one I would have chosen for her, but the exact look she requested. "It's perfect for your '80s party. I admire your dedication—most people would have just gotten a wig."

"I'm not most people," she snapped. "This is for my thirty-fifth birthday party. It's important. Fix it."

Scissors in hand, I snipped the teeniest, tiniest bit from the longer side. When I was done, I fluffed it up. Jenn stared at herself for a long moment, and then said, "*Now* it's perfect."

"That it is," I managed to say without rolling my eyes.

She left a substantial tip and promised to text photos of her big party—to which I was not invited. Usually, I would never expect an invite to a client's social event, but for some reason, Jenn's exclusion bothered me. I could feel an irrational anger brewing, the suffocating pressure of a slow rise in blood pressure.

I was being ridiculous. Time for a breather. My next client wasn't due for another half hour—I could swing a quick outing if I hurried.

"I'm going for coffee," I told my friend Heather. Normally a stylist, she was here on her day off, filling in for our receptionist, Roxanne, who was down with strep. "You want the usual?"

"Nope," Heather said, her eyes growing wide and bulging.

Heather never turned down caffeine. "What's up with you? Why are you making a frog face?"

She nudged her chin toward the waiting area behind me. "You've got a client."

"No, I don't."

"Yes," she hissed, "you do. He's a walk-in."

I turned, stomach sinking, as I was pretty sure I knew who it was.

Sure enough, Matt sat there, reading an old copy of *US* magazine. He looked thin and pale.

I felt Heather's hand on my shoulder. "You need backup?"

"Not yet. If you hear me scream, come running."

"You know I love you," Heather said, "but this is kind of messed up." She wasn't wrong. It was.

I walked over to my almost ex-husband. "Ready?"

He nodded and headed directly to the hair-washing station. Matt had done this a thousand times. I wondered how many more times he would.

I'd been cutting his hair for over a decade, but it wasn't habit that kept him coming back after we broke up. At least I didn't think so.

It was my touch.

And not in a pervy way. We had simply inhabited the same space for such a long time, my touch became one of those comforts of every-day life—a brush of the hand as I handed him a beer, a shoulder rub after a long day, a kiss on his arm as he held me while we stretched out on the couch, watching HGTV and dreaming about the new house we'd never have.

He missed my touch and I missed his.

I perfected the water temperature and drew Matt's head back. He closed his eyes, thinking of . . . What? Happier days? It hurt to specu-late, so I didn't. Shampoo, conditioner, head massage. This was where it got a little dicey. Matt loved the feel of my fingers running over his scalp. It relaxed him . . . in all kinds of ways. It would be odd if I didn't do it, so I'd begun to rush it after we'd separated, giving him the same businesslike attention I'd give Jenn with two *n*'s.

I ran the pads of my fingers over his scalp, pressing hard enough to cause slight discomfort.

Still, he groaned.

I'll admit, it stirred something in me. How could it not? For ten years of my life, that sound was a precursor to other, more satisfying sounds. Helpless against a swirling mix of imagination and memory, I softened my touch.

"Ally!" Heather's voice cut through my thoughts. She gave me that frog face again and mouthed, *Stop it!*

Swatting away the familiar feelings, I pressed harder, moving faster, trying to get it over with. I dumped conditioner on his head and rinsed it away.

Afterward, I guided Matt to my chair, though he probably could have found it blindfolded.

"Kylie had a sore throat this morning, and a headache," I said as I grabbed a comb.

Matt stiffened. "And she's in school?"

I ran the comb through his hair, still blond and thick, though Matt had recently turned forty. "I had mixed feelings, but I sent her. Haven't gotten a call from the office yet, so it was probably the right decision."

"Probably," Matt said, and I could feel his shoulders loosen. "She needs to be in school or she can't go to play practice, right?"

Kylie had scored the role of Veruca Salt in her school's production of *Charlie and the Chocolate Factory*. We were thrilled in front of her and terrified behind her back. What if she got sick on opening night? "That's the director's rule. Maybe the incentive helps her manage the pain?"

Matt sighed. "I hate that she has to manage anything."

"I know. I keep telling myself she'll be a stronger person in the long run."

"She will. I tell myself the same thing."

Matt was actually agreeing with me. I knew when an opportunity presented itself. "Have you changed your mind about helping me pay for Dr. Indigo? I really think she might be able to help."

Matt thought for a moment. I'd like to say I was above subtle manipulation, but I started to massage the back of his neck and tops of his shoulders. He was full of knots.

"I can swing something," he said. "But probably less than you'd like."

"Anything is helpful. Thanks."

"You don't have to thank me. I feel guilty is all."

I needed to change the subject before he changed his mind. "So, same cut as usual?"

"Shorter," he said. "Cleaner and more businesslike."

I laughed. Matt taught history and political science at the local high school. He'd been there so long I didn't think anyone would mind if he showed up on campus with neon-green hair and a forehead tattoo. His usual look was that of a carelessly rumpled intellectual with a touch of absent-minded professor. "What's with the conservative do?"

"I . . . I decided to try online dating," he said, wiggling in the chair a bit.

My hand froze. "What? Why?"

He shifted his gaze to the ceiling. "Because I need something to look forward to."

I didn't know what to do with that answer. I didn't know what to do with this at all. And if I was being honest, I wanted to pass the dating hot potato into the future. Not the near one, but the one residing years and years ahead.

"So," Matt continued, "I want to take some photos where I don't look like a degenerate."

"I usually give you a good cut," I said, knowing I should keep my cool, but still unable to control my need to defend myself. "It's tousled. A good look for you."

21

"I just figured I should look like more of a grown-up," he said flatly. "Even if I don't always feel like one."

Was that an acknowledgment of something? Weakness? Or was it bait for our argument du jour? If it was, I wasn't going to take it. "Well, just be careful. Jenn says people misrepresent themselves on those dating sites all the time. It's not like when we were doing Ecouples. The pool is much larger and more unpredictable."

"I'm fully aware of that," he snapped. "I generally have good judgment."

"Yeah, you did. Past tense."

"Just because you disagree with me about dating doesn't make me wrong to do it."

We stopped talking as I got to cutting his hair. But Matt's discomfort grew, his wiggling intensified. If he wasn't careful, I'd accidentally snip off his ear, Van Gogh–style.

"Ally," he finally said, "I'm going to list my status as divorced, okay? I mean, I think a lot of women might have problems with dating someone who is separated. And, it's only a matter of legalities until it's the absolute truth, right?"

My heart instantly contracted. "We're not divorced. Lying doesn't sit well with me." I swapped out my scissors for an electric razor and ran it along the back of Matt's neck.

The stylist-client relationship required mutual trust. I'd built a career on it. It was kind of ridiculous to think my clients might spot Matt's profile online, but what if someone did? They all knew we weren't divorced. "I can't stop you from doing what you want," I said, "but I won't lie if someone asks. I don't mind bending the truth a little bit, but breaking it? No. I'm not a liar."

"It's a white lie, and not a big deal."

"Lying is usually one of the bigger deals."

I brushed the hairs from Matt's neck and shoulders, taking my time, wishing someone could whisk me away from this conversation. I didn't want Matt to date anyone. The thought of him touching some-one else made me want to scream. And the thought of him telling his story—our story—to some sympathetic woman was *really* too much to handle. I still thought of our experience as *ours*. We knew details about each other, so many details. That particular intimacy still existed, and I couldn't pretend that it didn't. But maybe that was my issue instead of his.

"Done," I said. "You look like an earnest, young congressional aide. Or a phys ed teacher from 1954. You'll attract Miss America, no problem."

"Come on, Al," Matt said, standing up. He was a tall man, much taller than me. He bent his knees until we were eye level so he could meet my eyes when he talked to me, like he did when *we* were first dating. "This isn't something I necessarily want. It's just something I decided to do. Loneliness is a bitch, and I need a nice woman to slap it around for a bit."

"I would refrain from using that analogy around women you want to date. It's not the best."

"Doesn't mean it's not true."

He left a mediocre tip.

~

When I got home that night, Mom and Kylie had finished dinner and were glued to an episode of *The Great British Baking Show*. Mom held Kylie tightly against her, Kylie's small head flush against her chest. My mom was a good woman, but not a demonstrative one. A problem solver, not a hugger.

"What's wrong?" I said, unable to keep the fear from my voice.

Kylie glanced at me and burst into tears.

"She's all right," my mom said, voice steady.

I hadn't mastered her ability to remain calm. "Are you okay? What happened?" I drew my daughter to me, and she sobbed into my shoulder.

"It hurts," she said. "It hurts so much."

"What hurts?" I asked, mind reeling. "Kylie, *what hurts?*"

"Everything. Every part of my body including my *soul.*"

Ah. The insistent hyperbole of preteen melodrama. It wasn't something medical. I gently pushed her away from me so I could look at her face. "Can you explain?"

"I missed a day of school last week, and two days the week before," Kylie said, hiccupping softly. "Mrs. Loftus said I needed to step down and let Lola take Veruca. *Lola*, Mom. She's the one who rubbed a hot pepper on Marly's ChapStick. *She's* the star now. And I'm an Oompa-Loompa. I'll be *orange*. With *green hair.*"

"What?" The anger I'd felt earlier resurfaced, red and hot and not exactly rational. "But you're going to be a fantastic Veruca Salt. I'm going to the school tomorrow. I'll march right up to that Mrs. Loftus and make her give you the part back. This is absolutely not fair. When I'm finished with her—"

"*Ally.*" There was a warning in my mom's voice.

"*Mom.*"

My mother put one hand on Kylie's shoulder. "Tell her the whole story, kiddo."

Kylie broke eye contact, staring at a photograph of my grandparents hanging next to the television. "I couldn't remember my lines today. My head was bothering me too much. And, well, Mrs. Loftus kind of had a point. I haven't had as much practice as the other kids, and we don't have a lot of rehearsal time left."

"And?" my mom said, her voice gentle.

Kylie frowned. "They bought all the candy for the play, and Mrs. Loftus can't guarantee that it's peanut-free. She's worried because

Veruca has to eat some of the chocolate. She doesn't want me anywhere near it."

I slumped with my back against the couch, the truth taking the fire out of me. It was all so unfair. Poor Kylie. Adults build fortress-like defenses against disappointment. Kids barely have the tools to construct a chain-link fence.

"Can I buy different chocolate?" I said weakly.

"They had special chocolate bars made," Kylie said. "So I don't think so."

"I'm so sorry, baby."

"Yeah," Kylie said, defeated. "I'm sorry too."

The three of us settled in to watch mild-mannered British people attempt to construct pastries worthy of the Queen. A few consistently succeeded, but most failed here and there. The allure of the show came from how creative they were in fixing their mistakes. One really young woman tried to frost her cake before it cooled, and the top turned into a muddy goo. She had a reserved, Brit-style teary-eyed meltdown, and then ended up slicing two inches off the bottom, adding that layer to the top, and covering the whole thing in chocolate ganache. A flash of genius.

Problems were solved by taking action. Worry never solved problems. Neither did fear. When the show finished, I took Kylie's hand. "Come with me."

After a pit stop in the kitchen to grab a big glass of water, I took her into the bathroom.

"Here," I said. "Drink this."

Kylie gulped the water down without question. I tried not to think about why she was so agreeable, but it was difficult not to. She constantly heard, *Drink this. Eat this. Take this supplement or pill or tincture.* She took everything, hoping each time that she was ingesting a miracle.

"Okay," she said. "What now?"

"Therapy. In just a second." I dashed off to the front hall and grabbed a package from the top of the mail stack. The box was light, so light for all the potential secrets it contained. I ignored the voice that told me sometimes secrets are better off staying hidden.

I ripped open the packaging, glanced at the instructions, and handed the specimen vial to Kylie.

She turned it over in her palm. "What do I do with this?"

"Have you ever heard the phrase *spitting mad*?"

"I don't know. Maybe."

"It means you're so mad, you could spit. I felt that way a whole bunch of times today. I didn't spit on anyone, but I think I would have felt better if I had."

"Wait. You want me to spit?" The corner of Kylie's mouth turned up. "This is the DNA test, isn't it?"

"Yep," I said, ignoring the tug of guilt when I thought of my mom in the next room. "You've got to fill this vial, so you might as well get some aggression out while doing it." I leaned over the sink. "One of my clients frustrated me earlier." I spat into the drain. "That's for you, Jenn with two *n*'s!"

"Mom!"

"It feels good. What made you angry today?"

Kylie thought for a moment. "Lola. She kept laughing with her friends when she got the better part."

I pointed to the vial. "Spit."

Kylie drew some spit in her mouth, but paused.

"This is for Lola," I said. "Spit!"

She did, and broke into a grin. "I'm sort of mad at Mrs. Loftus too."

"Spit!"

She did. Again and again. For the boy who broke her pencil in social studies class. For the gym teacher who yelled at her to speed up her PACER test. For the math teacher who gave a pop quiz on a Monday morning.

The vial was half-full.

"I don't know what else I have," Kylie said.

"Yes, you do."

"What?"

"How about peanut allergies?"

Kylie nodded. "To peanut allergies!" Spit. "To headaches!" Spit. "To itchy skin!" Spit. "To sore joints!" Spit. "To doctors!" Spit.

"Keep going," I said, but there was a lump in my throat, and it came out a whisper.

"To . . ."

"To what, honey?"

"To . . . this life," Kylie said, and filled the vial.

Then we sealed it up, filled out the forms, and, with shaking hands, I sent all of her anger off the next morning.

CHAPTER 3

To: StylistAlly@hairmail.com

From: YourPast@yourpastisapresent.com

Ms. Kylie Anderson,

Thank you for using Your Past Is a Present! Your
DNA results are now available. Since you've signed
up for "Share My Chromosomes!" you can easily
connect with members who share one or more seg-
ments of your DNA. Have fun exploring your family
tree! Remember—be sure to load your file into the
HealthPredictor* for medical information specific
to your results.

Kylie—your past is a present! Open it and explore
the unique mystery of you!

* Your Past Is a Present provides raw data, but
does not take responsibility for any outcome,
health or otherwise.

"This isn't the Oscars," Heather said. "You can peek inside the envelope before you announce the results to an audience."

I poured her another cup of coffee. "I think we should wait for
Kylie. My mom went to pick her up."

"Okay, Miss Avoidance. Aren't you curious, even a little bit?"
Heather said, tying her thin, pale hair into a topknot. "I would be."

Curious wasn't the right word. Maybe terrified? Or nauseated? Or
so apprehensive I might run into the backyard and bury my laptop in
the garden. I'd never let curiosity grab me by the throat before, not
to this extent. Sure, I wondered about my origins plenty of times.
Who wouldn't? But my mom had always made it clear that I was a
Stefancyk—I was *her* daughter. Blood was made irrelevant by devotion.
The people who put me into the world cut their ties to me, and Sophie
Stefancyk grabbed on to the fraying thread, wove it into something
strong, and tethered me to her life. I was someone else's for a mere
twelve months. And that time, so brief as to never make an imprint on
my tiny little person, really didn't matter.

Until it did. A couple of taps on my keyboard could reveal very
specific information about the people responsible for me being in the
world, and for the first time, I felt I had a right to know who they were.
My tribe. I knew, looking in the mirror at my dark eyes and olive skin,
that I wasn't Polish. I was Sophie's, that's for sure, but was I entitled to
have parts of me that were mine?

I'd only casually mentioned the DNA test to my mom, presenting
it as part of the overall strategy to help Kylie. Still, she glanced away,
hiding the shock I'd seen burst in her eyes, and muttered something
incomprehensible to acknowledge I'd said something. I quickly changed
the subject. Sophie Stefancyk was of the generation that felt adoption

was nothing to be ashamed of, but should still happen quietly and in secret, never to be spoken of again. I had scant details of how she'd come to be my mother, and I learned those not from her, but from the man who helped her do it, my adoptive father. It had been during one of my rare phone calls with Jim, and even that was an accidental, offhand remark that got me asking him questions.

"Hell if I know why she doesn't discuss it," Jim said, talking to me from his condo in Scottsdale. I think I was in high school at the time.

"Nothing to be ashamed of," he continued. "She got drunk one night at the bar and asked if I'd help her out. We'd been dating awhile at that point, so I did. It was hard for a woman alone to adopt a kid, and your ma really wanted a baby. I admired her a lot back then, still do. She doesn't talk much, but when she does, you know she means it. I wasn't planning on getting married, but I had nothing going on, so I thought, why not? This was the early '80s we're talking about. Different times. Soph and I lasted longer than I thought we would, and a lot of that had to do with you. Never saw such a cute baby, and you slept real good too."

My teenage heart had swelled with pride at the thought of being a good baby, that I didn't cause Sophie any trouble. That was how *I* saw adoption, that I owed my mom a debt I couldn't possibly ever pay in full. She never made me feel that way, but sometimes the strongest feelings form in those empty pockets of air lodged between facts and assumptions.

What I didn't feel badly about was my adoptive father's lack of presence in my life, but again, that was my mother's doing. "He just wasn't cut out for it," she'd said. "Some people just aren't. It's not anyone's fault, and definitely not yours." My dad had been a detective for the Chicago Police Department. When he was on the job, Dad worked nights and spent his mornings at Stef's Tavern, trying to decompress with a bottle of Bud and my mom's famous cheeseburgers. I was the result of flirtation and boredom on his part, and a shrewd observation on my mother's. She wanted to adopt, and she needed a husband to do so. He stuck around for the first five years of my life, and though she never said so outright, they fell into what could be called love. Like she said, though, he wasn't built for that kind of family life. After he left, Mom raised me, and he sort of supervised from afar, his Irish Catholic family already too populated to include me. We got an unimpressive check in the mail once a month. Sometimes, he'd write *Happy Birthday* or *Merry Christmas* on the memo line. That was pretty much it. After he put his thirty years in, he moved to Arizona with his girlfriend. I barely noticed. I was a Stefancyk, not a Cavanaugh, and it was mostly through an unexplainable sense of duty that I called him twice a year to tell him about the granddaughter he'd only met once, and the life his sort of daughter had made without him.

Mom made up for his absence by being steady and trustworthy and showing her love with a quiet devotion that kept me bolted to the earth when I wanted to take off into la-la land. Kylie and I were her life, and that's the way it was. Years of working behind a bar had taught my mother to carefully guard her true feelings, and she used that same emotional vigilance to hold our family together, even as her daughter's marriage fell apart. Again, I owed her one.

"I'm not doing this to find out about my biological family," I insisted to Heather.

She rolled her eyes. "You can't tell me it never crossed your mind."

"It might have, but what really matters is using this information to find out what I can about any illness Kylie might have inherited."

"Bullshit."

Just then, Kylie burst into the room. "What did you say, Auntie Heather?"

"Bullet. Your mom made me a bulletproof coffee, and it's going to keep me up until three a.m."

Kylie shot her a skeptical look before falling into Heather's arms for a hug.

Coming from such a small family, I'd always sought people out to fill in the missing spots. Kylie didn't have any aunts—Heather didn't have any nieces. This worked out perfectly, especially when I separated from Matt, which made my small family even smaller.

"We were about to learn all of your secrets," Heather joked, guiding Kylie to the kitchen table.

Kylie flushed. "What secrets?"

Ignoring the uneasy feeling in my gut, I fired up my laptop. "The DNA results came in today. Want to see the ethnic breakdown?"

She nodded and scooched next to me.

I took a deep breath and logged in. The breakdown of Kylie's heritage appeared. I wouldn't consider it mine. I *couldn't* consider it mine. Scientific data. That was all.

Your Past Is a Present!

YOU:

Scandinavian: 48.9%

Northern European: 21.7%

- British Isles/Ireland: 16.2%

- France/Germany: 5.5%

Southern European: 20.3%

- Italy: 18.9%

- Iberia: 1.4%

North African: 3.2%

Native American: 3.1%

Ashkenazi Jewish: 1.7%

Unassigned: 1.1%

Heather whistled. "You are truly a woman of the world, young Kylie. Way to represent."

Kylie pulled the computer closer and began studying the analysis.

"All those percentages represent people," Heather said softly. "Lots and lots of people who made you into you."

The concept was almost too much to process. I sat back in my chair, my emotions fogging my vision, preventing me from focusing on the specifics of the ethnic breakdown. *All those people* included the people who made me and then gave me away. None of those people included my mother.

"Why don't you read it, Ally?" Heather said gently. "It's historical data, that's all it has to be."

"You're right. It's not my life."

"Yes, it is, Mom," Kylie said. "You and Dad are on here."

Her innocent exuberance had me pull the laptop toward myself. I studied the numbers, pretending I was in a lab coat, a cool, dispassionate scientist, not a woman who was about to find out the answer to the central mystery of her life.

The "unassigned" designation caught my attention first. It was a little disturbing. What did that mean? That there was a small part of Matt's or my DNA that was homeless, wandering rootless and alone? That had to be mine. Nothing about Matt was a mystery. So even my DNA questioned who I was. Great.

With effort, I shook off that downer of a thought and glanced at my daughter, at her sandy-brown hair, so much lighter than mine, her strong nose, the shape of her delicate brow. I thought of her strength, her sense of humor, her passion. Which traits came from these mystery ancestors and which ones were uniquely hers? Which were nurtured by me and Matt and my mother, and which were designed by nature? And . . . did it matter?

It did. Because there was her illness. It was as mysterious as these nameless, faceless contributors to the creation of the girl sitting next to me. Getting help from these people seemed an impossible task. But, as Doctor Indigo said, it was a start. So what could I do but get over my drama and begin to sift through all of the data? I dashed off a quick email to Dr. Indigo, sending her the link to the DNA information. Then I drew the laptop even closer to me so I could have a better look at our past.

Matt's family came from Sweden, on both sides. Scandinavia made sense.

And the rest? It was time for a little detective work. The remaining big percentages had to represent my side. I did know that my biological parents were from Chicago. Given the ethnic mix of the city, in all likelihood, I was Irish and Italian. I let that settle in for a moment. Did that knowledge change anything? No. I already liked pasta and Guinness. I had dark hair, but my shoulders freckled after a day in the sun. These details were interesting, but didn't change my perception of myself one iota. Historical data, Heather said. That's all it was.

The smaller percentages also made sense if they belonged to me. North Africa was very close to Italy. I'd read somewhere that Irish immigrants worked the railroads out West, so maybe the Native American came through that?

"Look, Mom!" Kylie exclaimed. "They have a timetable! We had a Jewish relative somewhere in the 1770s. I wonder if that person was a girl or a boy."

The Ashkenazi Jew was the wild card, another lone DNA wanderer through the distant past. He was mine. Somehow I knew it. "I think a boy. I don't know why I said that, though."

Excited, Kylie wiggled in her chair, reminding me instantly of Matt. "Will I be on this someday?" she continued. "Like if my great-great-great-granddaughter tests her DNA?"

It was an awe-inspiring thought. "Yes, sweetie. You'll be a little dot in the first half of the twenty-first century."

Kylie's excitement turned down a notch. "That's actually kind of weird. Like, she won't know me. I'll be a stranger to her."

"At that point, she'll probably be able to stick a computer chip in her head and visit your memories. And anyway, I take a lot of photos of you. There will definitely be evidence you were on this planet."

Kylie snorted. "You never print those photos out."

"No one prints photos out," Heather said. "Who has time for that?"

"Well, I'll make time," I said to Kylie. "We'll make scrapbooks for your great-great-great-granddaughter, even though she'll probably be half alien or something."

Heather laughed and started telling Kylie about some science fiction movie she'd seen. I couldn't tear my eyes away from the results page. All those people over so many years—all those choices made, all those people falling in love, having babies, moving from place to place, living and dying and forming the basis of the lives we now lived. It was nothing short of a miracle, and something completely mundane at the same time. We were all here because someone got together with someone else—the simplest thing in the world, right?

I thought about me and Matt. Maybe not so simple.

He'd probably think this was all a waste of time. Still, I made a mental note to send him these results. It was his heritage, too, this map of our genes mixing it up.

"Grandma, take a look at this!"

Distracted, I hadn't noticed my mother come into the room.

"Let me put my eyes on, honey," she said, fishing her reading glasses out of her flannel-covered cleavage. I held my breath as she brought her face right up to the screen.

"It's the DNA test," I said, my voice flat.

"Uh-huh," she said. "I can see that."

"This one was for Kylie, but you can do one, too, if you want," Heather said, not realizing she was treading into dangerous waters. "Do you want to know where your ancestors came from?"

My mom straightened to her full five feet, three inches. "I already know. They're from Poland. I'm Polish." She looked directly at me. "And so are you. I raised you to be, so you are."

"I know," I said. "This is just . . . it's just a way to find out more medical information. It's for research. A tool."

"Tools can be dangerous," Mom said. She snapped the laptop shut. "My parents were Josef and Gloria Stefancyk. Their family was from Warsaw. I'm Polish. You're my daughter, so you are too."

Kylie looked puzzled. "But, Grandma, you adopted mom. There isn't any Polish on my chart."

"Not another word."

I knew I should back down, but I didn't like the sharpness in her tone. "Mom, it doesn't change anything about us."

"That's where you're wrong, Ally. It does. Go ahead and use this information for whatever you need to help Kylie. I get that it could be useful, but I don't want to look at it. I know you didn't come from my body, but your DNA sure wasn't the one cleaning up your puke when you got sick, and reading to you every night." Mom crouched in front of the fridge and dug out a can of sparkling water. "I need you to listen. When I said not another word? I meant it. At least not in front of me."

~

I heard her, but it didn't change the fact that I thought there should be another word about it. Lots of words, for that matter. At dinner that night, there were hardly any words at all. My mom ate with us, stoic and grim, barely responding as Kylie described her day.

I knew I should let her work through it, and that I should be gentle with her—I'd forced my mother to confront information she'd rather remain buried—but part of me wondered why she faulted me for simple curiosity. I was thirty-eight years old. At some point, didn't every adopted person wonder about where she came from? I'd think the urge to uncover that mystery would be almost primal. Part of me was hurt too. Didn't my mother trust the strength of our relationship?

Mom brought her plate to the sink. "I'm going out to the garage," she muttered. "To work on that lamp."

Kylie perked up. "Can I help?"

"Not tonight," she said, shrugging on a faded hoodie. "Some other time."

"You have homework anyway," I said as Kylie slumped down in her chair.

"We're sorry, Grandma," Kylie said. "We didn't mean to hurt your feelings."

After a pointed glance my way, Mom crouched next to her. "You didn't, honey. It's just that . . . I'm old. I like things to stay the way they are, and I don't like to be reminded that they could be different. Your mom is a Stefancyk. I hope looking at those numbers can help you, but it doesn't add anything but complicated thoughts to my life. Do you understand what I'm trying to explain?"

"Yeah," Kylie said. "I mean, I guess."

She briefly touched the top of Kylie's head. "Your mom is my family. You're my family. I'm not going to let those numbers tell me otherwise."

~

Later, after I'd tucked Kylie in for the night, I curled up with a mug of tea and my laptop. I wanted to start the process of sifting through the health data before our visit with Dr. Indigo at the end of the week.

The first thing I did was copy the link and email it to Matt. I wanted to call him, to pore over this material with the one person who should be just as invested in it as I was. But I doubted my phone call would be welcomed. And the thought of discussing his dating life was about as appealing as lasering Jenn with two *n*'s nether regions.

I knew why people tried to "stay friends" after a romantic relationship went bust. It temporarily allowed them to hold on to the one kind of intimacy that lasts—the one built of familiarity. In many ways, that type was the hardest to lose, because it took the longest to build. I'll admit, I clung to the idea of friendship with Matt. Maybe we couldn't be in the same place for more than ten minutes without arguing, but we still cared for each other, we still wanted the best for each other.

And wasn't that friendship?

Maybe. The thing was, friendship implied mutual respect.

Did I respect Matt's decision to move on with his romantic life? Did he respect my choice to continue seeing Dr. Indigo?

A whole lotta no. To both.

So we aren't friends, then, I thought, sadness echoing through me. We were just two people with something in common, which was barely any kind of a relationship at all. That conclusion made me want to add whiskey to my tea.

Instead, I took a deep breath and dug further into the DNA results. Underneath the ethnic breakdown was an image of a family tree generously dotted with colorful leaves. Each one represented someone who shared a fraction of my or Matt's DNA, and was willing to share that information with anyone who was interested.

Kylie, you have 1,526 relatives in the Past Is a Present database! 1,526!

My heart nearly leaped out of my chest. Talk about a big family!

I scrolled through quickly. There were pages of cousins—second, third, fourth, and beyond—from all over the world. All these photos of strangers reaching out blindly to those who shared their blood—their optimism warmed my frosted heart. I went back up to the top and started reading down the list of names.

Huh.

I didn't think I was comprehending what I was looking at, so I read the relationship designation again. And again. Then, sent the link to Heather and called her.

"What does this mean to you?" I said, trying to hide the note of hysteria in my voice. "Am I reading that right?"

"Oh, my friend. Yes. You are. Holy shit."

I could feel my blood pounding through my veins. "That's . . . a close relative, yes? Like, really close. Almost uncomfortably close."

I heard Heather gulp her beauty drink. She drank warm milk with coconut oil every night, claiming the concoction kept her from getting wrinkles. "Yep. Kylie's great-aunt."

"She could be Matt's aunt."

"She could be, but don't you know all of Matt's aunts?"

"I do. But what if there was a secret love child or something?"

Heather laughed. "I've met Matt's family. That seems unlikely. No, honey, she's *your* aunt. It's pretty clear."

"I figured. I just wanted a freak-out partner."

"You've got one."

"Do you see where she lives?"

"Willow Falls. We could drive there in less than an hour, like, if we were doing the speed limit and missing every light. Wow."

"Uh-huh. Wow."

Heather gasped. "She could be your biological mom's sister."

"Or my bio-dad's."

"Oh my God."

"My body feels weird," I said. "Kind of tingly and warm."

39

"That's your blood pressure going nuts. You are, like, *gaining close relatives as we speak*. Of course your body is reacting." Heather gasped again. "Her name, though. Micki Patel? Could the test be wrong?"

I thought about that possibility for a moment. "They allow DNA in court, right? So it's got to be pretty foolproof. And that's probably her married name. I mean, in all likelihood she's in her sixties, so chances are she's married, and might even be a mom."

"And maybe even a grandma." A pause. "You could have cousins, and great-cousins. Is that once removed or twice? I never could understand how that worked."

The thought of that stole my breath.

"Ally?"

"Yeah?" I choked out.

"Are you going to tell your mom?"

Good question. This went beyond rejecting the notion of another family in the abstract—this was a real live blood relative. I studied the photo of the woman. She took the camera straight on, grinning directly at whoever was taking the picture. Her hair was an unnatural shade of red, and she wore too much makeup. But there was something about her eyes I liked, something familiar. They were brown and warm and the slightest bit guarded, just like mine.

"I don't think so. How could I do that to her? She'd be so hurt."

"Do you think she'd be the kind of hurt that lasts, though? Or do you think she'd get over it when she finds out you were only satisfying a curiosity?"

"You know Sophie. Which do you think?"

"Yeah."

Heather was my best friend. I could say anything to her, so I did. "What if, hypothetically, I contacted this woman just to talk to her. Just to set some facts straight, if she even has any information. Like, family medical history."

Heather gasped. "You're going to contact her? Out of the blue? You have no idea who she is. I would do one of those search things beforehand. You know, find out if she's got any arrest warrants or foreclosures or anything. What if she's a con artist with a criminal record? What if she goes after your money?"

"Now you sound like Jenn with two *n*'s. And I don't have any money."

"Well, okay then. Maybe she's rich and you can go after *her* money."

"We're just talking in the abstract. I don't think it's going to go anywhere."

"It's not just talk. You have this . . . this open door right in front of you. I've known you for years, and you have never been able to resist an open door."

~

I found her in the garage, futzing around at her makeshift workbench. Even in a relaxed state, my mother had a strength about her, a confidence more earned than ingrained. Her silver hair held back in a neat ponytail, she bent over a midcentury lamp, oblong shaped and constructed of white iron spindles, which lay in front of her, wireless and hollow. Matt and I bought it two years ago at a flea market in Iowa, during happier times. We'd planned to get our HGTV on and refurbish it, but that sad little lamp sat in the basement, gathering dust until I claimed it during the Great Property Division six months ago. My mom, after years of being the default handywoman in our house, took on the project when she realized I probably wouldn't get to it until Kylie graduated from high school.

"I'm going to put a coat of paint on this tonight, and then I'll rewire it in a few days," Mom said, all signs of her early anger gone. "Let's hang it above Kylie's bed. It'll look nice there. The light will refract through the whole room."

"Mom—"

"No more," she said softly.

"How did you know what I was going to say?"

"Because I'm a mom. And you're a mom now. You know how much can be crammed into that one word."

"I think we need to talk about this."

She turned around and rested her back against the workbench, arms folded. "Why?"

"Because I think you're taking this DNA thing all wrong."

"I think I understand it pretty clearly. I also understand *you*. What I don't think you understand is *me*."

"Well, I won't understand anything if you don't explain yourself."

She drew up an old stool and motioned for me to sit down. "I learned a long time ago that bringing up painful memories only brings pain, but tonight, I'll cough it all up."

"Gross image."

"True, but the stuff I'm hauling up from the archives isn't pretty."

That chilled me for a moment, but curiosity won out over apprehension. "Bring it."

She stared at me for a moment before saying, "I told you that I got you from an agency. That's not exactly true."

"You've barely told me anything."

"You've barely asked."

"Something told me I shouldn't."

"You should listen to that voice."

I gently pushed at her arm. "Go on, Mom."

"I was almost thirty years old when I started looking into adoption. A single woman who worked in a bar and didn't have much of a pot to piss in. How well do you think that went over with the state?"

"Got it. You weren't a very desirable candidate. So you married Jim."

"I did. I always liked Jimmy, and he was willing to help me out. Still, being a married woman didn't help nearly as much as I thought. They said I should take in a foster kid, or adopt someone already in grammar school, but I didn't. I wanted a baby. Maybe that makes me selfish, but it's the truth."

Mom's fingers twitched, and I knew she wanted a cigarette, a habit she'd given up twenty years before. It was one of the only surefire signals she was stressed. I wondered if it was because of what she'd already revealed about herself, or because of what was going to come out of her mouth next. "So, what happened?"

"You sure you want to hear it?"

"I do."

"Well, okay. You hear things, working in a bar. All kinds of things. What did we have to talk about besides bill collectors and politics? Gossip. One day, Jimmy brought in a friend whose niece had a baby. Cissy Ricelli was her name. I didn't know the family personally, only heard of them, and what I heard wasn't good. There were criminals in the city and there were lowlifes, and the Ricellis belonged to the latter. The woman was wild and could barely care for herself, much less a kid. She couldn't get out of bed in the morning, and there was no one else to watch the baby. No one knew who the father was."

Emotion clogged my throat. "He could have been anybody."

"Don't do that," Mom said. "She was looking for someone decent to adopt the kid."

"She was looking for money," I said.

"What does that matter? I got you, and from that first day, you were mine. I got a lawyer to make it all official. You were a Stefancyk. Jimmy was . . . Jimmy. He meant well. But you and me . . . it's always been you and me. I know it hasn't always been a piece of cake. I'm not an easy woman, but I'm not hard either."

"You're a good woman, Mom. I've always known it."

My mother doesn't know what to do with tears. She swiped awkwardly at the ones that filled her eyes. "I don't give a crap what you do with that stupid DNA test, especially if it helps Kylie. It gets to me, to think about those other people who had you for the first year of your life. I don't like feeling those feelings. But, I do understand why you did it, and I guess I should be thankful you held off pressing this issue until now."

"This doesn't have anything to do with us. I just want to know who's in my blood. I didn't think I did, but I do. I'm sorry."

Mom took both of my hands and squeezed. "It has everything to do with us, but you do what you need to do, Ally. You always have. I want you to remember one thing, though. Love is stronger than blood. Don't you ever doubt that."

~

Before I went to bed, I googled the heck out of Cissy Ricelli. Nothing. What was Cissy short for? Cecelia? I tried that. Then Christine and Christina. There were plenty on Facebook, but no one appropriate in the fifty-five to seventy age range.

What had happened to her? I thought about the few details I knew. She was a party girl in the late '70s, early '80s, from a fractured family with criminal tendencies. Great. How often did a story like that end well?

A flash of sympathy surged through me. Did she regret giving up her baby? Did she have other children?

Oh, wow. I could have a sibling. Or even more than one. I had to admit the thought was strangely exciting. The loneliness of being an only child stays familiar. It runs too deep to completely fade.

Kylie, you have 1,526 relatives!

Some of them were mine. Their DNA popped up in my Roman nose, my dark hair, the slight bend of my ears. Love might be stronger than blood, but blood was pretty tenacious—the stuff coursing through my veins had been through the wringer, and it had stories to tell.

And suddenly I needed to hear them.

I positioned my trembling hands over the keyboard. I could do this. No one needed to know. All I wanted was a phone call. Maybe a meet up for coffee. One conversation. What could it hurt to ask?

Past Is a Present Message Center

Kylie Anderson to Micki Patel:

I'm your niece, or at least this DNA test thinks I am. My name is Allison Stefancyk Anderson. I'm the biological daughter of a woman named Cissy Ricelli. My father's name is not known. I'm not sure where you fit in, and I don't want to cause you any stress or bring up painful memories, but if you are willing, I'd like to talk. I live in the Chicago area.

CHAPTER 4

Before Kylie got sick, I thought the world worked mostly in an orderly, organized manner. I mean, the sun rose and set, the earth turned on its axis, we had answers for questions like, why do kangaroos have pouches, and how did the Red Sea get so salty? Okay, we still weren't sure about life after death or the true size of the cosmos, but as a species, we kind of had it going on. We had experts and trusted authorities and people-in-the-know. And the people who knew things could give me clear, easily digestible answers, often with a simple Google search. I didn't question much, though, because I didn't need to. I knew how to cut hair, and Matt could teach kids about things like gerrymandering and the Electoral College, and we had a daughter we were pretty good at caring for. The major stuff made sense, and when that does, how much thought do you really give anything else?

Then Kylie woke up one morning, looking like she'd gone a few rounds with Muhammad Ali in his Cassius Clay prime. Her eyes were so swollen she couldn't open them, her face ruddy and bruised looking, her lips puffy and cracked—a frightening caricature of how she looked when she burst out of me, when my body put the squeeze on her.

I panicked. We already knew her system really didn't like peanuts. Had she accidentally ingested any? She could breathe with ease, and the symptoms seemed different from her previous reactions. I took her to the pediatrician instead of the emergency room.

Diagnosis? An allergic reaction.

We returned to the traditional allergist. She suffered through another round of scratch tests and blood work and endless doses of Benadryl. We discovered that, in addition to peanuts, now her body also took offense to cats, grass, dust, mold, and strawberries. The doctor prescribed a stronger antihistamine. It worked for a while. The puffy eyes returned to normal size, her face regained its natural paleness. Life made sense again.

Until the headaches started, and the dry mouth, the ugly, itchy rashes, and the aching joints. The questions became more difficult to answer.

Life started to make less sense.

But someone had to know something, right? I googled until I felt like I'd gone to medical school. I joined Facebook groups and chat rooms, and posted on Reddit as often as a millennial. I dragged Kylie to doctor after doctor, so very hopeful, until one specialist asked to speak to me alone and said, "We don't have names for all the autoimmune disorders we're seeing. Your daughter is inflammatory, but so is half the country. We can't keep up with all the permutations of these illnesses, so we try to fit them into ones we've already identified. You can guess how effective we are at treating those cases. I'm sorry, Mrs. Anderson. We'll try, but at this point, we might be talking trial and error."

It was mostly error.

But still . . . I hoped someone had the answer. Optimism isn't a choice when it's your kid's future at stake, it's a strategy.

~

"This is just like Girl Scout camp."

Kylie sat a respectful distance from the odd-smelling sticks burning on a metal plate on the floor of Dr. Indigo's office. The doctor sat next to her, wearing a shapeless black dress cinched at the neck, kind of a sleeveless hemp/cotton Hefty bag. I sat across from her, cross-legged and pretending the position didn't pull at my tight hips.

"Should we hold hands?" I joked, but the doctor shook her head once and said, "That will come later."

Kylie shot me an *Is she for real?* glance, and then returned her gaze to the fire. Because even though this was ridiculous, the orange-red flames were kind of mesmerizing. Still, we'd driven all the way from the burbs for a reason, and sitting around an office campfire wasn't it.

I leaned forward, the flames warming my face. "Did you get the blood work back?"

"Shhh," Dr. Indigo hissed. "I asked that you try to clear your mind. I don't think you're giving it much effort."

"I don't know how to stop thinking," Kylie whispered. "I've tried meditation before, and it's impossible! There are lots of ideas living in my brain, and they have idea babies all the time, and it's too crowded for me to clear them out."

Dr. Indigo smiled faintly. "You don't need to get rid of them, you just need to calm them down for a while."

"What do you do when you feel pain?" I said. "You usually deal with that really well."

"Thoughts are different," Kylie said. "Pain is just . . . pain. I'm used to it, so after a while it feels the same to me. Thoughts change. They go in all kinds of directions."

I guess it was hand-holding time, because Dr. Indigo wrapped hers around Kylie's and said, "I have a way of looking at the problem that might help. Did you have quiet hour in kindergarten? Can you remember that far back?"

"I can," Kylie said. "And, yes. Mrs. Shipley had us lie down on mats for twenty minutes. We didn't have to sleep, but we couldn't talk, and we had to be still."

"That's what you need to do with your mind," Dr. Indigo said softly. "Tell it to settle and quiet. The ideas have every right to be there, but they have to lie down for a while and not bother you."

I knew what she was doing. There was value to meditation. But . . . BUT! Kylie's current headache was going on day three. If she hadn't already gone through a CAT scan and MRI, I would for sure think she had a brain tumor. Meditation was a bridesmaid treatment—we needed to bring in the bride!

"Doctor—"

"Shhh, Mom," Kylie interrupted. "I'm telling my thoughts to chill out."

My daughter's eyes were closed, and her features relaxed and peaceful. It was as if someone had come with an anxiety eraser and smudged it all away. I shushed.

We sat there, breathing in and out, in and out. Then Dr. Indigo said to Kylie, "Now that your brain is settled, we can focus on calming some of your body's systems. They're upset and overreacting. They're acting irrationally."

Oh, for heaven's sake! I was trying to be open-minded—really I was—but a few ideas started acting up in *my* brain, including one borrowed from my mom. *Quack!* it squawked. *She's a quack!* Oh, there was no way I'd ever tell Mom about this, or Matt. Maybe I'd tell Heather. Maybe.

Dr. Indigo continued, her voice low and almost hypnotic. "Kylie, I want you to imagine that you are walking a dog."

What?

"What kind of dog?" Kylie asked.

"A big one," Dr. Indigo said. "Almost bigger than you."

Kylie grinned. She was only borderline allergic to dogs, and she'd always wanted one. Matt and I always said no—why risk it? I guess an imaginary pet was better than nothing.

Dr. Indigo continued, "Can you see it in your mind?"

"Yes. I'm walking him in a park. It's sunny, and the different color leaves look pretty. Like today."

"Good. Okay, so you are walking along, enjoying the beauty of nature, and a squirrel runs across your path. The squirrel isn't bothering you, but your dog becomes very agitated. He's barking and pulling hard at the leash. You're having difficulty controlling him. Even though the squirrel is long gone, your dog won't calm down. You become upset as well. Your heart pounds fiercely, you start to sweat, your mind races. Your dog picks up on your distress and reacts, becoming even angrier, turning his rage on you. It's getting really hard to handle him now. He's dragging you, and your hold on his leash is slipping."

Kylie made an anguished noise. "Is he getting mean?"

"He is," Dr. Indigo said. "Very. It's like he can't control himself."

"I don't know what to do," Kylie squeaked.

"He's barking so loudly it hurts your ears."

Kylie gasped. "I don't like this."

Neither did I.

"Your dog's just snapped at the air," Dr. Indigo continued, her voice growing stronger, "and then at the leash, his teeth just an inch from your hand."

I could picture it. Skinny, exhausted Kylie hanging on for dear life as a fierce, anger-mad German shepherd tugged hard against his leash, teeth bared, drooling, ready to pounce.

"What do you do?" Dr. Indigo's question was for Kylie, but I couldn't help myself—I took it.

"Let it go, honey," I whispered. "Let go of the leash and run."

"I don't know . . . What if he comes after me? I'm not sure, Mom."

"What do you do, Kylie?" the doctor repeated. "Do you hold on or let go?"

"I—"

"What do you do?" Dr. Indigo insisted.

Kylie sniffled. "Let go, I guess."

"Enough," I said. "She's *crying*. This ends right now." I held my arm out, and Kylie—her eyes wide open now—scooted over, burrowing into my side.

Silently, Dr. Indigo rose and flipped the light switch. She placed a metal snuffer over the fire plate and resumed her place behind her desk, gesturing for us to sit opposite her. Displeasure oozed from every crevice on her face.

"Kylie's blood work showed inflammatory markers consistent with an autoimmune disorder," she began. "Which one? It's not clear. We do know that autoimmune issues have some commonalities—the immune system is attacking its host, the person it's meant to protect."

"I know what an autoimmune disorder is," I snapped.

"Well, then you understand that Kylie needs to learn to calm the dog." Dr. Indigo stared at me, like she was waiting for my brain to catch up with hers.

I stared right back—I didn't need to catch up, I was already there. "And how is she supposed to do that? Calm a dog that's bigger than her? An *uncontrollable* dog."

"She'll learn that there are plenty of ways to settle it down. Ways she hasn't even thought of."

"What ways?" Kylie said. "There were two. I could try to hang on, or I could let go."

"There was another way," Dr. Indigo said, smiling at Kylie. "Do you want to try to figure it out?"

"No," Kylie said, her voice flat.

Dr. Indigo's smile turned down a notch. "Help. You could have asked for help."

"From who?" I said. "The trees?"

"From the dog," Dr. Indigo said.

"Aren't you an allergist?" I said, not bothering to hide the irritation in my voice.

"I am."

"Shouldn't we be focusing on her allergies and health issues? I thought that's why I was here. I didn't come to see Mr. Miyagi, I came for help."

"How many doctors have you been to already?" Dr. Indigo asked. "And how much have they helped?"

I had to admit, she had a point.

~

"I failed," Kylie said on the drive home. "I couldn't calm the dog."

I inched the car forward about three feet. It was the fastest we'd gone since we left the wellness center. Chicago traffic at the height of rush hour tested my every last nerve, and I didn't have much patience left after that doctor visit. "You can't fail at meditation. No one does. Don't you pay attention in yoga?"

"I'll be the first one, then." She sighed. "So the dog is my sickness, right?"

"I think the dog is your immune system, and it's attacking you for no real reason. Or maybe it's overreacting to a reason, but doesn't realize it. I think. Right?"

"Dr. Indigo is smarter than us."

"We're plenty smart."

"Then *why* couldn't I calm the dog?" Kylie's frustration was palpable.

I slammed on the brakes—damn Uber drivers!—and looked at my daughter. Her face was red, and tears were collecting in the corner of her eyes. "Because you weren't prepared. Neither was I. Why couldn't I stop the dog either? Because it's really stinking hard to control an angry, vicious dog! Almost impossible. Stop beating yourself up."

We drove in silence until we got home. Matt's ancient Chevy truck sat like a beached whale in the driveway.

"Dad's here," Kylie said. "But it isn't his day. That's okay, right?"

Anxiety wrenched my stomach. "Yeah. It's fine."

"Why do you think—"

My phone made a doorbell noise. Some kind of app notification. "I've got to look at this. Might be something important."

"Uh-huh," Kylie said. "I'll wait for you."

My daughter knew me well. I didn't like surprises when it came to Matt. And I didn't feel like explaining anything to him. I didn't feel like being around Matt at all. Today felt like a failure. *I* felt like a failure. And I didn't want him adding to the doggie-pile of mortification I was already suffocating under.

I made a pretense of studying my phone. A notification *had* come through, from Your Past Is a Present. Maybe a response from Micki Patel? I could feel my heart beat in my throat, pumping blood into my warming face. I clicked on the app, which took an eon to load. "Come on, come on . . ."

"What, Mom?"

You have a new report from Your Past Is a Present!

Are you ready?

Based on your DNA, Kylie, you are unlikely to have smelly pee when you eat asparagus.

I stared at the message for a moment, deflated.

"What is it?" Kylie asked, a note of worry in her voice.

"A notice from the DNA place."

"What did they say? Does everyone in our family get sick?"

"Oh, honey, no. They said you can eat all the asparagus you want, and your pee won't smell."

She crinkled her nose. "So, my people don't get smelly pee? That's like, our thing? Well . . . I guess I've got that going for me."

"Better than nothing—" I said.

"Because it's something," Kylie finished.

We sat for a moment until I realized how badly I was procrastinating. "I guess it's time to see your dad."

Kylie put her small hand on my arm. "I'm not going to tell him about the dog," she said. "If you're worried about that."

"You can tell your dad anything at all. I don't want you to think that way. Don't worry about me."

"I'm not. I'm worried about Dad."

"Why?"

"Because he'd *destroy* the dog if it was hurting me."

"He'd feel badly about it afterward," I said. "But yeah."

"I need to learn to calm the dog myself," Kylie said. "So it's not anyone else's problem."

"Honey, it was just an exercise. The dog is imaginary."

"The doctor said my systems were attacking me. That's the dog. I know what she was talking about. I'm not dumb."

"I never said you were. I think you're very smart."

"If that's true, then I'm going to learn to calm the dog."

"I don't think it's an easy thing."

"Mrs. Loftus says anything that's too easy usually isn't worth doing," Kylie said.

"I'm pretty sure she stole that from somewhere. And I'm not sure if I agree with that."

"Well, I do. The hard stuff matters."

In dealing with Matt, I was about to do some of the hard stuff. Did it matter? Would it accomplish anything?

"I'm going to go say hi to Dad," Kylie said. "You should come inside too."

She was right. I had to stop being such a chicken. After she dashed into the house, I pulled the car up farther, parking next to Matt's. I sat there a few minutes longer, telling myself I had to wait until the end of whatever song was playing on the radio, and then finally headed inside.

Matt wasn't in the house. My mom was—studying a Pottery Barn Kids catalog like it held the meaning of life. Kylie had grabbed an apple and was sitting next to her, her small face scrunched up in thought just like Mom's. I kissed my mother's cheek, and she murmured hello.

"Where's Matt?"

"Where he belongs," my mom said. "In the garage. He's not allowed in the family home. The family home is for *family.*"

"Seriously, Mom." I shoved my arms back into my sweater and headed to the garage, being sure to let the door shut loudly on my way out. I wasn't a slammer, but I still wanted to make a point.

My mom didn't understand why, absent cheating, drugs, or abuse, two married people would decide to separate. Actually, she couldn't accept that her little girl had failed at anything, so it had to be Matt's fault. She'd already had one man turn away from her family, and though she probably always knew Jimmy wasn't going to stick around, she wasn't going to accept two. To Sophie Stefancyk, it was a crime punishable by banishment.

The banished one stood at my mom's workbench, staring at the lamp destined for Kylie's room.

"She's doing a great job with this," Matt said. He turned, and I got a good look at him. I could see the lines in his hair from when he combed it. He wore a neatly pressed light-blue shirt and a navy-blue tie. Khakis with a knife pleat. Brown loafers. Where were the concert T-shirt and worn-out jeans? The beat-up Converse?

"You look . . . professional." That seemed like a neutral word.

"I look like an overgrown Eagle Scout." He gestured to the almost-wired lamp. "Your mom is competent. I am *incompetent.* I don't know how to do any of this stuff."

"She would have taught you. If you'd asked."

Matt's mouth went flat. "Are we going to start?"

"I didn't mean anything by that. Just that . . . she would have."

He ran his hand along the wire snaking down the workbench. "I'm . . . on my way to a meeting."

"For faculty? At this hour?"

"No . . . uh . . . a date. I met her on Cupidworks."

Even though he'd prepped me for this, I still had to clench my jaw to keep my mouth from hanging open. Though our marriage was slowly dissolving, the outline was still there, watery and vague as it was. The rules still applied. But who would enforce them?

"I didn't mean to upset you." Matt looked more like a Cub Scout than an Eagle Scout at that moment. A little boy sorry he'd gotten caught stealing cookies from the pantry. Vulnerable and almost sweet, and . . . guilty? Maybe.

"It doesn't," I lied. "It's nice, I guess."

"It is?" He raised an eyebrow.

I exhaled loudly. "No. It isn't nice at all. I honestly don't know why you even told me."

"Because she lives in town. I thought you might spot us, or I might run into someone we know, and it would get back to you." He ran a hand over his face. "I don't know how to do this. There isn't a guidebook."

"It's just . . . embarrassing. Every part of it."

"I disagree," Matt said. "I think it's necessary. Isn't that what people do? Move forward? Dating Cassie is me moving forward."

"Cassie?" I only knew one Cassie who lived in our small suburb. "Cassie Flores?"

"Yeah."

"You're seriously going on a date with Cassie Flores." I'd cut Cassie's hair for about a year after I graduated from beauty school. She liked caramel-colored highlights and talking about her dog. That's all I remembered. But still. There was a *connection*, however slight. "I *know* her. That's not . . . that's not how we're going to do this. If you go on a date, it has to be with a person I've never come in contact with. That's it."

"That's going to be pretty difficult given my time constraints and the size of our town."

"Then it will be difficult."

"It's just a single date with a nice woman. I think you'd actually like her. She's a lawyer at some downtown firm, but she's not snobby. Her son is eight and just two grades below Kylie. She's running for the open position on the school board, just to give something back to the community. *Cassie runs marathons*, for heaven's sake. You have to be a semidecent person to run for twenty-six point two freaking miles."

"Or a complete psychopath," I said.

I watched the anger bubble up, and I watched Matt decide it wouldn't get the best of him. "Maybe we shouldn't talk about anyone we see unless it gets serious."

"Maybe we just shouldn't date yet. At all."

Matt sighed. "Okay. Subject change. I came to talk about the DNA test. I don't want to know how much it cost."

"I had a Groupon."

"I'm sure you did," he said. "Was it weird for you? I saw . . . Italian. Irish. I can't imagine what it's like to look at something that definitive."

"It was definitely weird, staring at those percentages." I wanted to tell him about Micki Patel and the message I'd sent. I wanted to tell him about my curiosity, my confusion, my anxiety. I opened my mouth and shut it just as quickly. Those thoughts were mine, and sharing them with Matt, such a normal part of life before the separation, now seemed dangerously vulnerable. As much as I didn't want to, I needed to start protecting the new me forming under my skin. The me without him. "I'm okay with it all. I mean, we did this to help Kylie."

"What did Dr. Indigo say about the medical information?" Matt asked.

"Nothing yet."

Matt frowned. "Why? Wasn't that the whole purpose of your visit today?"

"Only part of it. I'm sure she'll discuss the results next time. I plugged the data into the medical website. I have the results, but they don't make much sense to me."

"They don't need to make sense to you," his voice growing angrier. "They only need to make sense to the doctor who asked you to buy this test."

"I'll make sure she covers that next time."

"Do that."

Time to switch subjects again. "Did you check out your half of Kylie's DNA?"

"Yeah." He almost smiled. "The Scandinavian part . . . that's me."

"Did your family ever mate outside the tribe?"

"Apparently not," he said, disappointment underlying his words. "I kind of wish there was something in it that surprised me."

"Maybe the Ashkenazi Jew or the North African?"

We both laughed, puncturing holes in some of the tension. Matt was so pale he needed sunscreen indoors, and his hair was the color of hay.

"My parents weren't very connected to their culture," he said. "You know I grew up on Wonder Bread and bologna sandwiches."

"That's a sort of culture."

He made a face. "Doesn't feel like it. There should be a connection, and I felt nothing. It's just data on a page."

"That's okay," I said. "It doesn't have to mean a thing if you don't want it to."

Matt's expression softened. "I guess it doesn't. Hey, did you tell Sophie about the test? It might be weird for her too. She never seemed all that comfortable with talking about your biological family."

"I told her. She's not comfortable with it."

"Maybe you shouldn't have told her."

"Or maybe she should have told me some things a long time ago. Sophie hasn't been entirely honest."

"Maybe your expectations of people are too high." Matt leaned back against the bench and crossed his arms. His muscles strained against his shirt, and I fought down the urge to ask him to hold me up. I suddenly felt very, very tired.

"I don't think that's true," I said.

"Okay, maybe I should have said your expectations are unrealistic. You expect people to think the way you do."

"Is this your way of telling me you think I shouldn't give you a hard time when you want to parade around town with a woman both of us know, even though you're not divorced yet?"

"One doesn't have much to do with the other."

"We'll just have to agree to disagree," I said.

"I hate that phrase," Matt said as he headed for the door. "It's a cop-out."

"No, it means we can both be right."

"Or both be wrong, I guess."

~

It took my brain a while to settle that night. It felt like I'd just drifted off to sleep when Kylie bounded onto my bed, complaining of a nightmare.

"The dog," she whispered. "It was chasing me, and my legs wouldn't run."

She pressed her cheek to my bare arm. She felt warm . . . too warm?

"You feel okay, baby?"

"I'm fine."

Fine.

Great.

I tried to keep my breath steady until her body relaxed into sleep. Mine wouldn't. I stared at the shadows on the wall for a while until I gave up and padded into the kitchen. My laptop sat charging on the counter.

I fought the urge to try again with Micki Patel, and instead walked over to my mom's bedroom. The door was open a crack, just as it had been throughout my childhood. Her soft snores reached my ears, and I just listened for a moment. Usually, the sound of her breathing soothed whatever was jumping through my nervous system, but tonight, it wasn't enough. *Wake up*, I thought. *Talk to me.*

She didn't stir. Disappointed, I returned to the kitchen to make some chamomile tea.

When Kylie was a baby, I used to find a quiet house at 3:00 a.m. peaceful. Now, it was simply lonely. I poured a mug of tea, opened my laptop, and logged on.

There was a message waiting for me.

Your Past Is a Present Message Center

You have a connection!

September 17, 2:48 a.m.

Micki Patel to Kylie Anderson

My late sister Cissy, may she rest in peace, never stopped thinking about you. She hoped you were living a good life, and I hope you really are. Would I like to meet up? Of course! If I knew where you lived, I'd probably show up on your doorstep. We're family, honey. Since we are practically neighbors, I was thinking this Sunday at around 1 p.m. 959 Main Street in Willow Falls. Can you make it? Please say yes. And, who is this Kylie? Is she family? Bring her with you!

Love,
Aunt Micki

Love, Aunt Micki.
Oh my God.

I let that phrase roll around in my head. My Aunt Micki. Kylie's Great-Aunt Micki. My biological mother's sister.

Aunt Micki's *late* sister.

My biological mother was dead.

That stopped me cold. I felt like I'd dropped something valuable into a deep, deep well—there was only a split second to register the loss, and then it disappeared, forever gone. My throat seized up and my eyes watered. Was I mourning? Did I even have a right to? I grabbed my phone.

"I'm sorry!" I squeaked. "I know it's three a.m. I just . . . need you."

"Why do you think I keep my ringer on?" Heather said, her voice gravelly with sleep. "I've always wanted a middle-of-the-night phone call. It's so dramatic."

I started seriously crying then, huge, body-wracking sobs.

"Oh, Ally. What's wrong?"

I spilled everything to Heather.

"Feelings are okay," she said when I'd finished.

"Who are you? Mr. Rogers?" I sniffled. "I feel heavy. There are too many emotions crowding up my body. Guilt? Sadness? Pissed-offed-ness? I don't know which one is going to come out on top."

"I'm going to ask you a shitty question."

"Go."

"What are you going to do?"

I answered from the gut, no thinking things through. "Meet Micki Patel. I have questions and I want answers. I don't need to tell anyone."

Heather laughed. "You just told me. So that means I get to go with you."

CHAPTER 5

The drive to Willow Falls took only forty-eight minutes.

During which I thought I was having heart failure about 367 times.

"This town has got to be a set from a Hallmark movie, like, *Autumn in Harmless-Looking White People Land.*"

Heather talked nonstop, probably trying to distract me from my nerves.

"*You're* a harmless-looking white person," I said.

"Way to rub in my blandness. I'm going to get a tattoo. Or a nose ring. Something."

"Don't be a cliché. You're too old for conformity."

"Will you dye my hair pink?"

"You'll look like Frenchy from *Grease.*"

She laughed. "I'd rather look like Rizzo. At least she got some action."

It was easier to devote what coherent thoughts I could manage to Heather's life instead of what awaited me in Willow Falls. Since befriending her five years before, I'd listened to countless complaints about the horrors of living single, but not once did I see her take action to change her situation. I tried, encouraged, pushed, and prodded, but eventually I stopped trying to shove Heather into the world of dating, figuring she had reasons she wanted to keep to herself. And when my mind processed all the reasons that might keep someone from pursuing a relationship, I figured I wasn't helping the situation if I kept pressing. We buried the topic with humor, never discussing it directly. But now that my romantic circumstances were less than ideal, could I gently bring it up?

"This is probably the most dangerous thing I've done in ages, maybe longer," Heather continued. "Who knows what the mysterious Micki Patel is going to be like? Is she hiding something? Who is she *really*? I love this."

Love was not quite the word I would use. My stomach felt like it was turning itself inside out. I glanced in the rearview mirror to check on Kylie, who'd fallen asleep in the back seat. I'd had no intention of bringing her. Really, I hadn't. She had a rough night, her sleep punctuated by nightmares, so she clung to me like plastic wrap on Jell-O. Mom had to go to a wake, and Matt . . . well, it was *my* day with Kylie. Selfish, maybe, but it was too hard to give up time with my girl. Heather and I devised a plan—Micki would be the aunt of a client, and I was making a house call. I had the iPad with me, stocked full of the fashion games that could immobilize Kylie for hours. I'd sent a message to Micki, explaining the situation, and she agreed to the ruse. I ignored the nagging internal voice telling me I was being a hypocrite. I'd just given Matt a hard time for wanting to tell a white lie, and here I was, telling a whopper.

It'll just be the once, I told myself. *Kylie won't give it another thought, and everything will work out fine.*

But part of me still wanted to pull a U-turn and head right home.

"Maybe we should stop for coffee so I can gather my thoughts," I said, prompting a frown from Heather. "Or maybe I should stop at a grocery store for a pie or something. Why am I showing up empty-handed? What's wrong with me?"

"No stopping. Just keep driving. We're almost there, and this is too potentially life changing to put off."

Heather was taking pains to treat this like a lark, and I was playing along, but my stomach decided it wanted to be not only inside out but on fire too. "What if she's awful?"

"You're a hairdresser," she said. "You can handle anyone."

I told myself that she was right, and if Aunt Micki turned out to be horrible, I could always get in my car, drive home, and pretend it never happened.

Google Maps said I only had a tenth of a mile left, but we were in the heart of Willow Falls, on the main strip through the picturesque downtown. I passed O'Malley's Pub and spotted its address—955. Did she live above the bar? I almost smiled at the thought. Maybe my mom and Micki weren't so different after all.

"It should be on this block," Heather said, but she sounded just as confused as I was.

I pulled into a spot in front of a quaint bridal shop, its window display full of flowers and hope, and ignored the jab to my heart.

"Are we here?" Kylie asked from the back seat, her voice still rough with sleep.

"I think so," I said. "I don't see 959, but the annoying robot voice says we've arrived. Let's get out and take a look around."

Even though we hadn't been in the car very long, we got out and stretched like seasoned road trippers, and then took in the suburb of Willow Falls. It was gorgeous in the fall. The tree-lined main street was awash in gold, crimson, and bright orange, and the shops had already jumped into the Halloween season. Gourds were everywhere, and their slightly phallic shapes added an oddly humorous touch.

"Uh, Ally?" Heather stood in front of the bridal shop window. On closer inspection, only one of the dresses on display was white, the others were blue and pink and purple and even burgundy. Oddly, they looked like bridal gowns, not bridesmaid or mother of the bride dresses.

"I've never heard of something like this," Heather said, grinning up at a sign in beautiful calligraphy. "I might have to make use of it someday!"

The Not-So-Blushing-Bride: THE Wedding Experience for Women over Forty!

And hanging from the sign, tiny and barely noticeable, was a white plaque stenciled with the numbers 9-5-9.

Was this a joke?

"This is it," I said, mustering up some confidence.

"It is?" Kylie said. "I'm confused."

Heather just laughed.

~

An old-fashioned bell chimed. We walked in . . . and then stopped in our tracks, completely unprepared for the chaos in front of us.

There were dresses everywhere, some arranged neatly in rows, but most thrown over chairs or hanging from nails driven haphazardly into walls. In one corner, on what looked like a PVC pipe balanced between two brightly painted ladders, dresses of every color were hung low, their skirts brushing the floor. Sofas were placed in random spots, though it would require moving mountains of bridal magazines, shoeboxes, and accessory bins to find a seat. Makeup and hair products covered the small, low coffee tables assigned to each sofa. It was a room that needed riot control.

"Welcome! Someone will be with you in a minute!"

"Is that her?" Heather whispered.

It couldn't be. The voice was too youthful. Searching for its source, I explored the space further, stumbling upon a changing room half-hidden by a forest of silk and taffeta. In contrast to the surrounding chaos, it was simple and well lit, a small stage positioned in front of three large mirrors. A row of closed doors lined the opposite wall. A young African

American girl, dressed inexplicably in a gold patterned sari, motioned for us to join her. Since Kylie was so young, I wasn't good at guessing older kids' ages, but if I had to, I'd say she was fourteen? Maybe sixteen?

"Can you give me an opinion on something?" she asked, her smile open and trusting. "I mean, I'm usually okay with mine, but not always. I've only been working here for six months."

"Sure," Heather said from behind me. "We love our opinions and mostly trust them."

I gave Heather a look, tilting my head toward Kylie, who plastered herself to Heather, her small arm wrapped tightly around my friend's waist. Heather tried to back up into the next room, but Kylie held her in place. *Sorry*, Heather mouthed.

The girl in the sari knocked on one of the closed doors. "Bernie?" she called. "Are you ready?"

Maybe I wasn't so great at gauging kids' ages, but I could ballpark those of the elderly. The woman who walked out of the changing room was ancient.

And she was wearing a virginal, snow-white, full-skirted, taffeta dream of a wedding gown.

"Let me help you get in front of the mirrors," the girl said, and gave the older woman her arm for support.

Sure the scene was bizarre, but strangely enough, this ninety-year-old woman preening in a wedding dress was less Miss Havisham and more something timelessly beautiful. Fine-boned and birdlike, she must have been a stunner when we were sending boys overseas and rationing sugar. I helped countless women her age try to camouflage the ravages of time on hair, but hers was still thick, a silver cap adorning a small, well-shaped head.

The younger girl took a step back while the older woman made slow half turns in front of the mirror.

"You look nice," Kylie said, flushing.

"Thank you, dear," Bernie said, "but I was hoping for something more . . . dramatic. One of those mermaid skirts, possibly? I think something more form-fitting is the answer." She placed two wrinkled hands on her bottom. "A bride must show off her best assets on the most important day of her life."

Heather made a strange noise and covered it up with a cough.

"I can pull some more dresses," the young girl said, "but let's not toss this one to the side yet." She glanced into the other room, the disaster zone. "I have an idea. Hold tight."

She left, and a heavy, awkward silence fell like a veil.

"When's the big day?" Heather croaked, the laugh still caught in her throat.

"Soon," the older woman said. "Which one of you is getting married?"

"Neither of us," I said quickly. "We're here to see Micki Patel. Do you know her?"

"Of course I do. She owns this shop. Did you think Radha owned it? She's sixteen!"

My patience was starting to wear. "Can you tell me where I can find Micki?"

"She dashed off to the café for something or other. She should return momentarily."

Radha ran back into the room carrying an armload of accessories. "I've got a silk hat to try, and a tiara if that doesn't work. I found some nice drop earrings—they're fake but no one will know, they look so good, and—oh! Let me try this on you!" She jumped onto the small stage and opened a tube of red lipstick. "This is totally classic. You're going to look amazing."

"Hmph," Bernie said.

Radha gently applied the bright color to the thin lips of the older woman. Bernie closed her eyes, enjoying the sensation.

"Have a look," Radha said.

The splash of color brightened Bernie's entire face. She didn't smile at the mirror, but she did stare, fixated by the change in her appearance.

"That lipstick is a firm maybe," she said after a moment. "Possibly even a yes. Put it to the side."

Radha raised her arms, triumphant. "Yay! I knew we'd find something that worked."

Bernie opened her lipsticked mouth to say something, but just then a huge crash sent us back into the other room.

"Is it you?" said a blowsy from-the-bottle redhead. At her feet lay coffee to-go cups, their contents spilled over the floor and rapidly heading toward a haphazardly stacked pile of wedding dresses. She ignored the mess and looked from me to Heather. "Which one of you is mine? Oh, you're both so gorgeous! I'll take both of you!"

Heather peeled off her cotton wrap and dove to the floor, using it to soak up the coffee before it ruined the dresses. "Her," she said, pointing to me. "I'm just the support staff."

Frozen, I stared at my aunt. *Say something*, I told myself. *Say anything.*

"Do you have any paper towels?"

"Oh!" Micki said. "I do . . . somewhere."

"I've got it, Mom," Radha said. "No worries."

Mom?

Micki plucked the cups from the floor and disappeared into one of the back rooms. Heather helped Radha finish sopping up the coffee. I stood there, clutching Kylie's shoulders.

"You're cutting her hair?" she whispered. "This is a little weird."

"Weird can be good, right?"

"Uh-huh. Sure."

Micki fluttered back into the room, holding a wicker basket full of juice boxes and chocolate Kisses. "This is all I've got," she said. "My stash for bored flower girls."

Apple juice. That was one of the few fruit juices that didn't upset Kylie's stomach. She tentatively reached a hand out and took a box. The chocolate Kisses were nut-free—we'd established them as one of the few safe candies years before—but still Kylie didn't accept one until I plucked a Kiss and popped it in my mouth, putting the wrapper in my purse because I didn't spot a garbage can.

"I have a severe nut allergy," Kylie told Micki. "But these are okay for me to eat. Thanks."

"My pleasure," Micki said. "Eat as many as you want."

Kylie's hand snaked into the basket, and she took a few more and passed one to me.

There was the odd moment of silence that happens when a group of people suddenly realizes the awkwardness of their situation. Bernie had snuck into the room, still wearing the poofy wedding dress. She took a juice box from the basket and struggled to puncture the top with the straw. When she finally got it in, some juice splashed up on her bodice. Radha cringed and forced a smile.

"Um . . . do you have another room so we can get started?" I asked Micki, hoping she'd get the gist.

"Of course!" she said. "Let me get your friends settled." She desperately searched for a spot that wasn't covered in wedding paraphernalia. She gathered up some dresses and tossed them off the nearest couch. Radha cleared some veils off another, and we situated Kylie and Heather around a coffee table covered in piles of what looked like industrial strength Spanx. Radha and Bernie sat opposite, the two parties engaging in a staring contest. I figured it would only be seconds until Heather would come up with a way to break the silence.

Micki led me back into the changing area. She shut a pocket door, and we found ourselves alone, sitting together on the small stage in front of the trio of mirrors.

Do we jump right in? I popped another Kiss in my mouth, silently berating myself for not preparing better for this meeting. Why didn't

I have a list of detailed questions? Should I have practiced? I needed a shopping list!

"You hated oatmeal," Micki said, her eyes swimming with tears. She clutched my hands. "I knew I had to feed it to you, but you'd stick your tongue out every time I tried. I felt so guilty for forcing you. I'm so, so sorry. I was in my twenties. I should have known a better way to feed you."

A surge of emotion caught me off guard. I opened my mouth to comfort her, not realizing I was still sucking on the chocolate Kiss. Instead of offering words of support, I offered a long stream of brown-tinged drool that landed on her wedding ring.

"I'm so sorry!" I squeaked, glancing around for something to wipe it up.

Micki wiped her hand on her pants and smiled at me. "Don't worry about it. We're family."

Family.

I took a good hard look at Micki Patel. The tilt of her nose. The color of her eyes. The arch of her brow.

So similar to mine.

My hands started trembling in hers. Suddenly, I wanted everything. I wanted this woman to lay out my past as clearly as the DNA test. "My mother," I said. "Tell me . . ."

Micki swiped at a runaway tear. "She was older than me. Old enough to take care of a baby, if that's what you're thinking."

"I can't judge her yet. I don't know anything about her."

Micki smiled faintly. "Cissy was wild. Always liked a good time. Our mother died young, and we lived in a house full of men. We didn't have anyone really minding us."

"How did she die?"

"Your mother or mine?"

"Both, I guess."

Micki glanced at the carpet. "My mother by her own hand. Her life was harder than you can imagine, and she didn't have the kind of spirit that can overcome too much pain." She paused. "Your mother . . . well, my sister didn't treat her body right. She was always sickly. As she got older, her arthritis got really bad. She had a hip replacement and sepsis set in. Her body couldn't take it. This was four years ago."

I tried to think about what I was doing four years before. Kylie was six. Matt and I were still happy.

And the woman who brought me into the world was leaving it.

"Why did she give me up?" My throat nearly closed while asking the question, as if my body was trying to protect me from the answer.

"She was an adult woman who could barely take care of herself," Micki said quietly. "She hated getting out of bed in the morning, but she liked staying up late. She liked a drink and sometimes a drug, and she liked men, but hated responsibility. There was never enough money, and she didn't try too hard to change that."

I tried to picture this woman. I couldn't. "Do you have a photo of her here at the store?"

"No, sweetie. I'm sorry." She took my hands again. "Look, none of those things necessarily make someone a bad mother, but Cissy knew that they did make *her* one. I wish I had an answer that wouldn't make you feel awful, but this is all I've got."

"Sounds like she tried to give me a better life than she had," I said, grasping for something positive.

"I can tell just by looking at you that she succeeded," Micki said. "My sister and I weren't close—we ran with different crowds—but I loved her, sometimes despite who she was. She loved you in her own way. I loved you, too, and it broke my heart when you left."

"I didn't leave," I said quietly. "I was given away."

Micki's shoulders slumped. "Yes. You were."

"I have to ask you . . ."

"Anything," she said.

"Why didn't *you* take me?" I leaned forward, anticipating her response.

But Kylie screamed before she could answer.

~

A zombie had come through the front door of the bridal shop.

Gray-skinned, with a yawning mouth full of bloody teeth and a shock of matted yellow-white hair, the zombie inched toward us, groaning, his arms outstretched.

Kylie scurried to me and dug her forehead into my ribs.

"What the hell?" Heather said.

"Dad!" Radha shouted and ran over to the beast.

Dad?

The zombie laughed and accepted her hug.

"Sandy," Micki said. "Come and meet my . . . friend!"

"Just a moment," he gurgled. The zombie gently released Radha and yanked at his hair, which came off with a tug. Underneath was a brown, shiny head with some wispy black and silver hairs sticking straight up. Out came the bloody mouth piece. He carefully peeled off a fake nose. "More presentable," he said to me, in a lilting accent. "I would shake your hand if mine wasn't covered in makeup. I'm Sandeep Patel, Micki's husband."

Micki beamed at him. "Sandeep is a scream actor at the pop-up haunted house off Route 83. He's fantastic at it."

Sandeep returned her smile and then shrugged at me. His eyes were amused and friendly underneath the makeup. "It's a good retirement job," he explained. "Scaring the stuffing out of people pays fairly well."

"You scared the stuffing out of me," Kylie said, half under her breath. She'd returned to her spot on the couch.

"I'm surprised," Sandeep said. "You look like the fearless type. 'And though she be but little, she is fierce.' That's Mr. Shakespeare."

Kylie stared at the bloody teeth he'd set on the coffee table. "Um . . . thank you?"

We stood there, smiling at each other, waiting for someone to make a move. I didn't know what to do next—had I gotten what I came for? The details of my biological mother's life had set off fireworks in my brain, sonic booms bursting into a million questions—questions I wanted answered, pronto.

But those would have to wait until another time, when Micki and I could be alone again.

Still, I could scoop a question from the top of the pile. Every bit of information about this new family felt valuable. I went with, "How long have you been married?"

"Ten years. Sandeep was the office manager at the medical supply company where I used to work in sales," Micki began. "When we got married, I had a hard time finding a dress, or anything suited for an older bride. So when we retired—"

"We cashed out and opened this shop," Sandeep finished. "We're active people, and we didn't want to sit around in our retirement. We sensed a need and figured we were just the right people to fill it."

"So then they got me," Radha said. "They were in a good position."

Micki drew Radha to her and squeezed. She showed affection in a way I admired, impulsively and without forethought. "We began fostering Radha about a year ago. Now, we're trying out to be her parents."

"Trying out?" Kylie asked, puzzled. "Like I did when I tried out for my school play?"

"Very similar process," Sandeep said. "Radha must decide if she likes us enough."

"I like you plenty," Radha said, and I could tell she meant it.

"We're proving to her that we've got what it takes," Micki said. "To Radha and the state."

"So they can adopt me," Radha said.

Sandeep's smile tensed. "We hope," he said. "If it all works out."

Anyone could see Radha loved her prospective parents. But they were older—weren't there rules about that? I silently sent a good thought out into the universe—*please make it work out for them.*

Heather gave me a questioning look. We needed to get home. It was getting late, and Kylie had school the next morning. My feet wouldn't move, though.

"Mom," Kylie said, probably picking up on my hesitation, "we should probably go. Grandma's gonna be waiting for us."

At the mention of my mom, guilt struck hard, disorienting me for a moment. I heard her voice loud and clear. *What are you doing here? What did you learn that mattered?*

"We do need to get going," I said quickly. "Thank you for having us."

"No!" Micki caught herself and smiled. "I mean, you can stay for a while longer, can't you?"

"This is a difficult situation," Sandy said, placing a hand on his wife's shoulder. "Today we don't have to think about anything but how wonderful it is to discover new friends."

"She's not new," Aunt Micki said. "I never forgot."

"How do you know my mom again?" Kylie said, looking skeptical.

"I'd like to buy the lipstick," Bernie interrupted. "Before I get any older."

"I'll take care of it, Mom," Radha said. She'd been watching her foster mother very closely.

Radha took care of Bernie's purchase, while Sandy commandeered the conversation, telling a funny story about working at the haunted house.

"Can we go sometime?" Kylie said, apparently feeling very brave. She still closed her eyes during scary movies.

"Sure," I said, uneasily. I should have said maybe. Why did I open my mouth without thinking? Maybe I wasn't thinking anything through. Is that what was happening here? Was I falling into these people's lives without weighing the consequences? I glanced at Heather, who'd begun to chat with Micki about her clientele, at Sandy, who put his fake teeth back in to draw a laugh from Kylie. I imagined my mom sitting here, her dry humor adding a wonderful element to the group. Could that ever happen? My gut was speaking to me loud and clear—the Patels were good people. The thing was, this was way more complicated than developing friendships. It was reinventing a family.

"We're having an event next weekend," Micki announced. "A fashion show. I'd love it if you came."

She looked so eager, so vulnerable. "Maybe," I said.

"That sounds really fun," Kylie said, excited. "I live for fashion! Can we go, Mom? Please?"

A group of middle-aged women walked into the store, laughing and generally whooping it up. Micki looked torn—she wanted to talk more, but then she needed to attend to her customers. "I'll be with you in a moment," she called out, and the women spread out over the shop, enthusiasm lighting their faces.

"You will come back, won't you?" Micki said to me. "Maybe you could help with hair and makeup at the show. We always need more hands."

"Moooom," Kylie whined. "This is my dream. Pleeeaaase?"

A warning roared through my subconscious. I ignored it. "Okay."

Sandy held out his hand. "It was wonderful to meet you."

Micki leaned over the coffee table, grabbing my shoulders. "Sandy, she gets a hug."

My heart threatened to melt just as fast as the chocolate Kiss. There was a brief hugfest, Sandy and Micki squeezing me, Kylie, and Heather. Radha joined in, dragging Bernie with her, and then the whole group walked us to the door.

"Could you bring Bernie home?" Micki asked as we shared contact info and said our final goodbyes. "She doesn't live far, and it would save her the car fare."

"Be happy to," I said as Bernie eyed me warily. Her lipstick had smeared, a red streak bisecting her cheek.

We settled Bernie into the back seat next to Kylie. After giving us her address, she was contemplative on the drive home, quietly humming what I was pretty sure was "Fly Me to the Moon."

"Have you been married before, Bernie?" Heather asked.

Probably not the most tactful question, but I hadn't offered any better. I glanced at the older woman in the rearview mirror, interested in her answer.

"No," Bernie said dreamily. She began singing softly, "When I find my love, it will last forever," garbling the lyrics a bit.

"That's nice," Heather said, because . . . What could she say? At Bernie's age, forever generally meant into the great beyond sooner rather than later.

I stopped in front of a modest ranch home, the low brick building dwarfed by its oversized, overstuffed neighbors. Heather jumped out to help Bernie to the door.

"Her fiancé's name is Reggie," Heather said when she got back into the car. "And they don't plan on having any children, in case you were wondering."

CHAPTER 6

After dropping Heather off, I silently suffered the aftershocks of meeting Micki. I gripped the wheel, struggling to pay attention, my mind wandering everywhere but on the road in front of me. Had I really agreed to meeting up with her again? Did I know what the hell I was doing?

I was searching. Aunt Micki said my mother had been a sickly person. I needed to know more about that. In fact, I had a responsibility to Kylie to find out more.

That seemed like the right thing to do, so why did I feel so hollow?

My mother was why. I was going to keep this secret from her. Maybe I could meet up with Micki just once or twice more, get all my questions answered, and then fade back into my real life. I'd send her a Christmas card, and maybe call her every so often.

Satisfied, I walked into the kitchen fully confident that looking her in the eye wouldn't be a problem. She sat at our small round table, having coffee.

With Matt.

Gone was the animosity my mother had shown him only days earlier. The two of them were hunched over a number of catalogs spread neatly across the table, staring at them with intense scrutiny.

"Daddy!"

Matt held his arms out, and Kylie ran right into them.

"How're you feeling, munchkin?"

"Fine," she said, nuzzling into his shoulder. "Maybe my elbows hurt a little."

"Maybe it's your funny bone," he said, tickling her. Kylie let loose with a completely unrestrained giggle.

If someone took a photo of this scene, in all its Norman Rockwell–esque glory, the story it would tell would be one of such sweet familial harmony it would be the photo on Facebook you hate-like because it's so perfect, it brings up instant feelings of inadequacy. I couldn't stand it.

"What are you doing here?" I asked, so bluntly my mom looked up and frowned.

"Matt was on a run," my mom said, as though that should explain everything.

"And I happened to be close by, so I stopped in," Matt said. "Sophie told me about the remodel she's doing on Kylie's room. She's got some great ideas, but she needs help with the heavy lifting." He smiled at Kylie. "Your bedroom is going to look fantastic! We're going to take that room down to the studs and completely start over."

I glanced at my mother, trying to get a read on her. Why was she letting Matt help with this? Her eyes gave nothing away. My mother could out-poker-face Lady Gaga.

Excited, Kylie began flipping through the catalogs, oohing and aahing over linens and bookshelves and funky rugs.

Kylie slept in what had previously been my mom's office. We'd moved the ancient computer out and put pink-and-white-striped sheets on the bed. I hadn't done much else because our living here was supposed to be temporary. My mother's eagerness to suit that room to

Kylie's personality told me she wanted it to be permanent. My heart twinged when I realized Matt probably wanted the same thing. "Her room is fine as it is," I said, not bothering to hide the edge in my voice. "I don't see why this is necessary."

"Mom, please!" Kylie was very close to whining.

"It won't cost that much," Matt explained with a hint of embarrassment. "Your mom and I found some stuff on the IKEA site." He ruffled Kylie's hair. "I figure if I can get through a master's program, there's a good chance I can figure out directions for a harfenurgengurgen bookcase."

"That's not a word," Kylie said, laughing.

"Dads are allowed to make up two words per year," Matt said, feigning seriousness. "Didn't you know that?"

As Kylie and Matt had their moment, my mom turned to me. "It could be a family project," she said with a shrug.

"Are you sure you want *all* of our help?" I asked, raising an eyebrow. Since when was Matt considered a member of the family again?

"If you can paint highlights on someone's head, you can paint a few walls and some trim," Mom said, brushing off my intent. "We can all go to the paint store to pick out a color."

"No pink," Kylie said definitively. "And no yellow. Maybe blue or purple."

My mom smirked at her. "I can live with those colors."

"This will be good practice for when we sell," Matt said, turning to me. "If we want top dollar, we're going to have to do a major overhaul."

"Sell the house?" It hadn't occurred to me that this was a possibility. Sure, I'd been the one to move out, but we came to that decision together. My mom lived closer to Kylie's school, and she'd be around to help me out when I needed it. Matt didn't have any family close by, and it didn't make financial sense for him to get an apartment. Also, if I was being honest with myself, when Matt and I were constantly bickering, I welcomed the comfort of my mom's home. Unchanging and predictable, my mother made the earth beneath my feet feel steady. And though she'd been an overworked single mom, she managed to infuse her quiet version of warmth and love in every part of her house—it was the scent of my childhood, and it persisted, just as she had.

But my house with Matt offered another kind of comfort. If we still owned it together, it was something that bound us, a lesser vow than the one we took at church, but a vow all the same. I wasn't ready to renounce it. Not yet, anyway.

"Can I help them after school, Mom?" Kylie asked, excited. "I want to learn to decorate a room. It's like HGTV."

My mom beamed. "It'll be a good experience for her."

"Agreed," Matt said. "Though we might have to be a little flexible with our time. That's okay with you, right, Ally?"

"What?" They'd continued talking, but my brain was still spinning from the idea of selling my house, not to mention meeting Micki Patel, and I was a step behind everyone else. "What do you want to do?"

"Kylie wants to help," Matt explained. "You don't mind if I'm here on your days, right?"

Mom put her coffee down and watched as I struggled for the right response. It wasn't a big deal—just a couple of hours after school. Why did it feel like I was giving in to something bigger than I realized? The three of them gazed at me, expectant.

"She can help as long as she doesn't have a doctor's appointment," I said, regretting my decision before I even knew why. "And homework takes priority."

Matt's expression soured slightly. "I'm sure we can work around all of that."

Mom refocused her attention on the papers in front of her and a sketch I'd just noticed, done in Matt's hand. It was drawn on a notepad advertising a local real estate agent. Had he talked to someone about selling already? Who was I kidding? Of course he had. Matt would sell our small bungalow, and the house that I'd infused with *my warmth* and *my love* would belong to someone else. Some other family.

"I'm tired," I said. "It's been a long day, and I need to lie down for a while."

"It's Sunday," Matt said. "The salon is closed. What knocked you out?"

"I had a house call."

Sharp-eyed and suspicious, Matt studied me closely. "Where? You never make house calls."

I could feel the blood in me rising, its power pounding from my toes to the tips of my ears. It pushed aside all guilt and concern and need for approval. I stepped around my mom, opened the fridge, and grabbed a beer. "I was out, and now I'm home," I said, and before anyone could question me further, I picked up my bag and walked into the living room. When I got there, I realized how small the house was. I could go to my room like I'd intended, or the garage. Hiding out in my room seemed embarrassingly childish. Garage it was.

~

I knew it was only a matter of time before someone would come looking for me, but in the meantime I sat at my mom's workbench and fired up my laptop. I'd stopped googling Kylie's every symptom a long time ago—it only caused worry and anguish—and instead had picked up the habit of going onto her MyChart and obsessing over what she *didn't* have.

No lupus.

No thyroid disorders.

No indication of leukemia or other cancers.

No diabetes.

No problems with her kidneys or liver.

I lived in that bubble of information for a moment, ignoring the ANA test—an inflammation marker—that showed something was going on, and it didn't care if we stuck a label on it or not.

The last doctor had diagnosed Kylie with Sjogren's syndrome. Though her symptoms didn't coincide exactly with that inflammatory disease, it was the closest he could come. "Close only counts in horse races," my mom said, and I had to agree with her. The doctor focused on treating symptoms individually, but that felt like playing a game of Whac-A-Mole—we'd calm one symptom, only to have another pop up. I couldn't accept that this was the way it had to be. Which had led me to Dr. Indigo.

I logged into Kylie's health portal with the Integrative Spiritual, Health, and Wellness Center.

There was a message from Dr. Indigo.

> Kylie and Ally—Kylie's IgE was high but still fine for treating her peanut allergy. The DNA info showed genes associated with a higher risk for chronic inflammation, as well as a stronger susceptibility to OCD, anxiety, depression, and celiac disease. Take care, Dr. Lucinda Indigo.

That was it? We had another appointment on Wednesday, and though I had my reservations, I wasn't going to cancel. I would insist on going over Kylie's blood work and health data in greater detail. Dr. Indigo could meditate with Kylie until they both reached nirvana, but that could come afterward.

I heard leaves crunch under someone's shoes. My brief moment of peace—if I could even call it that—was about to be disrupted.

"Can we talk?"

Matt stood in the open doorway. He looked more at ease in running shorts and an old T-shirt, his hair rumpled, a day of stubble already scruffing his chin. This was the Matt I knew.

"Fine," I said, closing my laptop. I glanced next to me on the bench, and Matt took the hint and sat. I didn't want him looming over me.

"Sophie's worried about you," he said.

"Why?"

"She doesn't exactly know. She just knows she should be worried."

"She should save her worry for Kylie."

"Kylie said her elbows hurt today," Matt said. "Her elbows? Really?"

"Joint pain. I rubbed some aloe vera on them. Dr. Indigo suggested it. I'm trying to lay off the ibuprofen."

"I suppose that's a good move if it actually works."

I could hear the skepticism in his voice. Justified or not, it rankled. "Well, I don't want her getting an ulcer on top of everything else."

"I wasn't judging."

"What would you call it then?"

"Someone has to question things. You accept everything, Ally. You want to find a cure too badly to say no, or at least take a step back."

"I don't think we should be taking any steps backward."

Matt sighed. "That's not what I meant, but okay. We've got other things to talk about."

"Like?"

"Well, I'm sorry, for one. I shouldn't have questioned you about where you were today."

An apology from Matt. I glanced down, wondering if the earth might just swallow me up. Nothing happened, but the garage floor did need sweeping.

"I took Kylie to meet my biological aunt today," I said, figuring it was best to be direct. "We got invited to come back next Sunday, and I think we're going to go. I didn't want to bring Kylie today, but the whole thing got away from me."

"Seriously? Oh, Ally. What are you getting into?"

"I had questions I wanted answered. I figured I had a right. I told Kylie she was a client."

Matt went quiet for a moment, and then said, "So you lied about it. That seems a lot bigger than my white lie."

"I did lie. I know that makes me a hypocrite. You don't have to say it."

"Okay, I won't then. But I don't have a good feeling about this. You don't know these people."

"I met with them once, and I'll probably see them one more time. I have a few more questions. After that, I won't go back again."

Matt threw me a skeptical glance. "Next Sunday is mine. I was hoping to get a start on that room. I'm not sure we should start trading days so much. It shouldn't work this way."

I thought for a moment before responding. *How should this all work, exactly?* He wanted family time just as I did. The thing was, our understanding of family had shifted. Kylie was his family, but where did that leave me? What happened when a man and woman, to borrow from Gwyneth Paltrow herself, "consciously uncoupled"? Could you be family one week and not family the next? That was the trauma of divorce. The forced reimagining of we to I. The thought was depressing.

"You just met them," Matt reiterated. "Maybe you should go slow?"

"I just want to get to know her a little," I said, fully aware of how defensive I sounded. "It's also important to gather any information she might have about hereditary illnesses. Who knows what kind of valuable information she might have? There isn't anything wrong with that."

"No, but I can't shake the feeling that your judgment's off."

"I don't think so. Will you give me Kylie for Sunday or not?"

"I don't think we should make too many changes to our agreement. It's unstable."

"I agree, but it's just this once. I thought we were supposed to leave room for flexibility."

"We should save that for emergency situations."

We sat there, fuming and rigid, neither of us having the least bit of interest in being flexible.

"That Dr. Indigo," said Matt, changing the subject. "Do you think she's helping?"

"Too early to tell, but if I had to say, I'd say . . . a strong maybe."

"Then I have a compromise," Matt said. "If I let you take Kylie on Sunday, then you don't give me a hard time about tagging along to Kylie's next appointment with this doctor."

"Tag along?" That made it sound lighthearted, not the tense show-down it was likely to be. "Why?"

"This woman is treating my daughter. And charging a crap ton of money to do so. I want to see what she's all about."

I couldn't argue with that one. "Okay," I said. "Fine."

Matt hopped off the bench and turned to me, nervously moving his hands from his hips to his sides to his pockets. "This thing with your mom, well, I know it's not necessary," he said. "I also know we don't need to be spending the money. I remembered how much Sophie needs a project, and I think it would be really good to do something produc-tive with Kylie. She's been through so much, with the . . . sickness, and . . . the divorce. She needs to work on something fun that doesn't have anything to do with the challenges she's facing."

I knew he was right, but I thought I detected a slight note of con-demnation in his comment. I fought my lesser self, but hell, when divorce cracks open a relationship, the stuff that oozes out usually isn't pretty.

"You aren't doing this just for Mom and Kylie," I said. "What is it you need? What are you looking for?"

Matt broke my gaze for a moment, silent, probably contemplat-ing whether or not he should tell me something personal. Our shared history won out, because he met my eyes again and said, "I've been a teacher for seventeen years. I still try, honestly I do, but I think careers age like people, and mine is having a midlife crisis. I'm a little restless, a little impatient. Since you left, I've been waiting for some other purpose to show itself. The other day, when I saw the lamp your mom was working on, well, I felt so useless. I don't know how to do things, to really do things that matter."

"You're a teacher. You've been responsible for educating thousands of kids. That definitely matters."

"I'm not saying it doesn't. I'm just saying . . . I need something more. And this might seem like a stupid thing, a small, meaningless thing, but it's one thing I know I need right now. I'll see this project start to finish. It'll be something real, something tangible. Does that make sense?"

His sincerity touched something inside me—a spot I thought had hardened, but turned out to have a soft center. "Okay. I get it."

Slowly, as though I was made of spun glass, he put one hand awkwardly on my shoulder. "Thanks," he said. He looked like he wanted to say more, to add something to the rare civil moment, but he didn't.

He also didn't move his hand until I slid off the bench and made my way back into the kitchen.

And I kind of didn't want him to.

~

Search: Cassie Flores

I had a case of internet paranoia. There is a small part in all of our brains that secretly suspects everyone else has some kind of magical power where they can immediately see who was stalking them on Facebook.

Cassie Flores seemed like just the kind of person to have that power.

I logged out and logged in as my mom. She hadn't used her Facebook account since 2014. One solo photo acted as both her profile pic and the entire content of her feed—a shot of Mom behind the bar at Stef's Tavern, dressed in a Santa hat and ugly Christmas sweater. Her features were blurred by the glare of the twinkling lights bouncing off the mirror behind her. She could be anyone.

I typed Cassie's name in the search bar again, this time with more confidence. There. Her profile showed an attractive brunette with her arms around a large, menacing Doberman, the kind of dog police use in movies when they are hunting someone down.

The cover shot behind her was of a random sunset on a random beach.

Didn't Matt say she had a kid?

I scrolled down a ways until I spotted him, a cute, skinny, bespectacled boy, shyly holding up a medal he won in a chess tournament. *Second place!* Cassie wrote. *Next time we go for the gold!*

Gut instinct? I did not like Cassie Flores.

My gut was often faulty, though, so I continued my cyberstalking. Cassie leaned left politically, a plus for Matt. She could water ski, kick box, and, like Jenn with two *n*'s, she was really into CrossFit.

Awesome.

We shared a handful of mutual friends, no one I was all that close with. We both belonged to an informal parents' group from our school district, so I went to that page and searched for her name.

Bingo. A post from earlier in the week.

District 168 Parents: Open School Board Position

Bree Nguyen: OMG—Rich Jenkins resigned from the school board! Don't know why—maybe a certain set of newborn twins has something to do with his decision (Ha—wish you the best, Rich and Kelly!!! XO!!!)? Anyhow, there's an emergency meeting a week from Sunday at 6pm, in the school gym, to discuss a special election, as the district bylaws state a position can't go empty for longer than sixty days. I'd consider it, but Bill would have me committed—Whitman is in soccer, Math Olympiad, and fencing. Bronwyn has Mandarin class, ballet, Poms, and meditation. My evenings are insane. How about you guys? Any takers?

Gloria Morales: Raine has gymnastics, improv class, Girl Scouts, and she's dead set on trying out for Iron Chef Kids. I'd like to, but no freaking way.

Hallie Oakland: I'm giving up volunteering. I mean it this time. Carbs too. And wine. Red meat. Maybe chocolate. Definitely sugar of all kinds . . . I plan on being in ketosis for the next fifty years . . .

Bree Nguyen: Oh, come on. Being on the school board is like being the wizard of Oz. You hold all the puppet strings!

Hallie Oakland: Actually, getting a position is more like being on an episode of *Naked and Afraid*. No, thank you. I'll be busy committing myself to a new low-carb, no sugar, no booze, meatless, joyless lifestyle. And the last thing I need is the whole district judging my life choices.

Gloria Morales: We have choices? I do not know of what you speak.

Cassie Flores: What's the actual time commitment?

Bree Nguyen: One evening a week, Sunday afternoons, and special sessions when needed.

Cassie Flores: Elliot has chess and Science Scholars, but I think I could fit it in. I'll be at the informational meeting.

Bree Nguyen: Yay! You are exactly who we need on the school board, Cassie.

People "liked" the heck out of Cassie's comment. Sixty-two people, to be exact.

I sincerely did like Rich Jenkins. During his time on the school board, he'd developed a new drop-off system for all the schools that resulted in way less mayhem and possible vehicular homicide. He'd also lobbied for an allergy table in the cafeteria, but to my frustration, he couldn't garner enough support. So, Cassie, a woman who likely valued her dog over her kid, was going to take his place?

No way.

I quickly logged out as my mother, logged in as myself, and started typing.

Ally Anderson: Your right, Bree. This is an important position. I'm interested, so I'll be at the meeting too!

And before I could hit the "Edit" button . . .

Cole Flounders: Not to be a grammar nerd, but it's "you're," Ally. You are. Not the possessive.

Bree Nguyen: Well, the more the merrier, I guess. And, Cole, "your" a total nerd, that's why we love you!

I didn't bother editing my comment. I already had two "Likes."

CHAPTER 7

When I got to the salon the next day, Heather was sitting in my chair, balancing her laptop on her knees. Jenn with two *n*'s stood behind her, pointing at the screen and shouting out directives.

"I know you took the photo here, but with the sink in the background, it looks like a bathroom shot. Bathroom pics are a hard no! The kind of men you want to meet will think you're loose, or worse . . . poor."

"I am poor," Heather said. "Relatively speaking."

"That information should remain private and confidential," Jenn said.

I dropped my bag off at the front desk and hustled over to them. Was Heather actually on a dating site? I checked for signs of the apocalypse. "What are you guys doing?" I tried, and failed miserably, to not sound excited.

"I want you to even out my haircut," Jenn with two *n*'s said. "The party was fun, but now it's back to business. I don't have an appointment, but you don't start officially working for forty-two minutes, which leaves us plenty of time."

This was not unexpected. And I wasn't exactly sure what kind of business she was referring to, but I also thought it was probably best I didn't know. Too interested in what Heather was doing to allow a stopover for irritation, I hunched down to get a better look at the laptop screen.

Cupidworks.com

Wasn't that the site Matt was on? And Cassie too? I tried not to think about that and read Heather's bio:

Heather, 39

Status: single

Occupation: hairdresser/stylist

Interests: traveling, watching Netflix, yoga

Looking for: single male, 35–55.

The photo she'd chosen was taken three years ago on a weekend trip to Michigan. It was slightly blurry because the photographer had a bit too much pinot grigio. I know because that photographer was me.

"Do I get an opinion on this?" I asked, working hard to keep my tone neutral. Heather, in the five years I'd known her, had barely dated, barely shown any interest in romance at all. What prompted the change?

"Yes," Heather said. "You just aren't allowed to laugh."

"I would never laugh. I might laugh at some of the guys who come up, though."

Jenn with two *n*'s snorted. "Slim pickings. I keep telling Heather she should go on Buzz. The men on that site are of a certain *quality*."

I wondered what that meant to a woman like Jenn. CrossFit trainer? Hedge-fund manager? I couldn't imagine Heather with either.

"Those Buzz guys look like they hired a team of professionals to style their photo shoots." Heather sighed. "I don't want someone high maintenance."

"You won't find any bathroom shots or dick pics on Buzz," Jenn said. "I promise you that."

I reread Heather's brief profile. It was generic, mild, and could have belonged to any woman. It wasn't likely to attract anyone worthy of my friend. Still, I knew this was fragile territory, and I didn't want to discourage her. "What kind of guy are you looking for?"

"Nice," Heather said without hesitation. "Employed. A grown-up man."

"*Boooring*," Jenn muttered under her breath.

"Any guy on this thing would be lucky to have you," I said, ignoring Jenn. "But I don't think this profile communicates how awesome you really are. Let's start with travel. Everyone uses that. People who haven't been farther than St. Louis in twenty years type *travel* in their profiles. It's supposed to make you sound worldly and interesting, when all it does is say you couldn't think of anything else to put."

Heather hung on my every word. She knew I'd met Matt online, and even though it wasn't working out, Matt wasn't a bad guy. Our first date was one of the best first dates I'd ever had—we had a picnic in the park and laughed about how we'd lived in the same town and never crossed paths. It seemed funny then, but now I realized that the older you get the more your life depends on the patterns you set—we make our lives small in search of safety and convenience, and only branch out when absolutely necessary.

"So let's get rid of travel," Heather said, poking at her keyboard.

"And watching Netflix," Jenn with two *n*'s contributed. "Because that is code for sexy-time stuff. You don't want to attract all the pervs."

"Matt and I used to watch Netflix all the time," I said. "We weren't having sex while we were watching *Stranger Things*."

"Maybe that was part of the problem," Jenn said, failing to keep the comment under her breath.

"Okay, I took out Netflix," Heather said. "Now, don't tell me there's something wrong with yoga."

I smiled at her. "There's nothing wrong with it. You've just never done it."

She reddened. "But I want to. I bought a yoga mat at Marshalls last year."

"I think it's a bad idea to lie," I said, thinking of Matt's request and my trip to Willow Falls. "What if some amazing guy contacts you, and he's really into yoga? It could happen, and how embarrassing would that be?"

Heather paused and then said, "Fine. Yoga's out. But then . . . I have nothing. I'm a blank slate. How can I have no interests at the age of thirty-nine? What's wrong with me?"

I grabbed the laptop from her. "Nothing's wrong with you. You're just not thinking about this in the right way. You've got to be creative to stand out. Work this thing like you would a resume. So, how would you describe how you spend your time outside of work?"

"Well . . . I hang out with you, or with my cousin Viv. I grocery shop. I read *Vanity Fair* and celebrity biographies, and I don't think I've ever missed an episode of *Jane the Virgin*." She thought for a moment. "Maybe leave that detail out."

"Good move," I said. "What else?"

"I drink coffee by the gallon. I'm pretty good at making a huge dinner on Sunday nights so I don't have to think about cooking throughout the week. I knit, and . . . oh God! When I really think about how I spend my time, I'm so boring I want to fall asleep sitting up."

"Because that's not how you really spend your time," I said. "Hold on." I typed while Jenn and Heather stared at me. "Okay, read this."

They scurried around my chair to peer over my shoulder.

Cupidworks.com

Heather, 39

Status: single, but hoping that's temporary

Occupation: hair expert/stylist/good with scissors

Interests: laughing, being a kick-ass friend, cooking for a crowd, drinking caffeinated beverages until my nervous system revolts, and sometimes, when I'm feeling like getting my craft on, I knit.

Looking for: I actually want a nice guy. I really do. Age-wise, somewhere in the middle of life, 35–55, old enough to have a little wisdom and young enough to have the energy to do something about it.

"Wow, you're good at this," Heather said.

"I like making people look their best." A thought hit me right then that almost had me sliding off the chair onto the floor—I would need these skills for myself soon enough if I wanted to date. I buried my panic at the thought and saved Heather's new profile. "We'll need a better picture. The library actually has great lighting. We can go there after work."

"Books," Jenn said. "That is so perfect! She'll look so smart."

"She *is* smart," I said, and Heather squeezed my shoulder.

I spent the next twenty minutes leveling off Jenn's bob, eliciting an almost compliment. ("Well, I guess it's even now.") After she left, I found Heather sitting in the back room, surrounded by all the boxes of hair dye, staring at her computer screen.

"I don't know if I can do this," she said, sounding drained.

"I've got to ask. Why are you doing it? You've never seemed very interested in anything like this."

Silence. And Heather was no good at silence. I sat there, waiting her out. Sure enough, after an awkward moment, she said, "Can I tell you something? It's not good, but I want you to remember how you've known me for five years and use that as evidence that I'm not a bad person."

"I would never think badly of you," I said, but I felt a heaviness in my chest, like whatever she was going to tell me was already pressing down, taking some of my breath.

"Well . . ." Heather paused. She looked at me, and her eyes welled up. "Right before I started working here, I'd just broken up with my boyfriend."

"I'm sorry," I said, because I didn't really know what else to say.

"I'm sorrier. He was married, Ally. I dated a married man."

"But you didn't know, right?" I knew that sounded judgy, but I knew Heather, and her morals had more fiber than one of Kylie's kale and pineapple smoothies.

"Not at first, no," she said. "When I found out, I was in too deep. It continued for years. Lying. Sneaking around. But the worst was when his wife eventually found out. She showed up at the salon where I was working, *with her kids in tow*. Six-year-old twins. She just lost her shidoodle, shouting at me, telling the kids that I wanted to take their daddy away . . . I'll never forget the look on their faces. It was awful. I felt like the worst person in the world."

"You made a mistake. *He* was the worst person in the world. Or at least in our town."

"The thing was, I really clicked with him. Like I never had with anyone else. I went on a few dates after we broke up, but I never felt like that with any of them, so I gave up. Pathetic, right?"

"Nope. Just human." I poked my head into the salon to make sure neither of us had a client waiting, and then poured us each a cup of the super fancy coffee the salon's owner, Teresa, had delivered every Friday. "So," I said, "why are you ready to get back out there?"

Heather thought for a moment. "I think it was visiting Micki that did it. You had no idea she was out there in the world, but there she was, so nice and so willing to meet you. It got me thinking—maybe there is someone out there who I'm supposed to meet."

"I think there is absolutely someone out there for you."

She gulped down the coffee, which I'm sure was scalding. "I'm scared, though. Like really, really scared of the process. When I get nervous, my stomach acts up. What if I meet someone and throw up all over him before we even start getting to know each other? What if he's a narcissist or worse? What if he's married?" She sunk into her dejection. "This is a bad idea. I'm not opposed to risk taking, but this seems more like running headlong into speeding traffic."

"To me it seems more like you want to keep punishing yourself for a mistake you made years ago."

Heather gave me a dirty look while I slid the laptop away from her and revved it up. "I can't totally hate you if you're right," she said. "That's so unfair."

"The only people who think life is fair are babies and priests." I started typing. "I have an idea. Why don't I sign up with you? We can sift through these singles together. We can *both* analyze profiles for mama's boys, narcissists, and potential psychopaths."

Heather brightened. "You would do that? Seriously? Are you sure? I mean . . . Matt."

"We're separated," I said, typing some more. "On our way to divorce. And who says I need to find another relationship right away? I can use this as practice for when I'm really looking." I ignored the small voice telling me what I was doing was some passive-aggressive way to hurt Matt for his interest in Cassie, not simply doing something nice for Heather.

"It would be awesome to do this together," she said. "Thank you. You're a good friend, Ally."

"Uh-huh." I finished and turned the laptop around so she could see.

Ally, 38

Status: single and spectacular

Occupation: hairstylist to the (local) stars

Interests: alternative medicine, solving puzzles, taking leaps into the unknown

Looking for: If you have no expectations, I'm your girl!

Heather laughed. "Seriously?"

"Why not? Let's see who crawls out of the woodwork."

"I guess anyone could be waiting," Heather said, with unmistakable notes of awe and terror in her voice. "Anyone at all."

Teresa poked her head in the back room to announce that Heather had a client. She passed the laptop off to me and scurried into the front of the salon.

It was still open to Cupidworks. I couldn't help myself. I searched until I found:

Matt, 40

Status: It's complicated. Unfortunately.

Occupation: political science teacher/nerd/NPR addict

Interests: being a good dad and staying grounded in
this crazy world!

Looking for: I'd prefer to focus on what I'm NOT looking
for—stress, drama, and angst!

Matt looked good in his photo. It must have been a holiday or
family event—he was wearing a bright-blue polo shirt, and he'd tamed
his hair. He held his arm in an odd position, and it took me a second
to realize why.

I'd been cut out of the picture.

CHAPTER 8

I was finishing up an elderly woman's perm (couldn't talk her out of it) when my phone squawked the refrain of Pink Floyd's "Another Brick in the Wall."

"Kylie's school!" I said, tossing a curler into a bin. "Gotta take this!"

Heart pounding, I snatched up my cell. "What's wrong?"

"Mrs. Anderson?"

I paused for a second. "Yes?"

"This is Principal Dunning."

"Yes?"

"This call is concerning Kylie."

No shit, I almost said, but my terror shoved sarcasm to the side. "Is she okay?"

"Yes. She's fine." He sighed. "There's been an incident, though, and I wonder if it would be possible for you to meet with me at two thirty today? Right before the end of the school day? Kylie said you work in town."

"She's okay?"

"As I said, yes. She's fine."

"I'm sorry. I just needed to hear you say it again." I took a breath, hoping to bring my blood pressure back to a normal range. "Can you tell me what this is about?"

"I'd rather address this in person."

Of course he would. "Okay, I'll be there."

~

When Kylie was four, Matt won the Teacher MVP of the Year Award at his school. Along with presenting him with an impressively large trophy, the school had paid for us to attend a Chicago Cubs game as VIPs. Our seats were right along the first-base line, close enough to the field to smell the players' sweat. The day was sunny and warm, the sky an electric blue over the friendly confines. Though she was on sensory overload, Kylie loved everything about being at the ballpark, and we loved watching her enjoy it. As the game approached the seventh inning, someone brought us free refreshments—an armload of hot dogs, chips, drinks, and . . . peanuts. Matt deftly moved them to the side before Kylie noticed the cheerfully striped bag. She'd gotten hives from eating peanuts the year before, and we avoided them as a precaution.

As the top of the inning came to a close, we stood for the seventh-inning stretch, when a local celebrity takes the mic from the announcers to belt out "Take Me Out to the Ballgame" to a park full of fans more than willing to sing along. We joined them, Kylie between us, Matt and I singing at the top of our lungs, laughing, happy to be there with each other and our baby, happy in our city, happy to be alive.

I didn't notice anything amiss when we retook our seats. The game resumed. It was close, the Cubs barely holding a lead against the Braves, a real nail-biter. Matt and I leaned forward, trying to give our boys a little mojo.

"Mommy," Kylie said, pulling at my shorts. "My tummy hurts."

I moved her onto my lap, figuring she'd stuffed her face with too many hot dogs. "You'll be okay," I assured her.

She fidgeted, so much so that I put her back in her seat. "Do you have to go potty?"

Kylie shook her head, and then brought her hands to her mouth, gripped her tongue, and started tugging.

"That's gross, sweetie," I said, gently drawing her small hands away. "You'll get germs."

She stilled for a few minutes.

And then projectile vomited on the retaining wall protecting the field.

"Shit!" Matt was on his feet, scrambling for napkins.

I knelt next to Kylie, placed a hand on her back, and started making circles. "It's okay," I murmured. "It's okay."

Unhappy with this turn of events, the people sitting next to us started to make some noise.

My daughter didn't make a sound. She wasn't crying.

Why wasn't she crying?

I lifted her face. Red hives streaked her cheeks. Her sweet lips were distorted, puffy, and swollen. Her eyes were round with fear. "Tight," she squeaked, clawing at her throat. "Hurts."

Matt was dumping water on the mess.

"Help!" The word came out strangled, my voice choked by adrenaline. Frantic, I grabbed Matt's leg. "Matt! She's having some kind of attack! Get help!"

Matt took one look at Kylie and leaped over the two people sitting next to us, his figure disappearing as he sprinted for an usher.

I'd never felt so helpless as I did in that moment. My heart jumped against my ribs. My limbs jerked with the need to physically do something to save my daughter.

Someone a few rows back yelled for me to sit my ass down.

I sank into my seat, cradling Kylie on my lap. She blinked up at me, pleading for help with her eyes. A blueish tint colored her lips. I could feel the energy she was exerting to simply breathe. The swelling worsened, her features forming a grotesque mask.

"Oh God!" I cried. "Please help my daughter! Please! Oh, please!" I didn't know who I was asking. I simply didn't know what else to do. Every cell in my body sounded the alarm—emergency!

"Help's coming, hon," a woman's voice said in my ear. "They've got doctors here. Don't you worry." Someone else slipped a jacket over our shoulders.

I saw Matt returning, and I burst into tears. Three men followed close behind, dressed in fire-engine-red shirts, one carrying a large case I fervently hoped contained something that would keep my girl alive.

Because at that moment, I knew where my baby was, on the thin edge between life and death.

They took her from me. Gave her an injection of something I'd never really heard of before—epinephrine.

I don't remember the trip to the ER. I know I was in the ambulance. I know they let me hold Kylie's hand.

We learned a lot that day. About peanut allergies and anaphylaxis. About carrying an EpiPen with us, always. About how fast a child can slip something in her mouth without anyone noticing.

We learned that being careful wasn't enough. We had to figure out a way to be more than careful. And even then . . .

Careful only works when life is predictable.

And we all know how often that happens.

~

Matt was already waiting outside the principal's office when I arrived at Kylie's school.

"Do you know what this is about?" he said the moment I walked up to him. I knew that look—irritation flaring to disguise worry.

"He wouldn't tell me, but the fact that he called both of us here isn't a good sign," I said, heart sinking. "But if she'd had a reaction, they would have told us."

"It's in her plan," Matt agreed. "We'd be informed right away."

"It's two thirty-four," I said, fidgeting. "I'll give him until two forty, and then I'm going in."

Matt smiled faintly. "Calm down, tigress."

"Why do people say 'calm down' when someone is obviously not capable of calming?"

"What am I supposed to say? Go ahead and lose your shit?"

"How about 'redirect your energy'?"

Matt smirked. "Is that the kind of advice Dr. Indigo rakes in the big bucks to dispense?"

Before I could come up with a retort, the principal's office door flew open, and the man himself strode out. He'd been the principal for a little under a year, so I'd only met him once before, and not for anything more than a handshake and a quick chat about Kylie's school allergy plan. He was a robust man, tall and big-bellied, and when he walked up to us, he immediately did what I'd seen countless large men do in Matt's presence—size him up to see who was taller.

Matt won by an inch.

I was glad, for my gut was telling me that we'd need a leg up.

"Hello, Mr. and Mrs. Anderson. I'm sure you're curious, so please, come in," he said, ushering us into an office that could double as a shoebox. We shuffled around to find space and, once seated, stared at each other for a moment. Principal Dunning seemed to be measuring what he had to say, looking for the lightest comment to lead with.

"Why are we here?" I said, impatience getting the best of me. "You said Kylie was fine, but there had been some kind of incident."

Principal Dunning's smile was brittle. "Yes, at lunchtime. In the cafeteria."

My heart seized. "What happened?"

Principal Dunning sighed. "Another child at Kylie's lunch table was teasing her. She questioned the legitimacy of Kylie's food allergy. This girl had a peanut butter cup in her lunch bag and offered it to Kylie, as a test."

"Kylie would never have eaten it," I said, struggling to contain my anger. "She knows better."

"Kylie didn't accept," Principal Dunning continued. "But when she refused, the other child unwrapped the candy and began to rub it on the table, making a circle around Kylie's things. At that point, Kylie ran to a lunch aide, who removed your daughter from the room."

"There is so much wrong with this," Matt said. "So much."

"The staff has washed down the area where Kylie was sitting. I've also talked to the parents of the other girl," Principal Dunning said, smiling as if that took care of the issue. "It won't happen again."

"You're damn right it won't," Matt said.

"In the past, I've asked for an allergy table during the lunch hour," I said, struggling to hold my temper. "I was denied. I don't see how you can say no after what's happened."

Principal Dunning ran a hand over his ruddy face. "I don't think isolation is the answer."

I curled my hands over the edge of his desk so I wouldn't clench my fists. "Kylie has friends who will sit with her. Friends whose parents are very careful about what they pack in their kids' lunches. It's not like she'll be sitting there alone."

"Our school is all-inclusive," Principal Dunning said. "I feel strongly about this. If some children are allowed to sit at what appears to be a special table . . . well, I think you can see my problem."

"I think a possible lawsuit is a much bigger problem," Matt muttered.

"These things tend to work themselves out," Principal Dunning said, trying to sound sage. "This girl and Kylie might be best of friends in a few weeks."

Matt stood to his full height. "I don't want that child anywhere near my daughter. Do you hear me? This situation could have easily become tragic. If you can't see that, then I need to carefully consider whether my daughter's needs are being met by this school."

Principal Dunning also stood, and extended his hand to Matt. "I'm sorry you feel that way. I take great pride in how our district serves our students' needs."

Reluctantly, Matt grabbed the principal's hand and shook it. I got a tight smile and a "Thank you for taking the time to come in." The bell rang, signaling the end of the day. We were dismissed.

~

Kylie looked confused for a moment when she spotted Matt and me waiting for her after school, but a huge grin overtook her face as soon as she processed what she was seeing, and she ran to hug us both.

"We heard about what happened at lunch," I said, hating to cut into her happiness with reality. "Are you okay?"

Kylie frowned. "*That's* why you're both here?"

"Principal Dunning called us," Matt said. He shot me a look. "He was concerned."

"It wasn't a big deal!" Kylie started walking toward the parking lot, and we scurried after her. "Why does everyone have to make this into such a thing? I'm *fine*. Totally, totally fine!" She stopped at the start of a long row of cars. "Who am I going home with? Which car should I be looking for?" Kylie's voice cracked, just before the tears started to flow. "I just want to go home. I don't care to which one."

Matt and I both reached for her at the same time, and we ended up locked in a semiawkward group hug, my soon-to-be ex and I bent over our little girl, trying to shelter her from the world.

CHAPTER 9

When your kid gets sick frequently, there is a built-in assumption that plans rarely work out. I hadn't fully invested in the idea of seeing the Patels again, because part of me expected Kylie to wake up with a sore throat or a headache or aching joints. Instead, she bounced onto my bed like a Super Ball of energy, like it was Christmas morning and she'd heard Santa rustling in the living room.

She half jumped on my head, but I would never, ever tell this girl to tone it down, especially with the week she'd had.

"Morning, sunshine," I mumbled. "What's up with you?"

"Fashion! What am I wearing to the bridal show?" she asked, cheeks flushed with what I hoped was just excitement.

"Uhhhh." I hadn't given much thought to the fashion part of this whole thing. "How about the dress you wore for picture day?"

Kylie scrunched her nose. "Lola said stripes are totally not what people are wearing."

"Lola, huh?"

She blushed. "Some of the other girls said the same thing. Stripes are lame. Can't I wear something else?"

I'd spent fifty bucks on that dress, and I hadn't done laundry all week. The striped dress was going to have to work. Lola could stick it. "What if we paired it with some gray tights?"

"Maybe," Kylie said, using the same tone I did when I didn't want to say no at the moment, but planned to later. "I thought . . . can I get one of those dresses like Radha was wearing?"

"You want a sari?"

"Well . . . yeah. I thought maybe we could find one at Target this morning. If they don't cost a bunch of money."

"It's not the money, babe." I thought for a moment. How do you explain something like cultural appropriation to a ten-year-old? Did I even need to? I wasn't sure if there was anything wrong with her desire. Or Radha's, for that matter. Maybe I should ask Sandeep directly?

"Saris are special dresses that women wear in India. Sadly, I don't think Target carries them."

"Maybe your friend will make one for me."

"We'll see."

She knew what *we'll see* meant. It was right next door to *maybe*.

Still, she scooched next to me and lay her head on my shoulder. "Does Radha get to wear one because she's going to be Sandeep's daughter?"

"I think Radha chooses to wear one because she wants to celebrate Sandeep's heritage."

"But she told me that if she gets adopted, then she'll be Indian. Then she can wear a sari anytime she wants, and it will be okay, right?"

Wow. Being in a profession that requires me to talk to people all day long, I didn't think someone could stump me conversationally. "Well . . . ," I said, because I had no idea how to address something so complicated. "Radha is African American. Sandeep is Indian. Micki is Italian, I think. Radha will have a *lot* to celebrate when she gets adopted."

"They'll be a new family."

"Yes," I said. "They will."

"That's nice," Kylie said, snuggling into me even more. "When it happens, I hope we can celebrate with them."

"Maybe . . ."

Kylie sat upright. "Why maybe? I like Radha. I want to be friends with her for a long time. I can, right?"

I had a choice. I could further bury the truth under an ever-growing lie, or I could uncover it before the weight crushed not only the truth but also the trust my daughter placed in me. "Honey, it's just a little complicated. You know that DNA test we did? Well, it tells you about your relatives who've taken the test."

"Living ones?" Kylie asked.

"Uh-huh. Micki is the sister of the lady who gave me up for adoption. I'm sorry I didn't tell you the truth about that, but I didn't know what kind of person she'd be, and I was trying to protect you. I don't like to lie, and I shouldn't have done it."

Kylie grinned. "So, she's, like, related to us?"

"She is."

"So that means Radha will be too."

"I . . . guess."

"That is so cool. Did you tell Grandma?" Kylie's smile dimmed before I could answer. "You didn't. You didn't want to hurt her feelings."

"You are a smart girl. I never want to make Grandma sad, and I think she would be, if she knew."

"Maybe Grandma can get to know Micki and Sandy and Radha. Then she'd like them, and it wouldn't be a problem."

"Sweetie, *we* don't know Micki and her family. We only met them once."

"I know right away when I like people or not. And I like them. Grandma will too."

"That might be true, but let's keep it quiet for now, okay?"

"Okay," she said, and then, with the incredible talent kids have for compartmentalization, she packed up that topic and skipped to the next. "So today I'll wear the striped dress," she announced, "but only with the gray tights. And I want to wear your necklace, the one with all the colored beads. I can make it work."

"Yes," I said, hugging her to me, "you can."

She hugged me back, and I grabbed at this moment of peace, shoving aside my anxieties, turning my back on my fears. We held each other, mother and daughter, barely moving, just drawing our breath in and out, in and out. For this snippet of a Sunday morning, we lived entirely, and gloriously, in the moment.

Until the scent of bacon (turkey, uncured, nitrite-free) wafted through the air.

Kylie's head popped up. "Grandma's cooking breakfast!"

"Go get some before she eats it all!"

She dashed out of the room, and I took a few more minutes to myself, lost to my thoughts. If I was being honest with myself, I *was* looking forward to Micki's fashion show, probably more than I'd looked forward to anything in a long time. It could be the last time I had contact with her . . . or not. The possibilities were like branches on the Past Is a Present family tree, reaching out in all kinds of directions. I knew I could control which path I took, so the image cheered me, and I needed cheering. I'd spent the night tossing and turning over the meeting with Principal Dunning. Why hadn't I been more forceful? I should have walked out of there with his commitment to an allergy table.

I thought of a child drawing a peanut butter circle of death around my baby, and knew I had to do something.

The school board. The only way to fight power was with power. I had to run.

And I had to win.

⁓

Kylie had eaten a plateful (yay!) and scurried off to take a shower. My mom and I were loading the dishwasher together.

"Where are you off to today?" she asked.

"Hanging out with a friend."

"Heather?"

"Yep," I said. Even though that was technically true, I glanced away when I felt the blood rush to my cheeks. "So, why did you decide to get so friendly with Matt?"

Mom stiffened. Then she looked at me with her all-knowing bartender eyes, capable of performing an MRI on my heart. I hoped she couldn't pinpoint the guilt in mine, but it seemed I didn't have to worry. To my surprise, I sensed something clearly in hers, something she usually hid—fear.

"If I had to making a shopping list for life," she said, "I know what I'd write at the top—family. It's the most important thing. I was thinking about how I've been treating Matt, and I think I was wrong to shut him out. You chose him to be your family, and so you chose to make him my family too. I'm starting to acknowledge the pain of it all breaking apart. Then I figured, if it's painful for me, it must be hell for you. I let my anger get in the way of seeing that, and I'm sorry."

It felt good to be understood, but I still didn't understand *her* completely. Was she saying she wanted Matt and me to get back together? That we should stay together because family was more important than our problems and resentments and hurt?

"I don't know, Mom. It's all still pretty confusing."

"Sometimes having something real to work on can make things pretty clear. If you get a chance, spend some time with us working on Kylie's room. Maybe if you work toward a common goal, it might give you a model for solving your other problems."

It was practical advice. Sound and solid. I should have been grateful for it.

So why did I desperately want her to grab me like Micki had, to wrap me in a hug so fierce I felt breathless?

Guilt didn't just tap my shoulder, it shoved at me, hard and demanding attention. "I'll try to make the time to help, but could you keep an eye on Kylie when she's messing around with paints and power tools? The last thing we need is more doctors' bills."

~

The main street of Willow Falls was closed to traffic—sawhorses blocked the road, and an enormous, leafy sign hung overhead, proclaiming the town's fall festival. It was so picturesque I couldn't get annoyed at having to circle the crowded side streets, searching for somewhere to park.

"This place can't get any better," Heather said. "It's the freaking *Gilmore Girls* set. Why don't we live here?"

"We haven't got enough money to live here," I said as I pulled into a narrow spot a few blocks from Micki's shop. "But yeah, everything here is too cute, even the parking meters." The meters were each colorfully painted with a different design and yoked with a sign that boasted the grade school classroom responsible for the artwork.

"I can't even make fun of that," Heather said. "It's just too adorable."

"I really, really like it here," Kylie contributed. Her large eyes were even rounder than usual, trying to take everything in.

Excited, we walked quickly in the direction of the bridal shop, oohing and aahing over the sidewalk displays, food trucks, and giant pumpkins, which only seemed to get larger the closer we got to Micki's. The two in front of The Not-So-Blushing-Bride could have featured in a Grimm's fairy tale. Bright orange and bulging, with healthy stems curling upward, they flanked a long runway skirted in deep-green fabric. A small crowd had already gathered, clustered around a tent that housed a flurry of activity. Radha, dressed in a black turtleneck topped by a burnt-orange and burgundy sari, stood outside, holding up the tent's flap and motioning for us to come inside.

"We need help," she screeched when she spotted us. "Quick!"

Having done hair at countless weddings, fashion shows, and high school senior photo shoots, Heather and I were well versed in the particular kind of drama associated with women on the verge of being looked at by a lot of people. Still, when we entered the tent, the whipped-up energy nearly knocked us over.

There were middle-aged to elderly women, all shapes and sizes, in wedding dresses—some poofy, some not, some bedazzled, some not, some meant only for a reality TV show, some draping off aging bodies with such elegance and grace, the simple beauty of it almost brought a tear to my very jaded eye.

A single mirror hung over a table covered with every type of makeup and hair product on the market. As the ladies jostled for position, the mirror swung to and fro, hitting one woman in the face while she tried to apply lipstick. Another woman decided to spray her hair and created a toxic cloud of fumes. The close quarters meant that every bridal train attached to a dress was getting stepped on, which meant half the women were regularly stumbling forward.

In the corner, Bernie stood talking to another woman, wearing a mermaid-skirted dress more appropriate for a twentysomething, and yet the form-fitting style suited her. The woman she was talking to, buxom and gesturing wildly, was wearing a push-everything-up bustier over a long skirt. She was younger than Bernie by about thirty years, which put her at about sixty.

"This is awesome," Heather said.

"It isn't awesome at all," Radha whined. "No one is ready, and we're scheduled to start in fifteen minutes. Can you guys help with hair and makeup?"

After finding Kylie a place to sit, I picked up a brush and got to work. I teased and French-twisted, and, in the case of one woman with waist-length gray hair, I fashioned two braids I curled around her head, Princess Leia–style. She loved it.

"Me next," Bernie shouted from across the room.

"Over here," I said. "In front of the mirror."

She shook her head and motioned toward her legs, encased in the dress. "I can't really move all that easily."

I wove my way toward her. "How are you going to walk down the runway?" I said in her ear.

"I don't know," she said, seemingly unworried. "I do know this dress is perfect. I've found it, and I'm not getting out of it."

"I think it might be permanently adhered to your skin." I gently brushed her cap of silver hair and smoothed down stray pieces. She wore the lipstick Radha had picked out. I plucked a brown eyeliner from my purse and drew her some brows.

"You look gorgeous," I said sincerely. "Very Audrey Hepburn."

Bernie frowned. "I have a better nose than her."

I stifled a laugh. "Will Reggie be here? You don't want him to see the dress before the wedding, do you?"

"Reggie is in London." She sniffed. "There are more important things in the world to do than come to a small-town fashion show."

"Well, I can't think of anything better than being here right now," I said. "But, I haven't seen Micki yet. Where is she?"

Bernie smiled in a way that could only be described as wicked. "You'll see," she said.

Heather and I primped and glossed, shaded and contoured, until every woman was ready to be scrutinized by the citizens of Willow Falls. "It's Raining Men" started playing in all of its bouncy, '80s-inspired glory.

"Oh, for the love of all that is holy," Heather said. "I live for over-the-top shit like this."

"Auntie Heather," Kylie admonished.

"I meant stuff! I misspoke!"

Kylie smirked. "Uh-huh."

We took our places facing the end of the runway. The crowd had swelled, and people pressed forward to make room for newcomers. I positioned Kylie in front of me, my hands protectively on her shoulders. The music turned up a notch, and the first bride sashayed toward us—the gray-haired Princess Leia wannabe. Her dress looked appropriately futuristic.

Radha's voice rang out over the murmuring crowd. "Helen is wearing a modern dress by Micki's Originals, perfect for a second—or third or fourth!—wedding! The drape is . . . uh . . . drapey, and the length . . . goes to the floor. Floor-length! Yeah!"

Princess Leia winked at me, then her elbow shot out, hand on hip, as she struck the posiest pose better than any supermodel.

"Oh, she's *good*," Heather said. "It's all about the attitude."

"So cool," Kylie agreed.

The next one was the bustier-clad woman I'd seen speaking to Bernie earlier. She bounded down the runway, barely contained in her dress, grinning and waving to countless people in the delighted audience. Buxom Bride was popular.

"I'm worried," I muttered. "Think that fabric is going to hold?"

"I certainly hope not," Heather said.

The bride blew kisses to the crowd. She got lipstick on her hand.

"So . . . Leticia is wearing a dress by Beautiful Bridals," Radha said, sounding a little unsure of herself. She dropped the mic, swore, then plucked it off the ground. "Uh . . ."

I scanned the scene. Where was Micki? Where was Sandy?

Radha cleared her throat. "Okay . . . um . . . the boob part of the dress is covered in Swarovski crystals. There's . . . a lot of them on there."

The crowd laughed. With one final wave, Leticia sashayed back into the tent.

Three beautifully dressed middle-aged brides followed, their movements narrated by Radha. She continued to struggle, but managed to keep going, her voice losing its nervous shake by the third bride.

Way to go, I silently encouraged her.

"And now," she said, "we have beautiful Bernie in a mermaid dress designed by Micki herself. She put panels in it to . . . you know, suck everything in . . . not that Bernie needs it . . . not that anyone needs it. You know what I mean."

Everyone's attention shifted to the start of the runway.

No Bernie.

"This dress will . . . uh . . . make everyone jealous if you wear it. I mean, you'll look so good everyone will want to kill you. Wait, that's not what I meant!" Radha caught my eye, everything about her look saying, *help!*

Heather craned her neck. "What happened to Bernie? Do you think she's okay?"

"Let's go see," I said, already heading toward the tent. Radha droned on about the importance of smooth lines, and again I gave her credit for doing so well under pressure. The crowd already showed signs of impatience, though, and I wondered how long they would last before getting distracted by the fair's other delights.

Inside the tent, the group of brides circled Bernie, who looked miserable.

I swam through the sea of taffeta and silk until I hovered over her. "What's wrong?"

"It's too snug," she snapped. "I can't move."

"Really?"

Bernie shuffled a few inches toward me, the mermaid skirt hugging her legs so much she could only move an inch or two at a time. "See?" she said.

Heather was at my elbow. "Maybe we could cut a bigger slit in the skirt?"

115

"No!" Bernie said. "Micki would be despondent."

"We're going to take a short intermission," I heard Radha say. "Really short. Don't go anywhere!"

Radha poked her head into the tent. "Do something!"

Kylie tugged on my sweater. "Mom, help her!"

I thought for a moment, then grabbed two wedding dresses from the rack and shoved one at Heather. "Change."

"What?"

"Just do it. We're going to hold her up. Once down the runway, once up, and we're good. Kylie, take my phone and get some pictures."

Modesty out the window, I tore off my sweater, skirt, and tights and squeezed into what was actually a really simple, elegant Meghan Markle–style gown. Heather's was a nightmare—huge pleats on the waistline gave the illusion of a not-so-hidden pregnancy.

"You gave yourself the good one." She laughed. "But let's go strike a pose."

Heather took one of Bernie's arms and I the other, and we lifted her onto the mouth of the runway. She was surprisingly light, her bones feeling fragile under my hands.

"Don't let go," she whispered.

Radha noticed we were ready. "Surprise! We have three brides instead of just one. We are *so* lucky!"

Someone changed the music over to a Sinatra song.

Ever so gently, Heather and I lifted Bernie an inch off the ground. We walked swiftly, eyes forward, and I hoped no one could see my scuffed green suede boots underneath my skirt. Radha prattled on about our dresses, and we showed off Bernie as best we could.

"Turn me around once so everyone can see the train," Bernie muttered through her smile.

Panicked, I locked eyes with Heather.

No way, she mouthed.

"Do it," Bernie insisted.

"Move clockwise," I hissed.

Slowly, so, so slowly, we turned Bernie 360 degrees, giving everyone a good look at her tiny, ancient, satin-encased bum. Then we started the long walk back to the tent. My grip began to slide down Bernie's arm, so I slid my other hand around her waist, tugging a bit on the silky fabric.

"Ally?" Heather tilted her head toward Bernie's chest. "Wardrobe malfunction!"

The front of the dress dipped low, so low that . . .

A ninety-year-old nipple peeked out above the neckline.

Shock froze my reaction time. A young mother in the front row gasped and covered her son's eyes.

Bernie began to laugh, a cackle that turned into a roar as Heather and I struggled to cover her wrinkled bosom. People started to clap, the applause growing thunderous as we quickly escorted her back into the tent.

We lowered Bernie to the ground. My arms ached—I could hold a hair dryer up for eight hours, but a couple of minutes hoisting Bernie had pulled at my rotator cuff.

"Our little exhibitionist," Heather said, grinning. "What would Reggie say if he saw that?"

"Reggie would have loved it," Bernie said. She contorted her body, trying to escape the dress. "Now I need someone to unzip me before I crack a rib."

"I know you want to look beautiful for your wedding, but maybe this isn't quite the right dress for you," I said as I complied.

"Beauty is pain," Bernie said, shrugging. "It's going into the maybe pile."

"And now for the grand finale," Radha yelled outside. "You're gonna want to see this."

Heather and I dashed outside, holding our dresses above our ankles as we ran.

The crowd, probably still riled up from Bernie's nip slip, surged forward, excited.

The music screeched on again, abruptly switching from Sinatra to the theme from *The Walking Dead*.

The doors to The Not-So-Blushing-Bride opened slowly to reveal a zombie bride and groom—gray skin, tattered clothes, blood spilling out the side of their mouths. They held hands, lurching forward as the hushed crowd parted to let them through. The zombie groom boosted the zombie bride onto the runway, and then hopped on himself. The ghoulish couple lurched around the stage for a moment, and then shoved their hands into hidden pockets, drawing out candy that they threw to the cheering crowd.

It was in that moment that I fell in love with Micki and Sandeep Patel, and their almost-daughter Radha.

The spooky music changed again, to something with a strong beat.

Radha began to rap. Badly but in earnest. "Just because you aren't in your twenties, doesn't mean you can't be funky. Brides come in all ages and sizes, and we're still all prizes. Want a dress that's a source of pride? Come shop at The Not-So-Blushing-Bride!"

~

"This is tandoori chicken, and this is a lamb dish . . . What is it called, Dad?"

Sandy's grin still showed traces of zombie blood. "Rogan josh."

"Oh yeah." Radha doled out a healthy portion on everyone's plate. "I forgot about that one."

We sat crowded together on the only sofas that weren't covered in discarded dresses, accessories, and low-heeled wedding shoes. Micki and Sandy had mostly cleaned themselves up, and Bernie had changed into a cardigan and polyester pants. She picked at the aromatic Indian food, taking infrequent nibbles.

"You can eat with your hands, if you want," Radha lectured her. "Try to use your right hand. That's how it's done in India."

Sandeep beamed at her, but there was something sad in his smile. Bernie scrunched her nose up at the thought of not using silverware.

"Can I eat with my hands, Mom?" Kylie had already dipped her index finger into the beef stew I'd brought for her, warmed in Micki's microwave. She was used to bringing her own food to events, but it was sometimes hard not to feel a little left out. Which is why I was going to let her eat something so messy without a fork.

"Wash your hands first, but yes, you can."

As I watched Kylie weave her way between racks of wedding dresses, I thought about Radha's deep interest in her foster father's heritage. I wasn't sure how I felt about it. In one way, Radha's desire to be fully part of the Patel family was sweet and loving, and proof of how well they treated her. But then, Radha's African American heritage should also be a source of pride for her. I wondered if she'd reached a level of maturity where she could balance both. I definitely wouldn't have been able to at sixteen.

Radha's deep desire to connect with her potentially adoptive parents contrasted with my ambivalence. Micki and Sandy seemed so nice and sincere. Still, I wasn't sure what I wanted from them beyond information, or what they wanted from me. Was simply making the connection enough for either of us? I thought about my mom. The deeper I went into a relationship with Micki, the more I risked hurting her.

"I shouldn't be eating carbs," Micki said as she squeezed next to me on the sofa. She held a glass of white wine in one hand and a chunk of naan in the other. "They don't agree with my system." She continued talking while chewing on the garlicky naan. "How can I say no to something that tastes so good? We only have one life, right?"

"I dream about carbs. My daughter is gluten-free," I explained. "But I make cookies and pizza crust with special flour."

"And that peanut allergy. That's got to be hard. When I was a kid we lived on peanut butter and Wonder Bread sandwiches."

Kylie was deep in conversation with Radha. Everyone else was similarly distracted, so I took my opening. "So no one in your family was allergic?"

She shrugged. "I don't really know. We were a family, but . . . we weren't, if you know what I mean. Some of us had sensitive stomachs—my sister for one—but that could have been caused by a lot of different things."

"You said she was sick a lot. With what?"

"If there was a cold going around, Cissy caught it. She was always cold. Her joints hurt, but that could have been early arthritis. She didn't take good care of herself, which could have been the root of all her problems. I don't know what else to tell you."

"You told me what I didn't already know, so that's valuable."

"You've got your problems, hon, but I sense you know how to play the hand you were dealt. Strong people always find a way to make the most of the life they've been given."

"I guess. I don't know if I see it that way. I just do what I have to do."

She laughed. "What do you think that is? Lots of people do anything but what they have to do."

Micki set her wine down so she could squeeze my hand. Hers was cold from holding the glass, but her warmth came through anyway. "You're a good person. And a good mom," she said. "I like that."

Emotion pushed up my throat, and this question popped out, "Can you please tell me more about my mom?"

Micki's eyes clouded over. "She . . . I can't say she tried her best. She didn't. But I don't think she knew how. At least that's how I decided I would forgive her. The kindest thing she ever did was give you away. It hurts to admit that, but it's true. My heart broke when it happened, but it was good for you, at least I think so. You love your mom, right?"

"Yes. Very much."

Micki nodded. "And she loves you. An unhappy woman wouldn't raise someone as nice as you."

"That's sweet, but you don't know me yet," I said, gently. "I have my faults."

"I'm not talking faults, honey. I'm talking about heart. And you've got it. I'm sure you've got faults. Who doesn't?"

I wanted to ask her questions until I'd scoured her brain for every detail, but there was a sharp rap on the door, and a red-haired, barrel-chested police officer bounded in. He looked around the room, and discomfort immediately showed on his ruddy face.

"I'm kind of the proverbial bull in the china shop here," he said.

"We're durable," Micki said, laughing. "Are you looking for something in a nice chiffon?"

"I'm sure your chiffon would be nice, Micki," the officer said, "but I'm here in an official capacity. There's been a complaint lodged against you and the shop."

"Complaint?" Sandy said. "Who would complain about us?"

"Well," the officer said, reddening. "It's a complaint of public indecency."

"It was just a nipple," Heather said. "The human body is a beautiful thing."

"That it is," the officer said. "But it needs to be covered on Main Street, or the fine folks of Willow Falls will be rioting. In a polite manner, of course."

Bernie stood. She looked impossibly tiny. "It was my nipple, officer," she said.

This was not what he was expecting. His eyes automatically went to Bernie's chest, and then just as quickly he averted his gaze. "I'm assuming it was accidental?"

"It was my fault," I interjected. "I was trying to hold her arm, and I yanked on the fabric of her dress."

"Ah," he said. "So it wasn't premeditated?"

"No," Bernie said, "but it sure was fun!"

The officer took an envelope from his pocket and handed it to Micki. "Fun isn't against the law, at least last I checked. You folks enjoy your meal. Fully clothed, of course."

"We'll try," Micki said. After he left, she took the envelope he gave her and put it in the cash register. "It's the final payment for his fiancée's dress. I designed it myself."

"I'd like to see it," I said.

Micki grinned. "I was hoping you'd say that. Come on, it's in the back."

We left the others chatting away and eating food with their hands.

~

"It's beyond gorgeous," I gasped. It really was. The lines were simple—a sheath dress with a plunging neckline—but the subtle additions, embroidered flowers on the skirt and a deep-green velvet sash at the waist, gave it a uniquely personal quality.

Micki seemed embarrassed. "She's a gardener. I wanted to bring her life into the dress. I try to do that. I know it makes me sound . . . What's the word? Pretentious."

"Not at all. You're an artist! And what a wonderful thing to make a bride feel so beautiful on her wedding day."

"Every bride is beautiful on her wedding day. It's my job to make sure everyone notices."

Impulsively, I reached out and gave her a side hug. "I love that. I wish I had you around when I got married. My cousin spilled red wine on my dress before the ceremony even began. I guess it was kind of an omen."

Micki squeezed me back. "You never mentioned a husband. I didn't want to pry, but I wondered."

"We're separated. Things just got . . . hard."

"Things always get hard. If you're with the right person, you join hands and climb the mountain together. If you aren't, well, the hard thing gets even harder and then everything's so brittle it just cracks."

Brittle. That could definitely describe Matt and me. I always thought we'd had something like Micki and Sandy, but when it came down to it, we were tested and didn't make the cut. "Sandy is the right person for you," I said with a sigh. "I can tell."

She laughed. "Sandy's not my first try at this. He's just the one I got right. And I did try with the others."

"Others?"

"Two others. And don't say the third time's the charm—as far as I'm concerned, Sandy is the first. The first time I've had unconditional love, anyway."

I felt like I should say something, defend Matt. We did love each other unconditionally. How could that have not been enough? It hadn't been. Love can be free of conditions but still have limits. And we ran smack up into the wall of ours.

"You look so sad," Micki said.

"I think that's my default look," I said. "Instead of resting bitch face, I have resting depressed face."

"Well," Micki said as she led me out of the storeroom, "at least now when you feel overcome, you can bring up the image of our gal Bernie flashing the Sunday afternoon crowd at the fall festival. Free the nipple!"

CHAPTER 10

Kylie—Your Past Is a Present!

Report 23: Based on your DNA, you're more likely to
be a long-distance runner, not a sprinter.

"You're being weird," Heather said. "Just sitting in a car in the grade
school parking lot like some creepo."

"I'm sitting with you, so I can't be creepy. Creepers always act
alone."

"The Manson family didn't."

I gave Heather a look. "I can't decide if I want to go inside. There
are pros and cons. Lots and lots of cons."

"I don't understand why you're doing this. You have zero time for
yourself. Why spend it with a bunch of uptight school board prisses?"

I hadn't told Heather about the cafeteria incident for fear she'd hunt
down the offender and stuff peanut butter cups up her nostrils. I turned
around to make sure Kylie was asleep. She was still dozing, clutching
Sandy's zombie teeth in one hand, like a ghoulish stuffed animal. "There

was an . . . incident at the school. A kid teased Kylie about her peanut allergy."

"Teased? How so?"

"She drew around Kylie's place in the cafeteria with a peanut butter cup."

Heather went deathly quiet for a moment. When she spoke, there was a murderous edge to her voice. "And you think you can stop something like that from happening again if you're on the school board?"

"I don't know. I think so."

"Then what the hell are you doing out here?"

Another good question. Why was I sitting outside of Kylie's elementary school, unable to either go in or get out of the car? It was 6:10. We were late, though we'd hauled ass from Willow Falls to arrive on time. I needed to get inside, pronto, but still, I didn't move.

I wanted to be on the school board. I really did. I'd have a say in policies and procedures in a school system Kylie would be in for years, policies designed to protect the rights of those who needed protection. I had experience with kids who needed accommodations, and I always looked out for the underdog anyway. Because I was the underdog. Which was why I couldn't get out of the car.

I went to beauty school instead of college. I didn't have anything close to a fancy law degree like Cassie Flores, or even a four-year degree like most of the other women. I'd worked in the same salon for fifteen years. I was an (almost) divorced woman, camping out in her childhood home, for heaven's sake. Could I go in there and present myself with pride? I'd need to if I was going to compete with the likes of Cassie.

"Tell me one thing," Heather said. "How could you stop something like that from happening again if you got voted into this school board thing?"

"You know the allergy table in the lunchroom I was telling you about? That would change Kylie's life. The school doesn't think it's a good idea because it implies favoritism. They offered to put Kylie in an empty classroom as an alternative. She'd be eating alone every day. *Alone.* If I was on the board, I could push for the change."

Heather touched my arm. "If that's true, then I'm going to ask you again. What are you doing sitting in this car?"

"I need . . ." I swallowed down the sudden lump in my throat. "I need you to tell me one reason I deserve to walk in there."

"Oh, Ally." Heather turned off the ignition. "You are the most good-intentioned person I know."

"Isn't the road to hell paved with good intentions?"

"No, the road to *change* is. Good intentions become good actions with people like you. Now go. I'll sit here with Kylie, and if she wakes up, I'll take her to the park."

I took a deep breath, then flipped down the mirror to check my teeth for stray bits of food.

"*Go,*" Heather said, nudging me. "You are just as good as they are. Probably better. Stop limiting yourself."

"Everyone has limits," I said. "People get in trouble when they forget that."

"Since when are you such a cynic?"

"Since my kid got sick." I said it too sharply. Heather went quiet.

"Sorry," I muttered.

We watched some stylishly dressed women approach the school's gymnasium entrance.

"They're late too," Heather said. "Run to catch up. If you walk in with them, no one will notice. Go!"

I ran for it, just making it to the door as it was closing behind the women. They didn't pay much attention to me, and I swooped into the room, riding the coattails of their energy.

A group of about thirty people sat on folding chairs inside the cavernous gym. The clean, fresh scent of expensive perfume did not quite mask the aroma of kid BO and industrial cleaner permeating the place. Current board members, including Rich Jenkins, sat behind a long table. His slumped posture and darkly circled eyes gave the appearance of a man trampled by exhaustion.

"We should get started," said a woman wearing a baseball cap and a sweatshirt that had *Sundays are my Fundays* written on it. Maybe this wouldn't be too bad.

A woman bounced out of her seat. I recognized her from the Facebook group—Bree Nguyen. "Cassie isn't here yet. Let's give her a few minutes." The cluster of women surrounding her nodded enthusiastically in agreement.

Baseball cap lady wasn't having it. "We're already fifteen minutes behind. I've got to help my kid with his biology homework when I get home. Cassie can catch up when she gets here."

Bree was undeterred. "But, I really think . . . oh, here she is! Forget it!"

Everyone's attention shifted to the door. Cassie, dressed in a dove-gray suit and black heels, strode into the room with . . . her dog. Her sleek, humorless, rather dangerous-looking beast. Was that even allowed?

She gave Bree a little wave and settled into a folding chair up front, angling it to give her dog room and to give herself a slight advantage—she now sat between the audience and the school board, as if she was just inches from joining them. Rich eyed the Doberman warily.

Did she bring it everywhere with her, like the Louis Vuitton bag on her lap? That wasn't going to fly if Matt was going to date her. Kylie's reaction to dogs was mild . . . so far. But who knew when her immune system would go into overdrive? What if he licked her and she hived up . . . or worse? Maybe I should calmly talk to Matt and explain why it just wasn't practical to date Cassie.

Cassie slipped her phone out of her purse and turned off the ringer. She ran her hand inside her bag, and then, giving up on what she was searching for, tugged at the zipper, which stuck a bit. Confident Cassie was fidgeting.

After finally getting the zipper to slide, she shoved her purse under her feet, and placed a hand on her dog's flank, as if to calm him.

Or . . . to calm herself.

Ohh, I thought. *I am a terrible person.* That dog was probably a therapy animal! I'd read about them online—dogs trained to help people suffering from anxiety, depression, and PTSD. I looked at Cassie Flores, in all her glossy perfection, with different eyes. What was she suffering from? Bringing her therapy dog with her was putting it out in the open that she needed help. It was brave. And I was an ass for judging her.

"Well," baseball cap lady said. "I'm calling this meeting to order. Can I get an aye?"

The glum-faced members of the school board murmured their response.

Baseball cap lady welcomed everyone and said her name was Vera. "First topic of discussion: the vacancy being left by Rich Jenkins."

Rich smiled weakly.

Vera clapped her hands once. "Let's get a sense of who wants it, and then we'll figure out an election timetable. This position is up for a public vote." She smirked. "There's no way around that, unfortunately."

"I nominate Cassie," Bree shouted.

"Nominations aren't necessary," Vera snapped. "Cassie can throw her name in if she wants."

"I do, then," Cassie said. Her voice poured out of her like honeyed bourbon. "I've got significant leadership experience, and as a litigator, I excel in public speaking."

"You can save the resume for the election, Cass," Vera said briskly. "Your name is noted. Anyone else?"

I opened my mouth and immediately closed it. How in the world could I compete with a stunningly attractive, intensely intelligent lawyer who wasn't afraid to be vulnerable in public?

"I'm in," said a male voice from the back of the room.

Thirty heads whipped around in his direction.

"Oh, you certainly *are*," whispered the woman next to me.

He was what could only be described as dreamy. Imagine James Taylor in his sexy *Sweet Baby James* phase, all decked out in Timberlands, L.L. Bean flannel, and Warby Parker eyeglasses. A smidge of silver gleamed in his beard, just enough to make him human. The retro glasses slid a bit down his beautiful nose, and if he turned around, I'm sure his jean-clad butt would give Springsteen's a run for his money.

If the women in this room were doing the voting, he would win. Everything. Even things he didn't want.

"I'm a single dad," he said, his deep voice tempered by a natural shyness. "Janie McMurphy is my fifth-grader. She's a good kid, like I'm sure all of yours are, but she struggles with her schoolwork, and social situations are sometimes tough for her. I'd like to represent parents who have kids who don't fit the standard, you know?"

The women in the room made a chorus of sympathetic sounds. Vera did not reprimand him for campaigning early and took to staring at him instead. I glanced at Cassie. Eyes narrowed, she assessed her opponent.

Could the brilliant, therapy dog–loving, almost ex-husband–dating lawyer win against the soft-hearted single dad hottie?

This could get interesting.

I felt someone tug my sleeve.

"Say something," Heather said. I'd been paying so much attention to Hot Dad I hadn't noticed her come in. She crouched next to my chair, irritating the woman sitting to the left of me. Kylie stood next to her, rubbing her eyes.

"You were supposed to stay outside," I hissed.

"Kids are not allowed," Vera announced, bringing everyone's attention to us. "I'm sorry, but this is a board meeting. You'll have to leave."

Heather stretched to her full, not very impressive, height. "You don't let kids in, but you'll let someone's dog sit up front?"

"I'm sorry," I said, directing my comment toward Cassie. "My friend doesn't realize your dog's purpose."

"What purpose?" Heather said. "What are you talking about?"

"It's a therapy dog," I explained, my theory losing steam as I saw the horrified look on Cassie's face. "I . . . think."

"Riker is *not* a therapy dog," Cassie said. "I don't know why in the world you'd think a Doberman would work in a therapeutic capacity. I mean, who would think that?"

I could feel my face flame with the heat of a thousand suns. "I'm sorry—"

"I had his attendance cleared with Vera in advance," Cassie interrupted. "Riker was at the groomer today. He had his anal glands expressed, and I thought the process might be traumatic. I didn't want to leave him alone."

Sometimes, I wish I could stamp life's moments with an emoji. Every single person present was making the wide-eyed, shocked face, mouths formed into perfect *O*'s.

"Ew," Kylie said. "What's an anal gland? It sounds disgusting."

"It's necessary sometimes," Cassie said, her snippiness fading as she talked to my daughter. "He's a well-behaved dog, sweetie. Would you like to pet him?"

"I don't know," Kylie said, backing into Heather. "I'm sort of allergic."

Cassie smiled pityingly at her. "That's too bad."

"We are getting so off track," Vera said, slightly desperate. "Should we close the books on this race? We have two candidates, Cassie and . . . er . . . Janie's dad."

"Sawyer," said Hot Dad.

Of course that was his name. The audience sighed.

"Sawyer," Vera said. I thought I detected a note of huskiness in her voice. "Okay? Can I get an aye?"

"Nay," Heather said. "You have one more candidate."

Vera tossed her baseball hat on the table in exasperation. "And who would that be?"

"Me," I squeaked. "Ally Anderson."

"Stand up," someone said in the back. "We can't see you."

I stood quickly, and my knees cracked, obviously protesting my idiocy.

"Mom," Kylie said.

"In a minute, honey." I cleared my throat. "Uh. Okay. I'm a . . . mom. Of Kylie here." I nudged Kylie forward.

"*Mom*," she said again, this time with more vehemence. I could hear a noise, the sound of a motor purring.

"I work at Stylin' on Grand Avenue. I know, kind of an obvious name. I cut hair. There. At the salon."

"Mom!"

The sound grew louder, and I realized it was Cassie's Doberman. He was standing, teeth bared, ready to pounce.

"Get rid of that!" Cassie shrieked at me. "It's upsetting him!"

"What?"

Kylie pointed at the floor. Sandy's zombie teeth, still covered in fake blood, lay between me and the dog. They must have fallen from Kylie's pocket at some point.

"Oh, I'm so sorry," I said, reaching for them. The Doberman snapped at the air. I quickly drew my hand back.

Cassie moved to grab his collar, but it was too late. He lunged forward, barking like crazy.

Kylie screamed.

I did what any sane mom would do. I kicked the teeth toward him, grabbed my daughter's hand, and ran like hell.

~

"So now I know you wouldn't have my back in a zombie apocalypse."

Heather, Kylie, and I sat at my mom's kitchen table, recovering. Mom stood at the counter making hot cocoa (organic, free-trade, nut-free). We'd told her all about the Doberman drama, taking turns to give her each of our perspectives.

"I was thinking of Kylie," I said to Heather. "Kids first. And I think you can take care of yourself just fine. You're alive, right?"

Heather accepted a steaming mug from my mother. "Barely. Cujo would have feasted on my arm if Cassie hadn't gotten him under control."

"His anal glands were bothering him," Kylie said. "It's a thing," she added when my mom raised an eyebrow.

"Why would someone allow a dog into a school board meeting?" Mom joined us at the table, sighing as she slid into her seat. Her gray hair was pulled back from her face, revealing tired eyes, and she grimaced while she rubbed at a shoulder muscle. Mom had fallen down the Pinterest rabbit hole the night before while planning Kylie's new bedroom. Then she'd spent most of the afternoon with Matt, hauling furniture and measuring windows and talking through all sorts of pseudocontractor stuff.

"The owner is kind of a big shot," I explained. "Cassie Flores. She's a lawyer who throws her weight around when she can."

My mom grunted. "La-di-da. She's not too bright bringing an irritated Doberman into a crowd like that."

Kylie finished her cocoa and took the mug to the sink.

"Get ready for bed, little warrior," I said. "Pajamas, teeth, backpack ready for tomorrow."

"And meditation," Kylie said as she kissed Heather and Mom goodnight. "Radha taught me a mantra."

My mom scrunched up her face a little. "A mantra? For a ten-year-old? And who is this Radha person?"

Kylie glanced at me nervously, and I suddenly felt like a top candidate for Worst Mom of the Year Award.

"She's, um, going to be the daughter of Mom's client," Kylie explained, while my heart skipped a couple of beats. "She's completely cool. Like, the best."

Heather, likely noticing my tension, did her part to dissipate it. "What is it, this mantra?"

"You breathe in and think, *I am*. Then you breathe out and say, 'Present,'" Kylie said proudly.

Heather tilted her head, thoughtful. "Isn't everyone present? I mean, you're here. Everyone can see you. Doesn't that mean you're present without having to announce it to the world?"

"Not that kind of present, Auntie Heather. Like, where you *really* see things, *really* hear things, *really* . . . smell things, I guess. Though that might get kind of gross."

Heather didn't laugh, and I loved her for it. "Well, I guess that's kind of like having superpowers, if you can see things others can't. It takes a special person for a mantra like that to work, so I guess you're pretty special."

Kylie beamed. "That's what Radha said."

"Enough of the new age talk," my mom interrupted, giving Kylie another hug. "Off to bed with you. School tomorrow."

"I'll be in to tuck you in in a minute," I said.

I could hear Kylie chanting her mantra on the way to her room.

After Heather left for her apartment, my mom said, "Kylie's a good kid. She's got a pure heart. I can't wait until we can give her the new room."

"We?"

"Yes. It's a family project, isn't it?"

"I guess." I toyed with my mug. "You know that woman with the scary dog? Matt's dating her."

My mom went silent, her mouth a thin line. "Well," she finally said. "How are you with that?"

"Not great. But I decided to put my mind to other things. I'm running for school board. At least I think I am."

"You think?"

"It was kind of a weird nomination process. To be honest, I don't know if I have much of a chance, but I'm going to try."

"Look at the fools we have running for president. You have every chance to make it to the school board."

"Thanks?"

"You know what I mean. Did I raise you to be afraid?"

"No."

"You've always dived into the deep end headfirst. Why would this be any different?"

"I'm older, and I'm realizing other people have passed me up," I said. "I didn't go to college. I've had the same job for fifteen years."

Mom snorted. "That's what you're using to measure success? Look at me."

I did. At her sloped nose and blue eyes. At her straight hair and long, thin neck. So different from me, but so, so comfortingly familiar. I met the gaze of the eyes that had watched me grow into the woman I was.

"You've always been smart," she said, steel behind her words, "but you didn't always know what to do with it. Now you do. Don't let anyone tell you otherwise."

I couldn't look her in the eye anymore, so I hugged her, tightly and fiercely. "Thanks, Mom."

"You've got a quiet house now," she said, gently extracting herself from the embrace. "Use it for thinking. You need a plan. It's time for a shopping list."

~

I used the silence for one thing, but it wasn't thinking. It was snooping. First stop, Facebook. I went directly to the parents' group page.

District 168 Parents: New Post

Vera Pastorelli: We have three candidates for the open school board position: Cassie Flores, Sawyer McMurphy, and Ally Ackerman. A debate will be held the third week in October, and the election will take place the first Tuesday in November, just like in national politics. Best of luck to all candidates!

Ally Ackerman? Oh, no way.

Ally Anderson: It's Anderson.

Bree Nguyen: What is?

Ally Anderson: My last name.

Bree Nguyen: Oh. Okay. I'm sure someone will take care of it. It's just a typo.

Someone "Liked" Bree's comment. Seriously? I saw the little three dots pulsing at the bottom of the post. Who else was commenting? I couldn't wait.

Sawyer McMurphy: Thank you, kindly.

Who actually said stuff like "thank you, kindly"? Did he think he was a cowboy? I didn't care how hot he was, Sawyer McMurphy was a poser.

I watched the "Likes" rise on his comment, rolling like a slot machine. Sawyer McMurphy might have been a poser, but he certainly was a popular one. Ten "likes." Twelve. Eighteen? Seriously?

> Cassie Flores: I'd like to begin by thanking the current school board for this opportunity. I am more than prepared to devote my time, brainpower, and creative energy to making this school board the most dynamic, effective force for positive change within District 168. If anyone would like a "Cassie for School Board" T-shirt, I'll have them in sizes small through double-extra-large at the beginning of next week.

T-shirts. Ohhhkaay.

I had to follow that up. But what in the world was I supposed to write? I needed to type something, quickly, or everyone would focus on them and forget about me.

> Ally Anderson: Thank you. I want to saw that weather I win or loose, I will work hard for the students of District 168. I've have lived in the district all me life and I am a proud product of the school system myself.

I sat back and waited for the "likes" to come in.

One . . . and . . . nothing.

Then I reread my post. Oh no! I *had* to go over these things before I hit "Send." I stabbed at the computer, searching for the "Edit" button. Shit!

> Cole Flounders: I hope the school system's English program currently focuses more on grammar than in your day, Ally! Hope you don't become "loose"—ha ha!!

Bree Nguyen: Haha, Cole! Glad to see we've all got a sense of humor about this race!

While I was reading Bree's comment, Sawyer McMurphy racked up forty-seven "Likes."

I had to come back with wit, something sly and smart.

"Mom?"

Kylie stood in the doorway, rubbing her eyes.

I closed my laptop. Wit could wait. "Come here, sweetie."

She nestled into my shoulder. "My eyes won't stop hurting."

"Let me see." They were swollen and red, the puffiness distorting their shape. I ran through everything she'd been exposed to today, any possible culprit. The problem was, there were just too many. Stress? Something she ate? Something she touched? I hadn't let her get near Riker. Was it that she simply breathed in his vicinity?

I needed to get the eye drops and an antihistamine. I needed to get a cool washcloth to soothe her eyes until the meds kicked in.

But for the moment, all I could do was hold her.

CHAPTER 11

"We can't afford this."

Matt, Kylie, and I were sitting in my car in front of the wellness center. It was raining, the moisture bunching up the leaves and making Chicago hell on earth for mold allergy sufferers. Still, the majesty of the center was evident. And intimidating. I could see why Matt gazed at it suspiciously, grinding his teeth.

"Dr. Indigo is in the back," I said. "Her office is a little down-to-earth. Well, down-to-earth mother."

We made a run for it, the three of us huffing and puffing, though we hadn't run far. It always seems more taxing on the body to run in the rain. Shaking off the freezing drops, we followed the impossibly gorgeous receptionist up the old wood staircase, and Matt stared at me when I kicked at the door.

"Is that necessary?" he asked.

"It sticks," Kylie said. "No biggie."

She didn't appear to have any lasting anxiety from our last visit, or at least she didn't show it. I had no idea what Dr. Indigo had in mind for today, but I secretly hoped it wouldn't be too way out there—Matt didn't have the patience for it.

We paused at her office door. Dr. Indigo sat at her desk, motionless. "Why are you hesitating?" she said. "Come in."

We sat down quickly.

Dr. Indigo shook Matt's hand. "You're here to check up on me?" she asked, but there was a touch of humor in her question.

Matt cleared his throat. "Actually, yes. You're a board-certified allergist?"

She pointed to some framed documents on the wall. "Have a look."

Much to my embarrassment, Matt actually did. He scrutinized each of her diplomas and certifications, and then, when he was finally satisfied, took his seat.

"What I would like to know," he said, "is what you're doing to address Kylie's peanut allergy. That would seem like the place to start, right? With what we know for sure?"

"I agree," Dr. Indigo said.

"I thought you did desensitization therapy," I added, both emboldened by Matt's questions, and still haunted by the cafeteria incident. "Is Kylie a candidate? Can we get her started?"

I'd contacted the few doctors who administered the therapy in the Midwest—all had waiting lists of well over a year, and many of them were still conducting trials, meaning Kylie might get a placebo, unbeknownst to us. It was one reason I'd come to Dr. Indigo—when I called to set up the first appointment, the receptionist wouldn't tell me if she had a wait list. I figured it was worth the chance to see if she'd take Kylie on.

"I've already started Kylie on the therapy," Dr. Indigo said.

"What?" Matt shouted. "Without our knowledge? That's illegal!"

Dr. Indigo smiled. "I already began her therapy. I've yet to start the exposure. I would need your permission for that. And you'd need mine. I take very few patients in this area. I wanted to get to know your daughter, your level of commitment, and I needed to study her blood work again. After evaluating all of that, I'll decide when it's time we begin the exposure."

"What kind?" Kylie said. "Is this the one where you give me a tiny bit of a peanut so my body gets used to it?"

"Exactly," Dr. Indigo said, turning to my daughter. "It's one way for your body to learn to calm the dog."

"Oh," Kylie said, "but what if I can't? What if I have a reaction?"

Dr. Indigo's attention returned to me and Matt. "This is not without risks. I know you're aware of what those are."

My mind flashed to the ballpark, to Kylie lying in my arms, face swollen and lips blue.

"We're extremely careful," Dr. Indigo continued, looking at me directly. "We monitor for a reaction for hours, in office. You will continue the therapy at home, but I will pay close attention, and Kylie will continue to see me for complementary therapies."

"Like what?" Matt asked.

"Guided meditation, acupuncture, hypnosis, aromatherapy. I believe they help boost success rates."

I could almost feel Matt's skepticism flood the room when he responded, "And what is the success rate?"

"It's variable, but generally very high," Dr. Indigo said. "I can give you some literature."

"I don't know if I'm satisfied with that answer." Matt crossed his arms over his chest. "So there is no guarantee, but there is a risk of a reaction, perhaps severe."

"That is true," Dr. Indigo agreed. "But I think you need to look at the bigger picture. Kylie would be undergoing therapy that hundreds of families are eager to begin. Given Kylie's other autoimmune issues, I think her case will be an important part of my research."

Matt smirked. "So, it's important to *you*."

"What about the DNA test?" I asked. "Did it tell you anything important?"

"Kylie is susceptible to a number of autoimmune disorders," she said. "That is very clear."

Matt and I shared a guilty glance. We'd passed along these sucky genes to our daughter.

"Just because she's susceptible doesn't mean she's destined to suffer from them," Dr. Indigo explained. "Lifestyle always comes into play. Also, the more knowledge we have, the earlier the diagnosis, and the better and more effective the treatment.

"I have a theory," she continued, "however unproven. If we can get Kylie's immune system to address one problem properly with the desensitization therapy, there's a chance she might overcome some of the other issues, or her long-term prognosis can be improved. It's just a theory, but if the end result is just that she will not have an anaphylactic reaction to peanuts, I'd consider that a win. A big win."

"She's a guinea pig," Matt said. "This isn't based on science."

"Exposure theory is clearly based on science," Dr. Indigo countered, though she seemed unperturbed by Matt's skepticism. "My other theories are just that, but I operate a bit outside the norm. Ally knew that when she walked in the door."

"It's a risk," Matt repeated. "She could have a serious reaction."

"I'm very careful," Dr. Indigo assured him. "There is a process."

"It's expensive," Matt pushed.

"I want to do this," Kylie interjected. "I want to calm the dog."

"What dog are you talking about?" Matt said. "We don't even have a dog."

"I'll explain later," I told him, wanting to address what I felt were more important issues. "Could we start right away? Could we get . . . financial aid?"

"Yes to the first, no to the second," Dr. Indigo said, but she did look apologetic. "Perhaps a slight discount could be worked out, but it's simply not our policy."

"You said we might get a Groupon," Kylie said.

"I did," Dr. Indigo responded. "But even if I created one, I need you to understand this is a significant financial investment."

"We need to talk about this," Matt said, looking at me. "Privately. As a family."

I nodded, not wanting to correct him. Were we? A family?

"Imagine if Kylie could go into a restaurant and order without scouring the menu," Dr. Indigo said. "Playdates, school functions, summer camp—so many of the day-to-day activities you've had to monitor with a vigilance most people can't imagine. With this therapy, it's possible you could live without constant fear."

I could barely imagine it. The fear was too great, too all encompassing. "If Kylie could eat without worrying about every bite? Now, that would be something."

"I need a fee schedule," Matt said. "And a breakdown of costs."

"We can supply that," Dr. Indigo said. "But when you look at it, think about this, and what it would mean for your daughter if we're successful. It could change all of your lives. Permanently."

~

There was no guided meditation after our discussion. Instead, Dr. Indigo took Kylie into a closet-like space for acupuncture. The thought of getting needles stuck into random body parts would freak out most ten-year-olds, but Kylie simply shrugged when Dr. Indigo suggested it, and asked if she could listen to music during the process.

"Of course," Dr. Indigo said. "As long as it's *my* music."

"Great," Kylie said, but she dutifully followed the doctor into the treatment room.

Which left Matt and me sitting next to each other in the silent office.

"Kylie likes her," Matt said, sounding surprised. "Does the woman ever crack a joke?"

"Maybe once. But it was about hemp seeds and omega-3 fatty acids."

"Must have been hilarious."

"Yeah, I nearly peed my pants."

I relaxed a little. Banter was good. Banter meant Matt was relaxed and possibly open to Dr. Indigo's program.

I turned slightly, facing him. It was strange to see this new, put together Matt. He wore khakis again, and a soft-blue button-down shirt. I saw the faint outline of a stain, probably coffee, on the front, a splotch right over his heart. A reminder of the man he was when we were together. I resisted the urge to put my hand over the stain, to protect it from fading. "What do you think?" I said softly. "I've already done a lot of reading about this therapy. It was one of the reasons I came here. It *can* work. It definitely has for some people."

"I'm worried, Ally. What if it makes things worse? What if she has an anaphylactic reaction and the EpiPen fails to do its job? This is a risk. A serious one."

"Every day of our lives is a risk. Kylie could misread a label one day. She could kiss a boy who just ate a peanut butter sandwich."

Matt smiled faintly. "I don't want her kissing any boys until she's thirty."

"Good luck with that."

"I just want . . . It's just that I want to . . ."

I recognized that all-encompassing want. It gave ache to Matt's voice, the anguish that coated every decision like a protective film. Every day we woke up to the same thought—How do we keep bad things from happening to Kylie?

"This is a way of being proactive," I said. "I trust Dr. Indigo."

"Ally, the risk isn't the only thing stopping me up. Between the two of us, we have very little savings. Who knows if I'll even have a pension in retirement, given the state of Illinois and its massive financial shenanigans? I have a feeling we're talking a lot of money for a therapy that might not even work."

"But it might. More than might. It probably will."

"Where are we going to get the money? Our insurance is not going to cover this."

"We'll find a way."

Matt didn't say anything after that, but a strange sort of tension filled the space between us. Before, we'd argue about this, battering each other with this point and that point, a tug-of-war that didn't end until one of us, tired or just too sad, gave up. It seemed we'd gotten past the point of bothering to fight. My heart froze. Did this mean he really went his way and I went mine?

"So, I'll try to find the money on my own," I said.

"I'll help where I can, but it won't be much. I'm going to spend most of my efforts trying to keep both of us from ending up in the poor house, unable to help Kylie at all."

That was as close to a win as I was going to get, so I stopped talking and entertained myself with Dr. Indigo's odd collection of toys. I was just zoning out while playing with a sand garden when Matt said, "I heard you're running for school board. Are you sure that's a good idea?"

"Are you worried I'm going to give your girlfriend some competition?"

Matt squirmed. "She's not my girlfriend. I know this isn't . . . easy. But, hey, you've been a lot of things, but you've never been bitchy—why start now? Cassie's nice. That's all she is at this point. A nice woman I might spend some time with."

"Cassie has a Doberman. Didn't you notice?"

"I'm a long way off from introducing her to Kylie. And we're not even sure she's allergic. One step at a time."

This did not console me. A long way off still meant he intended to do it someday.

"I think you'd like Cassie more if you talked to her," Matt said.

Something told me this was far from the truth. "I'll talk to her at the debate."

"You can't fault me for trying to move on," he added quietly. "I feel like I'm spinning my wheels. I teach all day, and then I tutor in the evenings when I'm not monitoring the Poli-Sci Club or doing my part in some faculty subcommittee. I take care of Kylie when I have her. I stand at the kitchen counter eating Cheerios for dinner when Kylie's with you, sometimes because I don't have time for anything else, and sometimes because it's just too lonely to sit at the table by myself. Sometimes I sleep in my clothes because I'm too tired or too depressed to change. I ran out of toothpaste the other day, and I've been brushing my teeth with mouthwash because I can't find a freaking minute to go to Target. I'm trying to find a small bit of life for myself in this scenario, Al. You've got to understand that."

I was familiar with those feelings. All of them.

The question I always asked myself was, Did we have a right to feel them? We chose to separate. Sometimes, I could see my mom's point—with no infidelity, no abuse, no drug or alcohol issues, why wouldn't we try to work it out?

The fights all blended together at this point. Matt decided he didn't want more children; I did. He talked about moving out of state; I wanted to stay put. We argued about Kylie's medicine, her sleep, her activities . . .

All that came from worry, I know. If that was the source of our unhappiness, I could have dealt with it. But it wasn't.

It was the money argument that finally sent me packing. All couples argue about money when there isn't enough of it, and we were no different. Matt's teaching job sucked up all his time and energy. He worked hard to make himself invaluable to the school—coaching softball, volunteering to head committees and a variety of student clubs, and teaching summer school during what should have been his time to recharge. I'd decided it was up to me. I'd hit the upper limit with what I could make as a stylist, so the only answer was to find a new job, one that paid more money. The problem was, I didn't have a college degree.

It was time I got one. I'd jumped into the college search, researching local schools that offered programs for people who needed flexible schedules. *I could be a paralegal*, I thought, my brain whirring with excitement. Or I could go into marketing and public relations. Or . . . I could get into nutrition. I'd already learned so much about reading labels from Kylie's allergy.

"You're going about this impulsively," Matt had said when I shared my findings. "Take some time to think about this."

Later, he said it was too expensive, and we couldn't take on a student loan. He wondered how we would manage Kylie's care if I returned to school. "I don't think this makes the most sense," he said when I got my first acceptance letter. "I'm sorry, but at our age it just doesn't."

I heard all those things, and I knew what he said was grounded in some truths I didn't want to admit. But those truths were mild rumblings in my ear, drowned out by the alarm that shrieked loud and clear—Matt didn't think I could do it. He didn't believe in me.

And if I stayed with him, I'd have to stop believing in me too.

Which is why I didn't reach for Matt when he ran through his list of stressors. Part of me wanted to touch him, to make a physical connection to communicate the emotional one. But, part of me just didn't.

He was struggling to gain traction in his new life, but I was too. Pursuing a relationship with Micki, running for a position on the school board, even jokingly putting myself on Cupidworks—these were all ways to make me feel like a full person, to somehow sketch out the missing part. Matt and I had blown a few holes in our personalities when we let our relationship explode, and we were each desperately trying to fill them in.

"I do understand your need to date someone," I said softly. "What I'm having a hard time with is accepting it. We were together for ten years. It's hard to picture you with another woman in my imagination, so I can't imagine what it's going to be like when I'm forced to witness it in person."

Matt's hand rested on mine for only a second. "You've always had a hard time accepting when life dishes out something you find unfair. I've got to admit, though, that's one of the things I admire about you most."

Admiration. It seemed like a weak kind of compliment. I needed more from him, so I asked, "Do you still like me as a person? After all we've said to each other?"

"Just because a relationship changes doesn't mean a person does," he said. "We aren't the same people we were when we were together, but we're still us."

"Is that an answer?"

He laughed. "Yeah. It means I still like you. I'll always like you, Ally."

Kylie came in then, flushed but calm. She threw her arms around my neck, much to Dr. Indigo's surprise.

"What's that for?" I asked.

"Because you're smiling," she said.

~

Later that night, after dropping Matt off, helping Kylie with her homework, and putting her to bed, I sat on my mom's bench with a notebook.

Shopping List for Kylie's Exposure Therapy
Money

I needed lots of it. Thousands of dollars.

I wrote down: *More work hours.*

That's it. That's all I had.

Matt wasn't going to help much. I couldn't ask my mom. Heather was just as broke as I was. No bank would ever give me a loan—on paper I was a financial zero. I tried to expand my thought process. I tried to come up with a way.

After a moment, I added a line to the shopping list.

Find a way to calm the dog.

147

CHAPTER 12

"You have to answer him!"

Kylie practically climbed on Heather's lap to get a better view of her laptop. The three of us lounged in the back of The Not-So-Blushing-Bride, judging the men who'd contacted Heather via Cupidworks. Radha gave her opinion as she lugged dresses in the back for Bernie, who'd decided today was the absolute deadline for choosing a dress.

Ignoring the guilt buzzing in my ears, I'd impulsively called Micki and told her we'd come by on Sunday to help organize the shop. It hadn't quite recovered from the fashion show, and its usual state of disarray had turned into a state of emergency. She told us to make ourselves comfortable until closing time, then we could clean up without inconveniencing any customers.

I liked the women who came into Micki's shop. A bridal shop should always be a happy place, but Micki's took that up a notch. The brides who walked in the door were older—some were marrying late, some were on husband number two (or three, or four), some had been divorced, others were widowed. All had two things in common—appreciation for finding love at a challenging age and hope for the future. Micki celebrated their hope and added an element of fun—I'd yet to see a woman leave the shop who wasn't smiling.

"This dress is atrocious!" came Bernie's voice from the changing room.

Okay, except one.

But even Bernie had high hopes for her big day. I laughed to myself as Heather brought up photos of Bachelor Number One.

Heather jabbed her finger at the screen. "Look at this one. Think he ate a lemon before taking this picture?"

"Whole lotta nope," Kylie said. "Give him to another lady. Someone who doesn't look nice. They can be mean together on their first date."

"Next," Heather said. She ran through a few more, nixing them because they looked like they had severe halitosis, still lived in their mother's basement, or had the gleam of a serial killer in their smiles.

"What about that one?" Micki stopped short on her way to the changing room to relieve Radha and leaned over Heather's shoulder. "He looks promising."

Heather went quiet, a rare occurrence. "Nope. He looks like someone I used to know."

"Once you get to my age, everyone looks like someone you used to know. And what does it matter anyway?" Micki pointed to the screen. "Scroll back. That one. He looks like he'd get out of bed at two o'clock in the morning to change your tire."

Heather clicked. "Nah . . . too . . . earnest looking. And he's bald. I'm a hair stylist. Not gonna work."

"He likes bowling," Kylie said. "I think that's good. You could have bowling dates. Can I come?"

"We can find out where they're going to be and spy on them," I said, turning the laptop toward me. The man—broad shouldered and wearing a plaid button-down shirt, smiled directly at the camera, no sunglasses, no attitude, no defenses. If a picture could really tell a story, this one said *nice* from beginning to end. "He lives in Willow Falls, right here."

Heather glanced around nervously, as though he might actually be in the shop.

"His name is Mel," Micki said, musing. "Sounds familiar. I'm sure someone I know knows him. We don't have six degrees of separation in Willow Falls. We have two or three, tops."

"That means his full name is Melvin," Heather said, her voice flat. "Awesome."

Micki clucked her tongue, which I'd never actually heard someone do in real life. "Stop being so judgy-judgy. Mel is a perfectly fine name. St. Mel is the patron saint of single people. Isn't that a hoot?"

I laughed, but my brain immediately stuck to this clue about Micki. Had she grown up in a religious household? My mind scrolled through great nature versus nurture debates. Micki held a pen the same way I did, too tightly and with the middle finger curled in. She flattened her lips when in deep concentration, just as I caught myself doing when focusing on a particularly challenging client. We both had a fairly dramatic arch to our brows, and the wrinkle running from my inner right eyebrow to the bridge of my nose would one day mimic Micki's deep crevice in the same spot. That was nature at work, passing things along, deepening a connection between two people whether they were aware of it or not. I made a mental note to try to get some alone time with Micki. I wanted to explore these connections, to clarify them before my time with her had to come to an end. And it did, I admitted to myself. I couldn't keep up the ruse. When I'd told my mother I was driving out to Willow Falls for a client's event, she'd scoured me with her eyes and only said, "Sure thing."

"Send him a message," Kylie demanded, interrupting my thoughts. "Tell him you're awesome, and you're looking for someone awesome."

"I don't know if that will come across the right way, sweetie," Heather said. She hesitated, hands poised above the keyboard. "This is harder than I thought. Maybe I should think about it for a few days."

I slid the laptop away from her. "Want me to take charge?"

"I don't have a choice, do I?"

"Nope."

Heather turned away. "Do what you will. Just don't tell him anything really personal. Keep it light. Don't mention . . . anything. Tell him nothing. Maybe just say hi."

Cupidworks direct message:

Heather to Mel

Hi, Mel! Want to meet for coffee?

I hit "Send" and flipped the laptop around to show Heather.

"That's it?" she said. "That's all you wrote? He'll think I'm a cheer-leader or a gold digger or a totally jaded serial dater who doesn't even bother to engage."

"You're the one who said not to tell him anything," I said. "He's going to think you want to skip the small talk BS and meet in person. That means you're direct and wonderfully old school."

"Really?" Though she sounded skeptical, I detected a note of hope in Heather's voice.

"Really."

Micki grabbed a couple of dresses from the couch where we were sitting. "Okay, ladies, it's time to get to work. Operation Cleanup is under way. We might not make it out alive."

I took in the mess before us. "You might be right."

Heather and Kylie scooted off to the front of the shop with Micki. Before they could notice I wasn't with them, I logged on to Cupidworks, curiosity getting the better of me. A small number 1 next to my name told me I had a direct message.

To my surprise, my heart shuddered with equal parts alarm and dread. Who would it be? Every nerve in my body vibrated. I had to admit—anticipation for a situation I controlled held a certain kind of allure. I could respond or not respond. I had the ultimate say-so. Entirely. Up. To. Me.

I took a deep breath and clicked. A message box appeared. It was shaped like a heart.

Cupidworks direct message:

Matt to Ally

Be careful on here. Don't settle. Don't jump in without thinking. Don't accept anyone less than worthy of you.

You became less than worthy of me, I thought, my hope sinking. *And I of you.* I started typing.

Cupidworks direct message:

Ally to Matt

Then I couldn't think of anything to write. And in a moment rare for me, I didn't say anything at all.

∼

"Let's make a shopping list," I said, grabbing a sheet of paper and a pen from Micki's desk. "We need to organize this in a way that makes sense for your particular kind of client."

"A shopping list?" Micki frowned. "I don't have much of a budget."

"More like a list of things we need to do," I assured her. "My mom taught me how to do this."

She blinked at me, and glanced around to make sure Kylie was out of earshot. "Am I ever going to meet her? We never . . . had contact. Can I sit down with this woman who raised my niece?"

"She's my mom," I said. "Not *this woman*."

"I know, honey. I just want to meet her."

"I told Kylie who you really were, but I haven't told my mother I've been coming here," I said, ashamed to admit it. "It's not you, I just don't think she'd like it very much."

"You don't want to hurt her."

"No," I said. "I don't."

Micki frowned. "We can't have much of a relationship then, can we?"

My heart fluttered. "Is that what you want?"

"I don't have much family left," Micki said. "Sandy, Radha, even Bernie. Those are my people. I'd like you and Kylie and Heather to be my people too."

I wanted to say she barely knew me. I couldn't. Time didn't matter much when hearts aligned, and that's what was happening between us. I could feel it. "I want that too. I don't know how to do all of this. I love my mother very much, and I feel a hundred pounds of guilt on my shoulders when I walk into this shop. But I keep walking in, you know? That's mostly because of you."

She nodded. "That you want to is good enough for now. So, how do we write this shopping list?"

"We jot down everything we absolutely need to happen. Then we check them off while we do them so we stay organized."

"I don't know if I've ever been organized," she said, laughing, "but I guess now is as good a time as any."

That didn't come as a surprise. The Not-So-Blushing-Bride held a variety of products, but the stock was so jumbled, it was difficult for a bride-to-be to get a handle on what she needed. Micki had set up a one-stop shopping emporium—she offered makeup and skincare for the over-forty set; Spanx, lingerie, and hosiery; shoes; jewelry; hair accessories, including extensions and wigs; and of course, the bridal and bridesmaids gowns, many designed by Micki herself. She had a corner devoted to advertising materials from local florists and photographers, and a white, shabby chic bookshelf stuffed with hundreds of bridal and travel magazines. A Willow Falls lawyer specializing in family law had made a banner declaring 10 percent off on prenups for Aunt Micki's clients. The problem was, it obscured a destination wedding display when it should have been covering up the section of the store related to bachelorette parties. I tried to keep Kylie away from the penis straws, *Kama Sutras*, and feathered handcuffs. Given the clientele, that section also had information about Viagra; eco-friendly, nontoxic lube; and something called vaginal rejuvenation, a process I hoped I never had to learn the details of.

"Women come in here for the perfect dress," I said. "Everything else is necessary, but secondary. We need to set up everything in a U shape, your most impressive dresses hanging right by the door, then intersperse racks of dresses throughout, with bridesmaids dresses adding dashes of color."

Micki gave me a side hug. "My niece is so smart. Glad you aren't just a pretty face."

We got to work. Everyone pitched in, even Bernie, who sported a pillbox hat with a veil, a la Jackie O. "I'm trying it out," she said when I asked her about it. "You have to live with something for a while to know if you really like it."

Radha smiled but rolled her eyes when she heard that one. "She'll reject it," she muttered to me, "just like everything else."

Today's sari was purple with pink piping. I wondered where she got them.

Sandeep showed up a few hours later, in full zombie regalia, and pitched in. When we'd gotten the main room in some kind of order, Micki and I attacked the storage room, making a clean line of separation between overstock and her workstation, where she sewed dresses and made alterations. I noticed a familiar fabric in the stack next to her Singer.

"Do you make Radha's saris?"

Micki ran her hand over the fabric. "It's something we started doing together when she moved in."

I didn't know how to politely ask what I wanted to know, so I just let it spill out. "Can you really adopt her?"

"I hope so," Micki said. "I'm optimistic, but Sandy is more realistic. We're older than is usually allowed. On the other hand, it's definitely more difficult for a sixteen-year-old to find a home. Most of the older kids live in state-sponsored facilities, waiting for their eighteenth birthdays. Her birth name is Rolanda, by the way. She said she wanted to be called Radha after living with us for a few weeks, and we obliged. She's really taken to Sandy. He had a daughter, but his ex-wife took her back to India years ago. Deval is an adult now, and they only have sporadic contact. It's been hard on him."

I tried to imagine Kylie becoming a stranger to me. I couldn't.

"I really hope it works out," I said, squeezing Micki's hand.

"So do I," she said. "I mean, it worked out for you, right?"

"It did," I said, wondering if I'd only imagined the edge to her voice when she said it. "My mom is a good person. She gave me a lot of love, just like you're giving Radha. I can see how much she glows in your presence."

Micki smiled, but it was tempered by sadness. "I know how to do that now, give love. It's a very hard thing to learn if you didn't grow up with it. Sandy helped, that's for sure, but Radha is the first person I ever loved without having to hack through a wall of suspicion to get there. I don't want to lose her."

"Whatever happens, I don't think her heart will ever lose you."

We began sorting and organizing in companionable silence. I liked Micki Patel. I couldn't help but wonder—Was it because she was a genuinely nice person, or because of a deeper, blood bond? I gave a sidelong glance at her gold velour sweatshirt, her brightly dyed hair, her bold, colorful lipstick. In some ways, she was so different from me and my family.

"When you walked in the door today, I could tell something was on your mind. What's going on?" she asked.

And in others, so very much like us.

"A whole bunch of things. Matt, for one. He's considering dating, and I'm struggling with it. He came with me to Kylie's doctor's visit and tried to explain his feelings, but I just don't want to hear it, you know? And, more importantly, the doctor we're seeing for Kylie has a plan to help her body deal with her immune issues, starting with her allergies."

"So she can eat peanuts?"

"That's the start of it, yes. It might not work, and there are potential risks involved, so my almost ex-husband doesn't want to do it."

"I'm guessing those kinds of things don't come cheap either."

"Nope," I said. "That's his other issue. He's obsessed with saving for a rainy day."

Micki shoved a pile of fabric under a table. "If we save only for the days it rains, then we don't have any money to have fun in the sun."

"He's just being careful."

The side of Micki's fuchsia mouth turned up. "You're sticking up for him. So you're not done with him yet? Is that why you have such a problem with him dating? Is there something still between you two?"

"Won't there always be feelings there?" I said. "That doesn't negate the fact that we can't be in the same room longer than a few minutes without disagreeing about something."

Micki shrugged. "Some people are into that. Not me, but some people."

"Not me either."

"So what are you gonna do?"

I wasn't sure if she meant Matt or Kylie's desensitization therapy. Probably the latter. "I was going to try to get more shifts at work to pay for the therapy, but my boss doesn't have any to give. The salon is closed Sundays and Mondays, or I would try to go in on my days off."

She hesitated for a moment, and then said, "And your mother? Can she help?"

"She sold the bar she owned, but not for very much. She's helped me so much already that I don't want to ask for another handout. She'd do whatever she could in a heartbeat, but I don't want my needs to make her financially insecure."

"Aren't they Kylie's needs?"

"Still."

Micki lowered herself onto a white bench we'd uncovered in Operation Cleanup. She motioned for me to join her.

"What if you worked here part time?" she asked. "A lot of the brides need someone to consult about hair and makeup. Some of them would love to hire you for their big day. I think that would bring in some extra money. Sandy and I could help out with the rest. Consider it all the birthday gifts I never got a chance to buy for my niece."

"I couldn't ask that of you." *Or of my mother. She'd sell a kidney before allowing me to take money from a stranger.*

"Yes, you can absolutely ask. You're family."

"You just met me. I could be a con artist, for all you know."

"I know a lot of those, and I know you aren't a criminal. What you are is a good mom. That means something to me."

The few comments she'd made about her family swirled through my brain. Although my biological grandmother had died young, the family had still managed to produce someone as warm and giving as Micki Patel.

"Tell me," she said. "What was Kylie like before she started having health issues?"

I went silent for a moment. The thing about illness is it attacks the healthy memories, obliterating all but those that revolve around the sickness. It becomes all you can think about. Other memories—good memories—are swallowed up. The bad memories—the ones outlined in fear—invade the rest of the brain. You can call them up in a sensory storm—the feelings they bring on threaten to drown you yet again. Micki gazed at me expectantly, though, and I didn't want to disappoint her.

"Curious. Funny. Gentle. Just the loveliest child."

"And how did the illness affect her?"

"Well, we figured out she had the peanut allergy when she was really young, and it was terrifying. She was always a smart girl, way beyond her years. She's learned to be vigilant. We all have.

"She was doing okay, but then she started having signs of other autoimmune disorders. We've taken her to so many pediatric specialists, but it's been difficult to come up with a definitive diagnosis. Unfortunately, autoimmune stuff isn't an exact science."

"Few things are," Micki said. "Can they treat it, whatever she has?"

"They can treat symptoms but not cure the disorder. The doctor she's seeing now at the wellness clinic? She's got some unusual ideas. One is that if we help the body to eliminate one autoimmune issue, it might have an easier time with the others. It might be crazy, but then, it might not be."

Micki hugged me to her. I wasn't used to a lot of physical touch. My mother was a good woman, but not a very demonstrative one. When she put her hands on my shoulders, or patted me on the back, her gestures were meant to keep me steady in the world, not offer comfort from the challenges of it. Micki's hug engulfed me with sympathy. At thirty-eight years old this could have horrified me, but instead I sunk into it, into her softness, and listened to the thump of her kind heart. I wanted to cry, but I couldn't, so pleasantly suspended in the comfort of being heard and understood. Our relationship was too new to call this feeling love, but it could definitely classify as its precursor—trust. Micki seemed genuinely interested in my life, and this ease with which we fell into sharing our lives with each other could mean only one thing—we both wanted to make a real connection. That strong blood was talking to us, reminding us of what we shared.

"Lack of money shouldn't stop someone from something this important," she said. "Consider yourself hired. You are officially the hair and makeup stylist for The Not-So-Blushing-Bride."

CHAPTER 13

"How do I know if this is working?" I whispered it, but Kylie's eyes sprung open. She sat in a chair with me looming over her, my hands supporting her small head, and my fingers pressed into the tender hollow at the base of her skull. Dr. Indigo had decided today was all about relaxation techniques and reflexology. I wondered if we were all going to have to take our socks and shoes off soon. Good thing we were doing this by scented candlelight, as I'd forgotten to get a pedicure.

"Is the pressure light, moderate, or intense?" Matt said. He was there too. Again.

"Light to moderate," Dr. Indigo said, and Matt added a note to his phone. "Ally, why don't you sit down, and Matt can get a hands-on experience. It'll be good for you and Matt to get a practical feel for what this is like. These things take practice." She glanced from me to Matt. "Often when one family member is suffering, the others become stressed. It's only natural. This might be a useful tool for all of you."

Kylie slid off the chair while I stared at Dr. Indigo, deer-in-the-headlights style. She wore an emerald-green caftan with a neon-yellow pendant that could hypnotize even the most resistant client. Her hair coiled on top of her head like a resting snake. Still, it was safer to look at her.

Because looking Matt's way was out of the question. I was okay with touching his scalp at the salon, but the thought of him touching me sent cold, liquid fear spiking through my veins. And honestly, something even more primal.

"Sit down, Mom," Kylie said. "It doesn't hurt at all."

I took a deep breath and sat. Matt slowly got up from his chair in the corner of the room. I could feel his presence behind me, and his hesitation.

"Ally, lean back. Matt, let her head rest in your outstretched hands," Dr. Indigo said, all business.

"And what does this do, exactly?" he asked. There was a slight tremor in his voice. Was he nervous too?

"This pressure point is the most effective for relieving pain and tension in the body. You can use this with Kylie at anytime, anywhere that's convenient. Most people feel a sense of calm after a few moments, almost like a feeling of floating on air. Pain is lessened. Focus is regained. Balance is more attainable. I find it works just as well with pediatric patients as adults. It's not a miracle, but an adjunct to other treatments."

I leaned farther back. Matt's hands took the weight of my head. His fingers slid into place, pressing gently on the top part of my neck.

I held my breath. I couldn't help it.

"Am I doing this right?" he whispered.

Dr. Indigo tucked her hands underneath my head. Her touch was swift and professional. "Yes," she said, removing herself. "Press a little harder, but don't strain. Ally, close your eyes and try to relax. You're stiff."

Of course I'm stiff, lady. My almost ex-husband is cradling my freaking head.

"Okay," was all I said. I closed my eyes and tried to soften my tense muscles. Matt continued pressing.

I attempted to clear my mind, but then wondered if that was necessary. "Should I be thinking about anything in particular?"

"Let the thoughts flow, but don't judge them," Dr. Indigo said, her voice low and hypnotic. "Consider each thought as an object to observe, as impartially as possible. Accept the thought and push it to the side. Do not assign it too much importance. It exists, and you acknowledge it. Then move on."

Easier said than done. I closed my eyes again. My thoughts drifted from Matt to Micki and the bridal shop, to Radha and Bernie, to Sandy in his zombie uniform. What would he do after Halloween was over? Would he miss it?

I thought about my mom, and how much she would like everyone in Willow Falls. I thought about Cassie Flores and her crazy Doberman. I thought about Heather and her online mystery date. I thought about sweet Kylie trying to calm the dog.

I thought about how good Matt's touch felt. The pressure spot pulsed against his fingers, pushing a sense of calm through my veins, my blood, emanating from my skin, pulling my eyelids down farther, easing me into a deeper state of relaxation . . .

"Mom!" Kylie was gently shaking my shoulder.

I wrenched my eyes open to find Matt, Kylie, and Dr. Indigo staring down at me, amused expressions on their faces.

"You were talking in your sleep!" Kylie said.

Panic seized at my gut. What had I said?

Matt smiled faintly. "You told me to have a scooch."

Embarrassment flooded my face. I sat up quickly, pretending to rub the sleep from my eyes. "Oh." Matt and I had spent nearly every Saturday night stretched out as best we could on our crappy old couch. He was so tall I was always pushing my backside into his midsection to claim some space. "Have a scooch" was my warning that I was about to claim some real estate.

"How do you feel?" Dr. Indigo said. "Take a moment to scan your body."

I let the embarrassment recede. Starting at the top of my head, I just . . . felt. And observed. And then took note.

"Well?" Dr. Indigo said softly.

"I honestly feel lighter. Like I could float to the ceiling. I had a little bit of a tension headache when I came in. It's not entirely gone, but it feels . . . muzzled."

"That's good," Dr. Indigo said, and I felt like the struggling student who'd finally pleased the teacher.

Matt cleared his throat. "What if you're alone? Can you, um, do this to yourself?"

Dr. Indigo patted him on the shoulder. She liked Matt better than me. Maybe because he was initially so resistant. "You could," she said, "but like most things, it just isn't as effective without a partner."

We both squirmed at that one.

"You can find a trusted friend at school who could help you find the pressure point, Kylie," Dr. Indigo continued. "So, now that you're relaxed, are you ready for your first challenge?"

Matt and I glanced at each other, panicked.

"Right now?" I asked.

"Yes. I'm fully prepared in case she has a reaction."

Matt and I nodded, though I was pretty sure we were both contemplating grabbing Kylie and running out the door. "Okay," we both whispered.

She took Kylie's hand. "Do you like ice cream or yogurt? They're both dairy-free, but still good. I've got vanilla and chocolate."

What?

"This isn't a trick question," Kylie asked. "Is it?"

"I have to mix the peanut flour with something. You'll be doing this every night with your mom or dad," Dr. Indigo said. "Today, though, you'll eat it with me."

Kylie smiled. "If I pick chocolate, that means I'll actually get to eat peanut butter and chocolate. Seriously?"

Dr. Indigo smiled. "Peanut *flour* and chocolate. It might not taste very good to you because your body doesn't want you to have it. It might even taste disgusting. You might hate ice cream when the year is up! Are you willing to take that chance?"

"Oh, I'm willing," Kylie said. "Ice cream every day? Sign me up!"

While Matt and I held hands and prayed to whatever gods would have us, Kylie scarfed a bowl of ice cream mixed with the equivalent of one thousandth of a peanut. This tiny amount could change Kylie's life . . . or land her in the ER.

Kylie finished her ice cream, and then promptly vomited into the bucket Dr. Indigo had wisely placed at her feet.

Matt and I sprang to our feet.

"This is a normal response," Dr. Indigo said, placing a hand on the back of Kylie's neck. "Are you feeling like you can't breathe, Kylie?"

"I'm okay," she said weakly.

We helped her clean up and then stared at her, waiting for hives to form, for her throat to start closing, for her lips to turn blue. Her cheeks grew ruddy, and she complained about a stomachache, but no other symptoms surfaced.

I realized I was holding my breath for most of that time. Matt looked peaked. Kylie sat on the chair, swinging her legs, so innocent and kid-like I could cry. I actually think I did start to choke up, but then my baby said, "Can we stop at the Halloween shop on the way home? I think I want to be a zombie."

She was talking normally. She looked like . . . Kylie. Not a swollen, suffering version of her. Every muscle in my body unclenched in relief.

"If Dr. Indigo says we don't have to go straight home, then yes."

Kylie wiggled in her seat. "Awesome! I want blood makeup and those fake teeth that Sandy has, and . . ."

She went on, detailing her dream costume. I stopped hearing her words, my brain too occupied by the one thought that stole my own breath—Kylie was okay.

Dr. Indigo brought us into another room, one set up with a television, board games, and a bookshelf filled with titles. We had two hours to kill.

"Don't turn the TV on," Matt said to Kylie. He slid a board game out from the pile. "Monopoly? It'll take at least two hours."

Kylie scrunched her nose. "I don't know that game."

Matt opened the box and pressed the game board flat. "Do you like money?"

"Everyone likes money."

"Then you'll like this game."

"I wish we had that much money," I said.

Matt played banker, distributing funds. Kylie fanned hers out, a huge grin on her face. "Even if it is fake," she said, "a girl can dream!"

And just then, in that moment, I saw Kylie's future, and it didn't rely on dreams at all—it was reality. And it was good.

~

Dr. Indigo cleared us to go home, as long as Kylie didn't exercise for a few hours. We needed to keep her heart rate from elevating, because it could prompt a reaction. And we had to watch her closely throughout the evening for any kind of weirdness. I figured I'd watch her all night, staring at her sleeping form like that creepy vampire from *Twilight*. Dr. Indigo assured me that after the six-hour mark, we should be in the clear.

Matt insisted on hanging out with Kylie until then, so I brought us all back to my mom's house. We found her hunched over Kylie's light fixture on the workbench in the garage. She'd painted it a light lavender.

"This is ready," Mom said, mostly to Matt. "We should get to spackling and priming that room."

Kylie stuck her head out from between two bags of Halloween stuff. "I got my Halloween costume, Grandma!" She ran straight to my mom and grabbed her around the midsection. "And I ate one thousandth of a peanut!"

"Are you a squirrel yet?" Mom joked. "Can you eat a pound of peanut brittle?"

Kylie laughed. "Someday! I passed the first challenge!"

"We think," I said, feeling like a party pooper. "We've got a few more hours to go. But it does look good."

"Because it will be good," Mom said. She took Kylie's hand. "Want to go inside and see how this lamp looks in your room? It'll take some imagination."

"Yes!"

Matt didn't follow them inside. "My heart almost stopped when she puked up that ice cream. I almost tackled Dr. Indigo while she was mixing it up. I still don't like putting our daughter's life in the hands of someone we barely know."

"I trust her," I said. "Or I never would have done it."

"I wasn't—" Matt made a sound of frustration. "I wasn't judging your decision. I'm past that."

"Lucky me."

"Ally."

It annoyed me that he used my name as a warning. It wasn't his, it was mine. "What?"

"Today's visit was $360. I couldn't stop thinking about that on the drive home. I don't know how we're going to continue this. As much as I want to, it doesn't do Kylie any good if we're bankrupt."

"I'm figuring out a way. I took on a second job."

"Where? Another salon?"

"No, at a bridal shop."

"Seriously? That doesn't sound like something you'd be interested in."

A battle raged inside me. *Should I tell him?* "It belongs to my biological aunt. The one I found on the DNA test."

"Oh, Ally. And you still haven't told Sophie?"

"Not yet. I did tell Kylie."

"Even worse. This really isn't fair. Your mom deserves to know."

In my ongoing fantasy, my mom takes a drive with me to Willow Falls, meets Micki, and decides we should all be one happy family. I didn't know how I was going to make that happen, or if I even could. Would it be possible for my mother to see how a relationship with my biological aunt could benefit all our lives? I wasn't sure.

"I'll ease her into the idea. It might not be such a big deal."

"You're kidding yourself," Matt said. "Sophie will think it's a very big deal. Didn't you think this through?"

Anger spiked hot inside me. "It sounds like you're the one who is going to do the watching instead of the doing. At least I'm being proactive. It may not bring in enough, but it's a start. What are you doing?"

Matt's cheeks flamed. "I'm working very hard at my job. Next summer, I can teach classes."

"Next summer? We can't wait that long."

"I deserve to have a life. I'm not going to apologize for that. I'll do everything I can for Kylie, but for me that includes making decisions that affect the long term, not just the near future."

I let his anger dissipate into the crisp fall air before dropping my bomb. "Fine. We can sell the house."

"We can," he said, though his tone said the opposite. "It needs work if we're going to make enough on the sale to make a difference."

"I thought you wanted to."

"I do want to sell, but I don't want to get taken. If we sell as is, that's what's going to happen."

"My mom could help us out."

"She's already offered. I'm grateful for it, but I don't think either of you understand how long it's going to take on a limited budget."

The sound of Kylie giggling floated from inside the house. We took it in for a moment, that glorious sound.

"Do you think you've changed since we broke up?" I asked after a moment.

"We didn't break up," Matt said. "We separated."

"And how is that different?"

"Because we both still think there's a possibility it could be different," he said before heading outside. "Which is much worse."

CHAPTER 14

District 168 Parents: Discussion Topic

Vera Pastorelli: Is everyone ready for the big debate? This Sunday at 7:00 p.m. in the school auditorium, Cassie Flores, Sawyer McMurphy, and Ally Ackerman will discuss issues of vital importance to District 168. Following the moderator's questions, the floor will open to parents—please bring a list of your concerns!

Bree Nguyen: I have extra Cassie Flores T-shirts, for those who haven't purchased one yet. Go, Team Cassie!

Cole Flounders: I have an itemized list of questions pertaining to busing, curriculum issues, nutritional challenges related to the school lunch program, early college prep for highly motivated middle schoolers, mandatory meditation time at the start of every class, security cameras for the entire block, not just outside the school, and alternatives to physical education for those who find it oppressive. If the moderator position is still open, I'd like to be considered.

Vera Pastorelli: We've got it covered, Cole.

Sawyer McMurphy: I'm truly humbled. Best of luck to my fellow candidates.

Ally Anderson: It's Anderson.

Bree Nguyen: What is?

Ally Anderson: My name.

"Aren't you supposed to picture everyone naked?" Radha said as we began my first hair and makeup consult. It was Bernie. I figured I had to start somewhere.

"I never understood that," Bernie said. "That technique is supposed to put you in the right frame of mind for giving a speech? Most people look completely ridiculous naked. Moles, wrinkles, hairy bits. It's distracting, and it's dangerous for you to get distracted, especially during a debate."

The staff of The Not-So-Blushing-Bride had taken it upon themselves to help me prep for the school board debate. I was more than willing to let them—the thought of it sent my body into such a panic, even Dr. Indigo wouldn't be able to find enough pressure points to help me.

"Did you study?" Radha asked. "I mean, did you think about the questions they might ask you, and then practice the answer?"

Radha was a smart girl, and it filled me with sadness to know her potential had been buried under heartache before she started living with Micki and Sandeep. I'd asked her to be my assistant, and she'd jumped at the chance—Kylie was spending the day with Matt and my mom, HGTV-ifying her room.

"Sort of," I answered. "I'm not sure which questions I'm going to be asked. I just thought about the issues that are important to Kylie."

Radha frowned. "But what about stuff important to the other kids? I mean, I love Kylie, but not everyone is living her same life, right?"

"Narrow focus." Bernie sniffed. "Always a bad idea to limit oneself."

I thought about that for a moment. Had Kylie's illness put me in a tunnel? I was so consumed with fighting for her rights that there was definitely a possibility I'd shut out everything else. "You're both right. I need to think about all the kids' needs and think about how I would address them. At least the bigger issues."

"Bullying," Radha said. "There also might be some kids who don't get enough to eat at home. What is that called?"

"Food insecurity," I said, trying to keep the sadness from my voice. Radha seemed too familiar with the concept. "What else?"

"Rigor," Bernie added. "These kids spend too much time talking about their feelings when they should be diagramming sentences and learning their multiplication tables. Does anyone memorize anymore?"

"What do you think phones are for?" Radha said. "Why would we stuff our heads with stuff we could just google?"

Bernie rolled her eyes.

"Stop that," I admonished her. "I'm going to mess up your eyeliner."

"What about after school?" Radha asked. "Does everyone have a safe place to go if they can't go home?"

"That's a great question," I said. "I don't know, but I'll find out."

Radha hugged herself, pleased with her contribution. "Can we come to the debate? Like, is it open to everybody?"

I didn't know if it would make me more or less nervous to have friends there, but the hopeful look on Radha's sweet face convinced me that having a cheering section might not be a bad thing. I mean, Cassie had Bree, and maybe even Matt. Sawyer had . . . every other woman. Who did I have? "It's open to the public, and you're public. So, yes."

She jumped up and down. "I'm going to ask my mom, but I'm sure it'll be okay."

"That girl is going to be disappointed," Bernie said after Radha was out of earshot.

"Oh, I don't know. Micki and Sandeep seem like the types who like debates."

"That's not what I meant," Bernie said, gazing at me with disdain. "Micki and Sandeep are old. State agencies are judgmental."

I picked up a brush and started gently combing Bernie's soft hair. "Anyone who spends more than five minutes with the three of them knows they're a family. I'm optimistic."

Bernie responded by closing her eyes and leaning her head to the side, like a cat. I wondered how long it had been since she'd been touched by another human being. "Is Reggie back from London?"

"What?" She opened her eyes, bewildered. "I almost fell asleep. Sorry."

"That means I'm doing my job. Do you mind if I trim you up a bit?"

"Not too short," she said. "Reggie likes a true pixie, not a buzz cut."

I smiled to myself. "I'll be careful."

I cleaned up Bernie's cut, which had gotten shaggy, careful to leave longer pieces up front to call attention to her elegant, patrician features. Radha and Aunt Micki joined us, watching silently as I brushed foundation on Bernie's face. She didn't need much. I finished the look with the lipstick Radha picked out.

"Wow," Radha said with a giggle. "Bernie, you look amazing! Reggie is going to freak the freak out!"

Aunt Micki leaned over and kissed Bernie's cheek. "Beautiful. Just beautiful."

I handed Bernie a mirror. She stared at herself, shifting her head slightly to the right and left.

Her total lack of emotion made me nervous. "Do you like it?"

Silence. And then I experienced the rare thing known as an approving smile from Bernie. "I look fabulous," she said. "Let's take a photo so you can re-create it for my wedding."

Micki plucked a gown from the racks. "First let's get you all dressed up, so we can get the whole effect."

"I haven't chosen a dress yet," Bernie said, instantly panicked. "It won't be right."

Micki took Bernie's hand. "Let's just try this one. No obligation. A pretty girl needs a pretty dress. Radha will get some shoes and a veil. You'll look perfect."

Bernie reluctantly took the dress from Micki and trudged to the dressing room.

Before we followed, I pulled Micki to the side. "I'm sure she'll live to be a hundred and ten, but when *is* Bernie getting married?"

"Oh, hon," Aunt Micki said. She gave my arm a squeeze. "Bernie isn't getting married. She's been coming here to make wedding plans for the past three years."

"But what about Reggie?"

"Maybe he existed at some point, but I don't think so. From what I know, Bernie lives alone and has always lived alone. She's got a niece in Vancouver, but other than her, I don't think there's anyone but some of the ladies she knows from volunteering at the library, and maybe a few neighbors."

"There's you," I said, surprised to find myself getting choked up. "Radha and Sandy."

"Yes," Micki said softly. "We've got her back."

"Mom! Ally!" Radha called, "Come quick!"

I was vaguely aware that brides wore white to signify purity, and though I'm sure it meant something completely different in the days of old, it was absolutely true for Bernie—there was a simple purity to her beauty. She was resplendent in the long-sleeve sheath dress, the white satin matching her snow-capped head and bringing a subtle glow to her skin. Her makeup only served to highlight her finely drawn features.

The vision of her stole my breath.

"You're gorgeous," I said, tears springing to my eyes. "Utterly stunning." I took out my phone and got a quick photo. I wanted to remember this particular kind of beauty, made all the more poignant now that I knew Bernie's situation.

"Like, you should seriously be on the top of a cake," Radha said, awed. "Or at least on our Instagram page."

"What do you think?" Micki asked Bernie.

She turned to admire herself in the mirror, smiling at her image, turning back and forth. "It's . . . almost perfect. We'll get there. Let's keep trying."

~

On stage, we were lined up like Jeopardy contestants, Cassie, Sawyer . . . and me, the one the audience could dismiss at first glance. Cassie wore a business suit and a confident smile. Sawyer looked like he'd just stepped out of a Lifetime Christmas movie. I wore a black tunic with black leggings, the uniform I'd created for working at the bridal shop. I hadn't had time to change.

"Five minutes to start!" Vera called. She'd upped her baseball hat game—this one was bedazzled with orange and black rhinestones for the season.

As if trying to get their conversations in before the debate started, the crowd grew even louder. Bree Nguyen and the Cassie crew took over the entire first two rows. They wore matching T-shirts and matching expressions of superiority. A skinny bespectacled boy held tightly onto a leash that prevented Riker from taking out someone's carotid artery. From the way he looked up at Cassie—with a mixture of pride and excitement—I assumed he was her son.

My crew stretched out over the back row—Heather, Micki, Sandy, still partially dressed as a zombie, Radha, in a bright crimson-and-gold sari, and even Bernie, who'd insisted on coming. She still wore her newly made-up face proudly.

I suffered a stab of guilt. I hadn't told my mom about the debate, partially because she was fully immersed in transforming Kylie's room and partially because I had enormous potential to embarrass myself, and I didn't want her to witness it. The need to make her proud had grown stronger with age instead of fading. I wondered how much being adopted influenced this. Was some small messed-up part of me desperate to prove I was worth the trouble?

I shook off that depressing thought, choosing instead to be grateful that, with Micki there, I hadn't invited my mother. The room quieted a bit as Vera attempted to climb up on the stage. She got stuck, and Sawyer reached a hand out to pull her up. A hundred women sighed. I nearly puked in my mouth.

"I'll have someone turn the mics on in a few moments," Vera said to us. "So be careful what you say after that. Answer the questions as best you can, but if you get carried away and start hogging everyone's time, I'll tug on the brim of my baseball hat to let you know it's time to shut up. We've got an hour and a half before they need this room for bingo, so let's stay on topic, okay?"

We nodded, and she edged herself carefully from the stage, shooing off Sawyer's offer of help.

"I'm a little nervous," Sawyer admitted. "I'm not the best public speaker."

"I'm not either," I said. "But it's not like we're professionals, right?"

"I am," Cassie said. "My profession requires it. Just answer everything with confidence, even if you aren't sure of what you're talking about. People will give you the benefit of the doubt."

I wondered if that was true, but I had to admit that Cassie was being gracious in trying to help us out. "Thanks for the tip," I said, and Sawyer nodded in appreciation.

"Two minutes!" Vera yelled. The crowd's buzzing resumed as people finished up their conversations before the big show.

We three candidates stopped speaking to each other, content to stare at the crowd, and—in my case—freak myself out a little further.

I watched the door open at the back of the room. My blood stilled in my veins. Matt, Kylie, and my mom filed in, taking seats in the row opposite the Willow Falls group.

Fuuuuudge. Matt must have told them about it. For sure Kylie would notice Micki and the gang—it was only a matter of time.

One thought punched at my brain. *How do I make this okay?*

Micki and Mom sat mere feet away from each other. Oblivious. I caught Mom's eye, and she gave me a little nod.

Maybe the "client" ruse would hold. Maybe Kylie wouldn't notice them, and it wouldn't be an issue at all.

I kind of wanted to cry.

Sawyer nudged me. "You okay?"

I couldn't answer him because I was busy trying to construct a wall between my mom and Micki using only my brainwaves. It wasn't working.

"Picture them naked," Sawyer whispered. "It's supposed to work."

I was the one who felt naked and exposed. Why had I been so stupid? I should have told my mother.

I watched my potential nightmare play out in slow motion. Kylie jumped up and down in her seat, calling out to Micki. My mom glanced over to see the object of Kylie's attention, and then, puzzled, took in the eclectic group. Radha heartily returned Kylie's greeting, smiling and waving back. Mom waved half-heartedly, probably wondering how in the world she knew these people.

Micki stared at Mom, openmouthed. Mom noticed and leaned toward Matt, cranking her neck to whisper in his ear.

Shit.

"Let's begin," Vera announced, slapping at her podium until the crowd shushed. "This debate is in preparation for the election for school board member number eight. The three candidates are Cassie Flores, Sawyer McMurphy, and Ally . . . Ackerman."

"Anderson," I said into the mic.

"Anderson," Vera repeated, not missing a beat. "I have a few questions to begin, and then I'm going to open it to the floor. Keep it respectful. And if anyone revisits the topic of going all keto in the cafeteria, I'm cutting off your mic."

Micki said something to Sandy, and he put his arm protectively around her shoulders. She looked troubled.

Oh, I was a bad daughter. And a bad niece.

"Ms.—er—Anderson?"

"What?" Startled, I banged my knee against the podium, and the hollow sound rang out through the gym.

Vera glared at me. "I said we'd start with you. The first topic relates to student safety. The unfortunate reality is that every school needs to prepare in the event of an active shooter. Our district currently has a very limited plan in place—student drills and visitors must be buzzed into the building. What do you think could improve our policies?"

The only enemies I'd ever considered were the kid who'd brought a peanut butter cup to school and the bully who made fun of Kylie's hives. An active shooter? The thought chilled my body so much that my brain froze.

"Ms. Anderson?"

"I . . . uh . . . I think we should be more vigilant?"

"How so?"

How? How the hell did I know? Desperate, I went with the first half-decent idea that popped into my brain. "I went to drop my daughter's medication once at the school, and got buzzed in before I said my name or why I was there. Maybe we should be more careful when screening who comes in the school?"

Silence.

A woman in the front row, wearing a shirt emblazoned with Cassie's name, sent me dagger looks. It took a second before I recognized her. Barb . . . Barb Something . . . how did I know her?

Yes! She worked at the school.

Behind the front desk.

And I'd just thrown her under the school bus. The first few rows of women growled at me.

"Can I step in?" Cassie interjected smoothly. "There are currently special alarm systems that are easily installed and only activate when a shooter is in the school. The PA system alerts the teachers, who can then usher children into their classrooms and hopefully out of harm's way."

The ladies in the first few rows puffed up like they wanted to burst into applause. I watched Matt, who sat expressionless, which must have taken a great deal of effort. Cassie was good.

"Well, that's a mighty nice idea," Sawyer said. Had he suddenly developed a drawl? "I have one question—how much does it cost, and where will we get the funds?"

"That's two questions," Cassie said, smiling tightly. "I'm sure if we analyze the budget, we'd figure out a way to pay for something of such vital importance."

"Surely," Sawyer said, his voice dripping with honey.

"Moving on," Vera said.

We moved on through teacher evaluations and hiring practices and curriculum changes and meeting state standards. Cassie had an answer for everything. Sawyer had a question for all of her answers, but curiously no answers to any of the questions. I managed to squeak in a few passable points.

Until Vera opened up questions to the floor . . .

Cole Flounders popped his hand up. "I have a question. How do you feel your job experience will contribute to your performance on the school board?"

Oh, you little weasel, I thought. *You're a plant. A Cassie Flores plant.*

"I'll take this one first," Cassie said, with a confidence so strong it deflated mine. "My work as a lawyer requires exceptional problem-solving skills and a talent for public speaking. I excel in interpersonal communication and conflict resolution. I also have full faith in my ability to be a team player."

"Where did you go to school?" Cole asked.

Cassie paused. "Georgetown."

"Fantastic," Cole said. "I have no more questions at the moment."

"This isn't a trial," Vera said. "Sawyer and Ally? You'll need to answer the same question."

"I'll take it next," Sawyer said.

What did he do for a living? Every woman in the place leaned in.

"My job is in a nursery . . ."

That was all he needed to say. The thunderous sigh nearly took off the roof.

"Well," he continued, "I work with plants and trees."

Oh, *that* kind of nursery. Huh.

Sawyer cleared his throat. "I . . . move trees around. Put them into cars. I can explain how to care for the root system. Trees take a while to get settled, you know, just like most people."

That didn't get a laugh. The women were still trying to reframe their fantasy of Sawyer cradling a baby in his muscular arms.

"Ally?" Vera sounded bored.

"I'm a hairdresser." Someone snickered.

Really?

I didn't know what else to say. Why did I think I was qualified to do this? Unable to think, my eyes zipped over the audience, landing on

Kylie. She was wide-eyed, nodding slightly, confident I was going to say something to redeem myself.

"My job requires that I listen to people," I began. "If I don't, I could really mess up, which would affect someone's self-esteem."

They looked unconvinced. Kylie kept bobbing her head, encouraging me to go on. "Well, it might not seem like much, but I put myself through beauty school, earning the money by waitressing at night, so I know what hoops working parents must go through. Some of us work so hard we don't have the time to go to meetings or pay attention to email chains or Facebook pages. We have to trust the members of the school board to make decisions for the health and well-being of our kids. I know I'm not the most knowledgeable candidate, but I do know that I'll earn your trust by making decisions that will make things better, not worse."

Cassie Flores might have had a crew, but so did I. Micki, Radha, and Sandy whooped it up for me. My mom eyed them warily. *Shit.*

Vera pounded on the podium. "All right, all right. Anyone else got a question?"

Parent after parent took the mic and asked us questions ranging from mild to almost offensive. Someone asked about after-school care, and I gave a silent thank-you to Radha for suggesting I think about it. Another parent asked about the allergy table, and I was able to make a case for it, so maybe it still had a chance, even if I lost. After about twenty minutes of this back and forth, Vera announced that we were done. "Elections take place the first week of November. Best of luck to the candidates!"

Cassie's followers stormed the stage, twittering with excitement. She'd done a good job. Sawyer hadn't answered many questions, but he did have a lot of them, which some people might interpret as intelligence. I was proud of how I answered the allergy question, but it was apparent I had a lot to learn.

So learn it, I told myself. *Step up.*

I scanned the crowd, looking for my family. Mom and Matt stood in the corner, locked in a discussion so intense it made my stomach clench. Were they discussing the right shade of lavender for Kylie's room, or had she picked up on something? Kylie was talking to Bernie, with the rest of the crew casually drawing closer to my mom. I needed to do something—to facilitate, or deflect, or maybe try to build that wall again using my body—I wasn't sure what.

"We're likely going to lose," Sawyer said, interrupting my thoughts. "And we probably deserve to, but I'm in for the whole show. You?"

"Yep," I said, distracted, as I watched my two worlds begin to clash. "I am."

"Good," Sawyer said, before hopping off the stage with grace. Unlike Vera, he didn't need any help.

The crowd swirled around the other two candidates, obscuring my view of my mom. I struggled to spot Kylie, but when I did, what I saw stopped my heart.

Her hands circled her neck, our code for an allergic reaction. She was talking to Micki, who glanced around frantically.

Without pausing to think, I jumped off the stage, scattering Cassie's followers. I sprinted for my purse, feeling like I was moving through wet sand. I pushed people to the side, deflecting rude remarks. It didn't matter. I grabbed my bag and barreled through to Kylie, whose face was now the color of borscht.

"My throat feels tight," she said, panic seizing her voice. "And too itchy. Mom, I'm scared."

"I gave her some candy," Bernie wailed. "I thought it was fine."

"I didn't notice!" Micki said. "What can we do?"

"Call 911!" I shrieked, while rifling through my purse. "Matt! Matt!"

My hands shook violently as I readied the pen. "Matt!" I yelled again, my voice rasping. Images flooded my brain—Kylie at the ballpark, *dying, dying* . . .

Matt appeared, took one look at Kylie, and drew her to him, sinking to the floor, whispering comfort in her ear.

I shot her with the EpiPen, holding it in place. "Let's count slowly, okay? One, two . . ."

There was a chorus for the rest. Six worried faces stared down at us.

Kylie watched the Epi sticking out of her leg with a kind of fascinated terror.

Please work, please work, please work . . .

"You're going to be fine," I choked out. "When the ambulance gets here, they'll take you to the hospital where they'll make sure everything is okay."

"I don't want to go to the hospital," Kylie said, tearful. She bolted upright, the adrenaline in the medication rocketing through her small body. "Please! I don't want to go."

Matt kissed her head. "We won't be there long."

I eyed the door. Where the hell was the ambulance? The Epi only worked for fifteen minutes. If they took longer than that, and Kylie continued to react . . . would I Epi her again? I thought about the girl I'd read about who still died after three shots, and my heart thudded against my chest.

"Where the hell are they?" my mom said from behind me. I hadn't realized her hand was on my shoulder. It calmed me as much as I was able to be calmed.

"Can you stand outside? Steer them in the right direction?" I shared a look of understanding with her. She knew every minute counted.

"On it," she said.

Micki stepped forward. "I'll go with you."

My mom gave her an odd look. "Thanks, but I've got it." She walked off, but not before winking at Kylie.

"I'm better," Kylie said. "I don't need to go to the emergency room." She started to cry. "Don't make me go. I'm scared."

I let out a relieved breath. The epinephrine seemed to be working. Kylie would start to shake soon, but right now it had lessened the constriction in her throat, easing her body's overreaction to the allergen. Matt continued murmuring to her in an unending stream, soothing sounds, distracting her from the sirens I hoped I wasn't imagining.

"They're coming!" Radha said. "I hear them!"

Matt lifted Kylie, and I held on to him, acting as one unit as we carried her toward the door. The EMTs rushed inside, taking over, sliding our girl out from under our arms.

We could go with them, they said. Both of us.

My heart didn't let go of Kylie.

My arms didn't let go of Matt.

CHAPTER 15

It almost seemed cruel to walk into the pediatric waiting room in the ER, knowing that Kylie was one of the lucky ones. Thankfully, the parents and caregivers and siblings, hollow-eyed and exhausted, didn't make eye contact with me. We didn't know each other's stories, only that we were in a place that had potential for tragedy at every turn—acknowledging each other made real what we were there for. Everyone stayed in their individual bubbles of worry, a space of safety, however temporary.

My mother sat under an ancient television set blaring an old episode of *Blue's Clues*. The harsh overhead light deepened the worry lines on her face and left gray shadows under her eyes. She looked small and vulnerable. I could relate.

"Kylie's going to be okay," I said, settling in next to her. "Four to six hours of observation and we can take her home."

She grabbed my shoulders, and we silently held each other for a moment.

"I hate feeling so helpless," Mom whispered into my ear. "I hate not being able to fix this, with every cell in my body."

"I know. It's terrible."

We kept hugging, drawing strength from each other.

Until, looking over my shoulder, my mom stiffened and said, "Okay, who the hell are those people?"

Sandy, Micki, Radha, and Bernie stood huddled in the doorway. I suddenly felt like Ally in Wonderland—the walls of the room seemed to shrink, while my body grew larger and larger, puffed up with guilt and embarrassment.

"We had to come," Micki said as they shuffled in. She glanced at my mother. "I'm sorry, but we couldn't just go home after that."

"She's okay, right?" Sandy asked. "She was already texting with Radha, so no lasting damage?"

That was a tough question to answer. What did he consider lasting? Kylie would be more afraid now. Her body might react even more the next time she was exposed. She might have to discontinue her treatment. We just didn't know. Like with everything related to modern health issues, there were so many unanswered questions. "She's going to be fine," I said, too exhausted to give a detailed answer. "They just need to monitor her as a precaution."

Mom stood. "I'm Sophie," she said, reaching a hand toward a flustered Micki. "Ally's mom. And you are?"

Micki grasped my mom's hand and stared at it. "I'm, ah . . . a friend. Of Ally's."

How far should I let this go?

Mom was smiling, but it was strained. "How do you know her?"

"I was a client, and she does the hair for my bridal shop," Micki said, her words running together. "We really like her."

"And Kylie," Radha said. "We like her a lot too."

There was a moment of silence heavier than the weighted blanket Kylie used to help her sleep. I desperately wanted to escape to the warm hospital room with Matt and Kylie. When it wasn't a life-or-death issue, a hospital room could be surprisingly nurturing, a temporary isolation from the outside world. Total isolation sounded pretty good to me at that moment.

Mom crossed her arms over her chest, ex-bartender's eyes sharpening into knives that could cut through the bullshit.

I took a deep breath. Of all the things I'd learned from my mom, cowardice was not one of them. Kindness was, and keeping this secret was not kind. "Mom, this is Micki Patel. She's the sister of Cissy Ricelli, my biological mother. Cissy passed away, but I found Micki on that DNA thing, and we've hung out a few times."

"I see," was all she said.

I touched her arm. "I'm sorry I didn't tell you. Really, I am."

Mom shook my hand away. "And this is your family, Mrs. Patel?"

Introductions were made all around.

"Thank you for your concern for my granddaughter," Mom said, her manner overpolite.

"I'm really so very sorry," Bernie said. Her shoulders sunk with exhaustion, and her makeup had smeared and settled into the deep wrinkles around her eyes and mouth. "I didn't mean it," she said. "I would never hurt Kylie like that. I am a stupid old woman. But it was chocolate. I'd seen her eat chocolate before. How would I know it would cause a problem?"

"Accidents happen," I said, resisting the urge to scream, *You could have killed her!* Anger does no one good, and Bernie would never have consciously hurt Kylie. "Now we'll all be more careful. And Kylie knows she's supposed to read labels and ask questions before eating anything."

"She didn't want to hurt your feelings by turning you down," Micki said to Bernie. "She was just trying to be a good girl."

"Kylie is always a good girl," Mom said, but her voice sounded far away. Her mind processed most things quickly, but this wasn't most things.

Another awkward silence, this one worse than the last because now my mother knew what was up. I couldn't look at her.

"I don't feel well," Bernie moaned. "I'm spent, and I don't like hospitals."

"We can't leave yet," Micki said, with a nervous glance toward my mother. "Radha wants to see Kylie."

"I'll take you home," Mom said.

"Mom, it's far."

As I've said, my mom is not much of a hugger, but she grabbed my shoulders and pulled me toward her. The force of her grasp was less maternal and more Michael Corleone's iron grip on his brother Fredo in *The Godfather*. "I need a little time," she hissed. "I expect you to understand that."

"Of course."

Mom released me and turned to Bernie. "Are you okay with me taking you?"

Bernie nodded. "I'm so tired I'd go home on a horse if I had to."

"Let me get this young lady home," Mom said. She took my chin in her hand. "We'll talk when you get home."

Bernie cast me one more mournful look. I carefully folded my arms around her fragile shoulders. "Stop worrying," I whispered in her ear. "She's fine. No harm done."

"I didn't mean to hurt anyone," she whispered back. "Especially that sweet girl." Bernie pulled away from me and shuffled after my mom.

Micki watched them, wringing her hands. "Oh, this isn't right," she muttered, running to my mother and tugging on her jacket. "I have to say something. I just do."

Mom didn't turn around right away.

I held my breath. *Oh, please, universe. Make whatever is about to happen not be apocalyptic.*

Mom turned around. Her expression said . . . nothing at all. She could have been staring at a wall.

Again, the words spilled out of Micki so fast, I was pretty certain she wasn't totally in control of what was coming out. "I need to thank you for raising Ally. My sister couldn't, and you've obviously done a very good job, because Ally has a goodness in her that I'm pretty sure she didn't get from my side of the family, so it must have been what you taught her, and she was such a sweet baby, so maybe it was always in her, but with you watching her—"

Mom put her hand up. "I wasn't babysitting," was all she said, and then left Micki standing in the middle of the room, her mouth agape.

Sandy went over and hugged her to him. "She's in shock," he said. "We should have been the ones to take Bernie home. This is a family matter."

"But we're family," Micki said. Tears spilled over her cheeks. "I didn't mean to be disrespectful."

"You weren't," Radha said, a murderous look in her eye. "She was mean to you, and that wasn't right."

"It's complicated, hon," Aunt Micki said, swiping at her cheeks.

"Karma will get her," Radha said. "Right, Dad?"

"She did nothing wrong," Sandy said. "I know you're defending your mother, but we shouldn't force someone to think about things she'd rather not think about." This was the first time I'd seen Sandy frown. "This whole night, just wasn't . . . right."

"Can we just see Kylie now?" Radha asked, still disgruntled. "I'd really like to."

~

Kylie was nearly asleep, her limbs loose, eyes shuttered. "Hi," she squeaked.

Matt stood quickly, effectively blocking us from Kylie's bed. "She should rest."

"I promise we won't be more than a minute," Sandy said. He introduced his family to Matt, while Micki slipped by them, kissing Kylie while Radha ruffled her hair.

The scene felt warm and loving, and worked to ease the fear that had gripped my heart since I thrust the Epi into Kylie's thigh. What if it hadn't worked? What if it was worse the next time? This didn't feel like the end of worry. It felt like the beginning of a deeper, more serious kind of terror.

"We were worried," Radha said. "You could have, like, *died.*"

"Radha," Micki said sharply.

"Maybe we should clear the room out so Kylie can sleep," Matt said, gritting his teeth. I loved Radha, but I felt the same—the last thing we needed was Kylie obsessing about a near-death experience.

Goodbyes were said. Micki asked that I walk them out.

"We've really messed things up," she said as we got to the elevator.

"No, you didn't. I made this mess."

She hugged me. "Will Kylie be able to complete the treatment?"

"I honestly don't know. Part of me hopes so, and part of me is so afraid for her to do it. The risk is intensified now." I'd texted Dr. Indigo as soon as Kylie had stabilized. *Come tomorrow at noon*, was all she said.

The elevator door opened. Radha and Sandy kissed me quickly and hopped in.

Micki hugged me again, tighter this time. I felt a tug, and she shoved something in my pocket. "Take this and shut up about it."

She was gone before I could protest.

The check was for seven thousand dollars.

On the memorandum line she'd written: *For 38 years of missed Christmas presents.*

~

We got home at three in the morning. Matt carried Kylie to her bed, and we tucked her in with a minimum of fuss. My mom, curiously enough, wasn't home yet. This unsettled me. Apologies should be made quickly, before unchecked anger grows to unmanageable fury.

"Do you want some tea or something?" I said. "I'm putting the kettle on for myself."

Matt rubbed at his face, as though he could wipe away the exhaustion. "Some coffee would be great. You've still got that press, right?"

"You'll be up all night if you drink coffee. You get that heart pounding thing."

"I know, but I have to go to work tomorrow. Mandatory faculty meeting at seven a.m. I might as well stay up."

Everything about that sounded difficult. "I'm taking Kylie to Dr. Indigo tomorrow. I thought you might want to come with."

"Really?"

"Yeah." I really did want him there. This would be an important appointment. Would we continue the treatment or give up? Was there an alternate plan? It was one thing to have our hopes crushed, and another to have them simply deferred. What was that poem about a dream deferred? Wasn't that awful too?

"I've got mandatory training at school," Matt said, his voice weary. "They're changing the grading platform again."

"Oh. Okay."

I busied myself in the kitchen, leaving the light dim. The glaring overheads of the emergency room had dried out my eyes, and I wanted them to rest, even if my body couldn't. Matt checked his phone, texted someone, and then shut it off.

"Cassie?" I said.

"What?" He smiled slightly, sheepish. "She's a compassionate person, Ally, and so she was worried. She wanted to know how Kylie was doing, that's all."

Sometimes feelings are so undefinable, you go with the first recognizable one you can grasp. This one I managed to hook was sadness. I poured his coffee, added a dash of milk like he preferred. I watched my tea steep, wondering how we'd gotten to this point.

"I thought happiness was something that just happened, and you went along for the ride," Matt said softly. "We met, we got married, had Kylie. I didn't think I controlled any of that, it was just life being good to me."

"And now?"

"I see happiness for what it is. A goal. And people have to work toward goals. Cassie might be great for me, or she might not, but I'm going to work to find out."

Matt had always been contemplative and analytical. I knew that part of him, and I knew it well. What I hadn't realized was how much I was going to miss it.

"She did a good job tonight," I said, offering my olive branch.

"You did a better one."

"I couldn't answer half the questions. You know that's not true."

"I didn't mean during the debate. You got that Epi in Kylie faster than it took for me to blink. We knew this day could come, but I had no idea how intense it would be. Our little girl." His voice broke. "I don't think I've ever been so frightened in my entire life."

I put my hand over his before I could overthink it. "She's okay," I said, tears rasping my voice. "She's okay."

"Who would have imagined that an old lady offering a piece of chocolate to our kid would result in a life-or-death situation?" He slid his hand out from under mine, and curled his palms around his coffee mug. "I would give anything to eliminate the risks in Kylie's life. For the most part, I can't do that. I can only control the things I can control. Ally, I don't want Dr. Indigo to continue with the desensitization treatment. The exposure could prompt an even worse reaction. What if the EpiPen doesn't work? What if we don't make it to the hospital in time?"

Those thoughts haunted my every minute. Matt had a point, but I couldn't think straight enough to make a definitive decision. I was so tired I felt like every process in my body had slowed, my heart and brain especially, the two things I needed to evaluate the situation with any clarity.

"Let's see what Dr. Indigo says."

"Her interests are not necessarily ours." Matt stood and rinsed out his mug. "I want you to promise me you won't proceed. You don't always think things through before you act. Promise me, Ally."

"I can't promise anything. I need to talk to the doctor first."

"She's not Kylie's mother."

"Neither are you."

CHAPTER 16

"Well, this is pretty fancy-pants. You're moving up in the world, Miss Kylie!"

I needed a voice of reason, so I ended up bringing Heather to our doctor's appointment. I figured she was smart, she loved Kylie, and she wasn't afraid to tell me no. She'd also insisted when I'd told her about the hospital visit.

"Maybe I'll meet a rich doctor," she continued, eyeballing the ritzy greystone.

"I don't want to burst your bubble—"

"You're my friend. You're supposed to protect my bubble."

I laughed. "Okay. I'll let it pop naturally."

Heather snorted. "That's what he said."

I glanced at Kylie in the back seat, but she was staring out the window, her face drawn and pale. "You okay, little warrior?"

"I guess. How long do we have to stay here?"

"As long as it takes."

"It didn't work, Mom. Why do we even have to come back?"

"I don't give up, and neither do you. Let's see what Dr. Indigo has to say."

Kylie sighed. "She'll say I didn't calm the dog."

"Just because you couldn't calm it yesterday doesn't mean you can't ever calm it."

"Never gonna happen."

Heather nudged me. "Let's go in and see if the dog is even around. Maybe you don't have to calm it anymore. Maybe you just have to calm the cat. And that would be a whole lot easier, right? Cats are totally chill anyway."

Kylie wasn't taking the bait. "I'm missing play practice today."

"I already texted Mrs. Loftus," I said. "Don't worry about it."

Kylie didn't respond. Instead, she got out of the car and slammed the door. I got it. The anger that comes from not being able to trust your own body.

The gorgeous receptionist didn't bother walking us upstairs. We swept by her, past the stylish but perpetually empty offices, onto the cold landing outside Dr. Indigo's door. I kicked the door open, and we were immediately confronted by a cloud of incense.

"Well, I've got to say, I'm disappointed," Heather said. "This looks like my first apartment after high school."

"Kylie?" Dr. Indigo appeared. She wore a long navy-blue knit dress with a black collar and thick purple belt at the waist. She looked like a bruise.

Then Dr. Indigo did something that surprised me—she knelt down, grabbed Kylie, and held her tightly.

"I'm so glad you're okay," she said, showing more emotion than I thought possible.

"I couldn't calm the dog," Kylie murmured into her shoulder. "I tried, but I was so surprised. My throat felt all swollen, and I got scared."

Dr. Indigo leaned back on her heels. "That's a completely normal response. Your mom calmed the dog temporarily with the Epi. The treatment you're doing is teaching your body to calm it naturally." She looked up at me. "We are continuing treatment, aren't we? This is a stumbling block, not a wall. We can start up again in a few weeks. This isn't the end. Not even close."

"It isn't?" Kylie beamed. "I want to. I was scared before, but now I'm not. We can keep coming, right, Mom?"

I thought about Matt and his reservations. I couldn't make this decision by myself. We'd have to discuss it. "We'll talk about it with Dad."

Kylie deflated a little.

"We can discuss this further next time," Dr. Indigo said, obviously sensing she shouldn't push. "Now, what did Kylie eat to cause her reaction?"

"I'm not exactly sure," I said, embarrassed. How much peanut had she ingested when she ate the candy? I was too caught up in the moment to ask Bernie for a piece to analyze. "I'll get a piece of the candy for you as soon as possible."

Dr. Indigo nodded. "Okay, since we're not doing the treatment today, let's focus on relaxing your body. You've been through a trauma, Kylie."

Kylie's eyes grew large, her imagination luxuriating in the word "trauma." But Dr. Indigo wasn't being melodramatic. It felt like trauma, just thinking about my daughter lying terrified on the gymnasium floor, a shot full of adrenaline possibly the only thing saving her throat from closing up. "You, too, Ally. And . . ." Dr. Indigo glanced at Heather.

"I'm Heather. The friend. I'm stressed, too, but for a lesser reason."

Dr. Indigo lifted an eyebrow.

"Online dating," Heather said. "It makes me nauseous."

"Well, everyone can benefit from relaxation techniques," the doctor said after a moment's hesitation. "Would you like to join us?"

Heather grinned. "I thought you'd never ask."

~

We were stretched out on the floor, heads touching, our feet splayed out—as she gazed down at us, I'm sure we looked like a slightly lopsided star to Dr. Indigo.

"What happens to our energy when we're stressed out?" she asked.

"When I'm stressed," I said, thinking about how I'd avoided seeing my mom that morning, "I feel like I don't have any energy at all."

"I feel empty and listless," Heather said. "Like, all my emotions are far away, and it takes too much energy to retrieve them."

Dr. Indigo nodded. "Kylie?"

"I don't know."

"I'm not trying to cause stress, I'm trying to help you alleviate it," Dr. Indigo said. "Let's approach it like this. When I say the word 'stress,' what's the first thing you think of?"

"Scared," Kylie said. And more heartbreakingly, "Alone."

The doctor smiled. "Good answers. I think a lot of people feel this way. What do you think most people do when they're completely overwhelmed by stress?"

"Drink heavily," Heather said.

"Distract themselves," I said.

"Try not to cry," Kylie said.

"And do any of these work?" Dr. Indigo asked.

"No," we said in unison.

The doctor began to circle us, clockwise. "What most people assume," she began, "is that because we suffer individual stressors, we must deal with those stressors individually. This is simply untrue. As human beings we can share energy with each other, and we can give each other positivity, and we can help drain unproductive energy away."

"And how is this done, exactly?" Heather said. "I'm kind of an experiential learner."

"I'm glad you asked," Dr. Indigo said. She lit some candles and a stick of incense. It wasn't her regular patchouli, but lavender mixed with something sweet but not cloying.

"Close your eyes," she began. "Breathe in. One, two, three, four. Breathe out. One, two, three, four. And again. And again."

We inhaled and we exhaled, again and again, counting the beats. Just when I felt like I might fall asleep, Dr. Indigo continued.

"Kylie, what are you stressed about?"

"Getting kicked off the school play. I've missed a lot of days."

I couldn't believe she hadn't chosen the exposure incident. The normalcy of her answer gave me a quick jolt of reassurance.

"Ally," Dr. Indigo said, "Kylie is going to take a deep breath. When she exhales, she'll be exhaling her stress. When you inhale, you'll be taking some of it in, to help her out."

I could feel Heather stiffen. I was sure she was struggling to contain her laughter.

"Kylie, I want you to think about all of your worries about the school play. Swirl them together and breathe them in. Hold them for a minute. Ally, be prepared to take them in. Exhale, Kylie. Now."

I could hear Kylie breathe out. Almost instinctively, I inhaled deeply. I imagined taking all my daughter's fears and drawing them into my body, where my adult defenses could pick them apart, one by one. She was no match for everything being thrown her way. But I could take it.

"Those fears might not be entirely gone, Kylie, but they're much weaker now that your mom has taken some of them. Do you feel a little lighter?"

"I think so," Kylie said. "I don't think I'm worried as much."

"Good," Dr. Indigo said. "Okay, Ally, what can you release to Heather?"

I didn't want to burden anyone with my problems, least of all my best friend. I wracked my brain for something mild, something innocuous.

"I can take it, Ally," Heather said quietly. "Hit me with your best shot."

"Trust your friend," Dr. Indigo said lightly.

There were too many things I couldn't say out loud. I was worried for my daughter's future. It was a primal worry—deep and body numbing and too overwhelming to hand off to someone else. The worries I had for myself seemed almost inconsequential. I couldn't give Heather my fear of being alone for the rest of my life, or the fear that I'd hurt my mother in my search for my past, or the fact that Mom was halfway down the slide into old age.

"I'm afraid I'll lose the school board election," I said. "I'm afraid I'll make an idiot out of myself."

"Chicken," Heather whispered.

"Gather up those fears," Dr. Indigo said. "Take them in, hold them for a moment, and then breathe out, long and slow. Heather, inhale Ally's fear."

"Gladly," Heather said, and inhaled theatrically.

We lay there breathing normally for a moment, until Dr. Indigo turned to Heather. "Your turn."

Heather was quiet for a moment. When she spoke, I felt like I was hearing something very personal, from a place she rarely revealed. "I'm afraid . . ."

"Keep going," Dr. Indigo encouraged her.

"I'm afraid . . . I'm afraid I'm never going to be as good of a person as I want to be."

I reached out and took her hand. "You're plenty good."

Dr. Indigo snapped her fingers. "Don't judge her fear, Ally. Now, Kylie, you're going to take Heather's fear. What are you going to do with it?"

"Stomp on it," Kylie said, without hesitation. "Squish it. Destroy it."

"Okay, Heather, are you ready?" Dr. Indigo said. "Get that fear in your lungs. Kylie, be prepared to take it in."

Heather drew a breath and exhaled sharply. Kylie inhaled, coughed a little, and inhaled again.

"Oh no," Kylie said. "Did I cough it out?"

"You still have it," Dr. Indigo assured her. "Go ahead and start stomping."

"I did it," Kylie said after a minute. "It's obliterated!"

"I can feel it," Heather said, a bit tearful. "You did that for me. Thank you!"

"We're stronger together," Dr. Indigo said. "I know you've heard that many times before, but sometimes we need to experience things to understand the truth of them."

"That sounds a little cheesy," I said, "but I get it."

"I can't eat cheese," Kylie said, and we all laughed.

CHAPTER 17

"Do you guys want to take a drive?" I asked once we were back in the car.

"Why does that sound like we don't have a choice?" Heather said. "Where to?"

"Bernie's house. I want to see if she has any more of that candy."

"She feels bad, doesn't she?" said Kylie from the back seat.

"She does."

"I want to talk to her. To tell her it's okay, and I'm not mad."

"That's a good girl you've got there," Heather said under her breath.

"Of course, sweetie," I said. I glanced in the rearview mirror, and Kylie's eyes were already drooping. She was asleep before we got on the highway.

Traffic was brutal, and we pulled up in front of Bernie's house an hour and forty-five minutes later.

"Isn't that your mom's car?" Heather said. "Oh, wow. Do you think she decided to give you up and move in with Bernie? That could totally be a reality show. Bernie could complain and pass judgment, and your mom could sit there and stare at her with nothing-escapes-me eyes. The whole show could be about how long it takes before your mom goes off the deep end."

"My mom loves her own house too much. And she already has us to drive her crazy." I had a strange sense of foreboding. It *was* completely bizarre that her car was still there. Why hadn't I noticed it was missing? I'd been tired, so tired, when I hauled myself out of bed, and then Kylie decided she wanted to go to school, so in the hustle to get moving, I hadn't knocked on her door before we left for the day. Also, part of me was too afraid of what she'd say about Micki. Mom had texted, twice, to check in on Kylie, but her messages were clipped and pointed—I figured she also needed some time before talking about what I'd done. But apparently she wasn't alone in her room—she was with Bernie.

Bernie's house, a box-shaped one-story ranch, looked perfectly respectable from the street, but when we got to the door, I noticed the brown paint had nearly peeled entirely from the wood. The railings were wobbly, and some of the cement was crumbling.

"Miss Bernie lives here?" Kylie asked. "I thought she'd live in a rich-lady house."

I hushed her as the door opened.

"Mom?"

"What a surprise," she said flatly, but then smiled at Kylie. "How's my girl?" She ran her hands over her granddaughter, as if to make sure nothing was broken.

"I'm good," Kylie said. "The peanut didn't win."

"Of course it didn't." She looked up at me, her expression grave. "This woman is a friend of yours? You need to come in here and have a look."

It wasn't the smell that hit me, bleach mixed with cheap air freshener, it was the emptiness of the space. Bernie's living room could hardly be worthy of that name. There was a couch, a threadbare rug, an old television set with an actual dial that needed to be turned. An antenna, covered in aluminum foil, reached toward a yellowed ceiling pock-marked with moisture bubbles.

"Where's Bernie?" I asked, my voice a whisper because my heart blocked my vocal cords. *This is what she comes home to every night?*

"She's in her bedroom," my mom said. "Come on, I want to show you the kitchen."

"Mom?" Kylie sat on the edge of the couch. "I don't think I want to go in the kitchen."

"I'll hang with you, Miss Kylie," Heather said. "Go," she told me.

Kylie must have had a sixth sense, because the kitchen was much worse. It wasn't so much dirty as empty and broken. The faucet dripped into an old porcelain sink, and two of the cabinets were missing doors. The refrigerator sounded asthmatic. Enough floor tiles were missing that it was like walking through a minefield, not a kitchen. An old per-colator was the only indication that anything food related was actually ingested in this room.

"She doesn't have anyone to help her," my mom said, in a way that told me she'd already made up her mind to do so. "The basement rail is missing, some of the lights aren't in working order, there's no food that I can find, save a few cans of soup, and the shower door has come off its hinges in the bathroom. These things aren't hard to fix. It'll just take a little time."

"Mom, she's a proud person. I know you understand that."

"When I dropped her off last night, the house was completely dark. I didn't like the feel of it, so I walked her inside. I saw . . . the state of things. I couldn't leave her to this, so I slept on the couch. I don't care much about her pride right now. I care about her safety, and this screams accident-waiting-to-happen. I think she understands that on some level."

I hadn't seen the whole house, but I could see that Bernie had been living in a neat, tidy hellhole. Had Micki ever seen this? I had a pretty small family, but I still had people in my life who would notice if I'd taken up residence in what was essentially a haunted house. A lump of sadness settled in my gut—Bernie truly had no one. No wonder she'd invented Reggie.

"I have to work," I said, "but I'll help you as best I can."

"You have enough on your plate with running for office. Maybe I'll ask Matt. He's really coming along with his remodeling skills."

"Matt is . . . handy?"

Mom smiled wryly. "I wouldn't exactly say that, but he's getting there."

"We need to talk," I said. "You know that, right?"

Mom hesitated for a moment, then said, "I'm not sure what upsets me more, that you did it or that you didn't tell me."

"I'm sorry for both. Well, one more than the other."

"Look, Ally, when you decide to keep a secret from someone you love, what you're really doing is saying you don't find that person trustworthy. I thought I was, in your eyes. It breaks my heart that you don't think so."

There was probably nothing she could say to make me feel worse. "I'm so sorry. I am. I trust you more than anyone."

"I don't feel like debating that," Mom said. "At some point, we'll talk about it, but I can't deal with all the emotional repercussions right now, so I'll deal with your friend's problem. It can be fixed."

"We don't need fixing," I said. "Do we?"

"Can I make you some coffee, Ally?" Bernie stood in the doorway. Dressed in a fleece robe and worn slippers, she looked even tinier than usual. Still, her hair was neatly combed, and she wore the lipstick Radha had picked out for her.

"No, thank you. Actually, I was hoping you still had some of that candy you gave to Kylie at the debate."

Bernie's eyes filled with tears. "I don't know. I'll look. Maybe." One tear escaped, rolling down her gaunt cheek. "Please tell me she's still okay."

"She's sitting in your living room," I said, taking her small hand. "And she's fine. I'd just like a sample of the candy to give to her doctor."

Bernie disappeared for a moment and returned with a small baggie full of mini-chocolate bars. "I bought it from the bins at the specialty grocery store. You can have all of them."

I thanked her and slipped the bag in my purse.

Bernie grinned at my mom. "Sophie is going to help me with my house. She slept on the couch last night to make sure I was okay. Wasn't that nice?"

"My mom is a solid person. Very capable."

"Trustworthy," Mom said, her eyes boring into mine. "I'm going home to get some things I need. I'll come around later today and get started."

Bernie's face shifted, as though she'd just remembered something unpleasant. "Oh, I—I'll have to know how much it's going to cost before we start anything. Maybe you could draw up an estimate, and I can think about it."

"I don't have anything going on," my mom lied. "And you're a friend of my Kylie, so you're a friend of mine. Friends don't charge friends."

Bernie looked like she'd swallowed a chicken bone. "I suppose they don't."

"Bernie?" Kylie called from the living room. "Can you come here?"

Bernie stood up quickly, happy for an excuse to leave the room. "She sounds perfectly well," she said before scurrying off.

"Don't look at me like that," my mom said. "I can finish Kylie's room next week. Bernie is a nice woman, probably just getting by on social security. I can do a good deed every so often."

I kissed her on the cheek, and was grateful she didn't brush me away. Then I picked up Bernie's purse and walked down the hall to her bedroom to return it. Truth be told, after seeing the rest of the house, I wanted to get into that bedroom to check it out.

It had the same feel as the other rooms—that of an estate sale on the last day, only a few overlooked items left in a house that once held things that truly mattered. The bed was neatly made, but the silk bedspread had dulled to a muted pink, and pillows had flattened with time and use. The dresser held no framed photographs, perfume, or jewelry, only a very utilitarian-looking brush and a pillbox that was empty when I checked.

The closet ran the length of one wall, hidden by folding doors. They were open a crack, and a flash of white caught my eye. Fully aware and slightly mortified that I was violating Bernie's privacy, I justified opening the door with the idea that I'd hang the purse for her.

I gasped. Inside, next to some uniformly hung slacks and blouses, were six wedding dresses, pristine and unused, and all labeled "Micki's Originals." A few veils were visible on the shelf above them, and four pairs of white shoes were lined up below.

Shocked, I sat on the bed for a moment. Was this where all Bernie's money was going? Did Micki know? Did she encourage it? Feeling sick to my stomach, I took one more look at the dresses, their bright hopefulness almost hurting my eyes.

There were all kinds of things I needed to do. But the list was long, and my ability to prioritize was not the greatest. So I took a deep breath and did what I usually did—I acted.

~

The shop was closed, lights out, displays darkened, but I pounded on the door anyway. I couldn't shake the feeling that I'd been stupid and impulsive—how well did I know Micki? Why hadn't I ever been to her home? Maybe I should have left things alone instead of forcing the past into the present.

I'd come alone, and the main street of Willow Falls had shut down, save O'Malley's Pub, but even the low hum of music escaping its closed doors seemed eerie. It was only seven o'clock, but in late October that looked like midnight. I needed to get back to Bernie's to take Kylie home to bed. Frustrated, I gave the door a sharp kick.

This time it opened.

I nearly screamed. It was Sandy, in full zombie regalia, holding a geometry textbook.

"Come in, come in," he said, ushering me in out of the cold.

I didn't move past the doorstep. "Is Micki here?"

"She and Radha are at home. What's wrong?"

"I—" Sandy looked so innocently concerned.

He held his free hand up. "Wait. Don't answer. I have to get this book to Radha before she loses her mind. Huge test tomorrow. Want to walk with me?"

I nodded, staying silent as he locked up.

We strolled down the block, Sandy picking up on my mood and keeping the conversation simple—Halloween was only a few days away, and his boss had asked him to play Dracula on the big day, a step up from his current position as a walking dead extra. "I'm not tall enough for Frankenstein, or I think he would have given it to me."

"You'll make a fantastic Count Dracula," I said as we turned the corner. A quaint, modest apartment building hugged the edge of the block, its front outlandishly decorated for Halloween—large fake spiders stuck to the brick facade, fake headstones on the small strip of grass in front, and a skeleton bride and groom hanging out on the front stoop.

"This is it," Sandy said. "We had a little fun with the holiday. The other tenants don't seem to mind."

It was the second time that day I was surprised by someone's living arrangements. Sandy unlocked the door, and we squeezed into a small foyer while he checked the mail. The building was clean but old, the wood heavy and the carpeting worn.

"Third floor," he said as we trudged up the stairs. "Micki says these stairs are what allow her to still eat carbs."

I laughed politely, but my thoughts wouldn't hold still. Looking at this place, it was ridiculous to think Micki was swindling old women. And with Sandy working an extra job, maybe I was headed in entirely the wrong direction.

Then I remembered the check for seven thousand dollars. Where the hell did that money come from?

"I'm home," Sandy called out as we entered the railroad apartment. "Look who I brought with me!"

"I hope it's the pizza man," Micki called out. "We're starving!"

Radha and Micki sat at a small half-moon table, flush up against the wall of a tiny kitchen. Radha, slightly disheveled in yoga pants and a too-small Harry Potter sweatshirt, was resting her elbows on a stack of paper. She held a calculator in one hand and a pencil in the other.

"Geometry was invented by people who really get off on being mean. There's a word for that, right?"

"Sadists," Micki said. She'd already gotten up from the table, kissed me on the cheek, and stood at the sink, filling a teakettle. "Sit," she said, though the only available chair was where she'd been sitting.

I sat. Full of nervous energy, Micki zoomed around the tiny space, putting together something for us to eat. Sandy disappeared into one of the other rooms, and Radha groaned over her inability to find the value of x.

I glanced at the table. Micki had been pulling apart an old photo album. She'd taken photos from plastic sleeves and made little piles. "What are you doing with these?" I said, my heart quickening when I realized they were probably images of people who were related to me, and possibly my biological mother.

"Radha has a family legacy project at school," Micki explained, placing an impressive charcuterie plate on the small circle of available space on the table. "We're her family now, so these are her people."

I swallowed. "And mine?"

Micki put a hand on my shoulder. "Yes."

Sandy had popped back into the room, face scrubbed of makeup. He'd heard our interaction, but didn't say anything, simply frowned at the photos and busied himself attending to the dirty dishes in the sink. Was he worried about Radha connecting too fiercely, only to be disappointed yet again? Was he worried about something I might see?

"Can I look?" I asked, finding myself suddenly shy.

"Of course!" Micki pulled a stool over so she could sit next to me.

I started sifting through the photos, oddly expecting to recognize someone, though that would be impossible. The sensation made me almost lightheaded—my unfamiliar past would become familiar. How would it change me?

"Are you certain you want to do this?" Sandy asked me.

No. But I was going to do it anyway. I glanced down at a photo and spotted a woman in a housedress, standing in front of a stove. "Who's that?"

"That was our neighbor, Hattie. She watched me and Cissy sometimes when Mom was busy." The tightness around Micki's mouth told me her mother was busy more than she'd liked. "She would lock me in the closet sometimes. I didn't like her. I don't even know why I have her photograph."

"It's your history," Radha chimed in. "I guess you kept it to remind yourself that it happened. Can I see her?"

I passed the photo to Radha, who carefully scrutinized Micki's mean babysitter.

"Excuse my French, but she looks like a total, high-grade bitch."

"She was," Micki said.

I flipped to another. A man this time, with a suit and hat reminiscent of Frank Sinatra.

"Uncle Joe," Micki said.

My heart stilled. "My uncle?"

The corner of Micki's mouth twitched. "One of my father's friends. He hung around for a while, and he was nice to me."

I tossed that one to the side, eager to find someone I was actually related to. I picked up another photograph, a Polaroid, and stopped short. It was an early '80s version of Micki. She sat on a sofa, cuddling a baby on her lap, her face bright with pride and love.

I scoured the photograph for details. The baby wore a pastel pink dress with yellow piping. Her cheeks were round and flushed. She looked happy. Cared for. Loved.

"Me?" I rasped.

Micki hesitated for a moment, and then said, "Your first Easter. I think you must have been nine or ten months old."

"Why is it you holding me and not her?" Of all the emotions running through me, the one that stopped cold was anger. "I want to see her. Now, please."

Micki shuffled through a pile of photos until she found what she was looking for. "There she is. Cissy. Your mother."

Only technically, but I didn't bother to correct her and focused on the photo. The image showed a shockingly thin woman in her forties, wearing cutoff shorts and a yellow T-shirt advertising a pizza joint. Her hair was the same shade of brown as mine, but frazzled and unkempt. She leaned against a kitchen counter, cigarette in one hand, glass of brown liquid in the other. Her smile was brittle and forced, and she had what looked like a purplish bruise on the side of her neck. It had obviously been many years since anyone could describe her as pretty.

"Life wasn't easy for her," Micki said. "Not at the start or the middle or the end."

Compassion was in my nature. But I did understand that, though life can be made difficult by the things outside of our control, it was our choices that could turn those difficulties into catastrophe. She chose to live her life in a certain way, so in a sense, she chose the consequences too.

"She passed on four years ago, right?" My voice sounded strangely flat.

"I'm sorry you never got the chance to meet her," Micki said quietly. "She loved you, in her way."

"Did she ever ask about me? Try to find out how I was doing?"

"Now, *that* wasn't her way. When she closed a book on something, she slammed it shut."

I glanced at Micki. "What about you? Did you ever want to know what happened to me?"

Tears filled Micki's eyes. "I couldn't take it, knowing any detail. I knew you went to someone good. I told myself to be happy with that."

"Were you happy with it?"

"No," she whispered. "Never."

With shaking hands, I studied the photo again, taking note of everything, trying to commit the scene to the part of my brain developed during the first year of life, the part that knew her. The sharp line of her jaw, the glasses with the large red frames, the fingers curled around the glass of something she probably shouldn't have been drinking.

Her fingers.

They bent unnaturally, her knuckles swollen into red, raw knobs.

"Rheumatoid arthritis," Micki said. "She got it pretty young. It was really bad, worse than if she'd gotten it later. She didn't have any insurance, so she couldn't afford any medications. I always wondered if I'd get it, because our mom had it, too, but not nearly as bad as Cissy."

"Sometimes, our moms give us all kinds of things we don't want," Radha said. I'd almost forgotten she was there. Her face had lost its usual animated expression, her features immobile, eyes dull. "My first mom gave me anxiety and trust issues."

"What have I given you?" Micki said. She pretended to joke, but her question held a great deal of seriousness.

"Love," Radha said. "You've given me love."

That comment stopped my heart from jumping down a rabbit hole of blame and bitterness. There was another part, powerful though small, that thought about things in a different way. My biological mother was irresponsible and self-destructive, but she gave me my mother. In her own way, she'd given me love.

"This is your grandmother," Micki said.

The haggard woman in the photo wore a floral dress, which, even in the saturated colors of the early '70s, I could tell had seen better days. She gazed at the camera with contempt, and I wondered who had taken it. She clutched a coffee mug with a smiley face on it, a stark contrast to her expression, one of complete and utter misery. I noticed the telltale swollen joints on her fingers, though they were not as severe as my mother's.

My mind instantly leaped to the DNA information, the increased risk for inflammatory diseases. I couldn't shake the feeling I was looking at Kylie's future.

I didn't want to think about that, so I thought about it in another way. This woman with the dark, haunted eyes and wary expression was our history. Her illness was proof of that genetic link. So was my biological mother's. So was Kylie's. It was terrifying but also exhilarating. The past, the present, and Kylie could write the future. Times had changed. Our awareness could mean early treatment, and that would make all the difference.

"She wasn't a good mom to you?" Radha asked Micki.

Micki sighed. "Nope."

Radha simply nodded. An unfit guardian was something she was familiar with.

"She yelled and swore at us, all the time," Micki said. "Slapped us around when we acted up. We weren't the best kids, I'll admit, but we weren't the worst."

"She had her own issues," Radha said. "That had nothing to do with you."

"Yes," Micki said, drawing her foster daughter into a side hug. "You're absolutely right."

We paged through the rest of the photographs still in the album. I'd thought it was a full book, but there turned out to not be very many. Radha took a half dozen for her project, but her mood seemed subdued. I wondered what demons she was wrestling with. I felt strangely numb. My demons were taking a nap, sure to rise later, sparking insomnia.

Sandy finished up the dishes and wiped his hands with a damp towel, lost in thought. "Sometimes the past is a very unfriendly place," he said after a moment. "As painful as it is, perhaps it's wise to free yourself of it. We all understand pain, so we have to respect those who desire to avoid it. Ally, you can choose to forget this ever happened."

"Sandy," Micki said, a note of warning in her voice. "Once you know something this important, forgetting it is impossible."

"She can't forget," Radha said. "It's her past."

"Radha," Sandy said gently, "would you like someone to force you to confront things you'd rather leave behind?"

She went quiet and stared at the photos on the table.

"Would you like some more tea?" Sandy said to me, his demeanor friendly but slightly more impersonal. "You are more than welcome to stay longer."

"I have to go back to Bernie's to pick up Kylie and Heather."

"Why are they at Bernie's?" Micki said. "Why didn't you bring them with you?"

After connecting the way we just had, questioning Micki felt like an affront. But the situation at Bernie's didn't seem right, and whatever the truth of the situation, I had to know, had to ask. "I stopped by Bernie's to get a piece of the candy she'd given Kylie. The doctor wanted it."

"She feels terrible," Sandy said. "We're all so glad Kylie is okay."

Micki looked puzzled. "It's not that you're not welcome, but why did you come to our place?"

I swallowed, hating to go on. "Have you been to Bernie's house?"

"No," Micki said. "I've dropped her off a couple of times, but I've never gone in. I guess that's kind of odd now that I think about it. She's never invited me in. People can be very private about the strangest things."

"She's private for a reason," I continued. "Her place is in bad shape. I don't think I've ever been in a house that seemed less like a home. It's very empty and depressing, and pretty unsafe."

"I don't like this at all," Sandy said.

"My mom's over there right now, assessing what needs to be done. She's going to help her."

Micki looked puzzled. "Your mom is over there helping?"

"Yes, but . . . that's not all. I . . . I opened Bernie's closet to return her purse, and there were wedding dresses hanging in it. Six of them. All Micki's Originals. She's got some shoes and accessories too."

There was a beat while everyone processed that information.

"Are you sure?" Radha said. "That sounds too weird."

"I know what I saw. I wish I hadn't."

Micki paled. "She's never bought anything but a lipstick. Why in the world?"

"I'm going to study in my room, okay?" Radha scooped up her books and left.

Sandy sat down in Radha's spot. "That poor woman. We considered her family, yet we never bothered to step foot in her house."

"She stole from us," Micki said. "There's no other explanation. I feel sick to my stomach."

I believed their reactions, ashamed at how I'd jumped to the conclusion that they'd swindled an elderly woman.

"We need to be understanding," Sandy said.

"She knows we don't make a lot of money," Micki said, growing angrier. "I told her. She knows. I'm very sorry if she needed those dresses to fill a need, but we've got to get them back. We're talking thousands of dollars."

"I just have a hard time believing a ninety-year-old woman carried six dresses out of our shop, and we didn't notice," Sandy said. "It's not adding up."

"She comes to the shop every day," Micki said. "I'll admit I don't always pay her the most attention. I give her to Radha. That girl has such patience."

We all suddenly sat up straighter, the answer coming to us at the same time. "Radha," we said in unison.

She wasn't in her room.

"Her coat's gone," Micki said, growing frantic. "And her backpack."

We scrambled. Sandy and I yanked our coats on, and Micki reluctantly agreed to stay in the apartment in case Radha came back. "Find her. Hurry!"

CHAPTER 18

When Sandy and I got to the street, we decided to go in opposite directions on the main boulevard. "If she wanted to take the bus into the city, she'd need to be on the central road." He took off before I could say anything.

I jogged down the mostly empty thoroughfare. It was almost eight o'clock, long after most people made their commute home on a dreary Monday. I kept aware, glancing around for Radha's slim form, her yoga pants half-hidden under her practical navy-blue coat.

The air bit into my cheeks—Illinois at the brink of November could be harsh and unrelenting. I thought about Radha, scared she'd lost another home, wandering the streets of a suburb she'd come to view as her own. She probably felt like nothing ever truly belonged to her.

"Radha!" I called out, knowing full well it was probably fruitless. "Radha!"

A serious-faced jogger gave me an odd look. Frustrated, I stopped in front of The Not-So-Blushing-Bride.

A light was on in the back of the store.

But the door was locked.

I dashed through the alley, my mind reeling with options in the event Radha was actually in the shop. *Do I confront her? Hug her? Listen to her? All of the above?* I hadn't had many interactions with teenagers since I was a teenager myself. Weren't there triple reverse psychology tricks that were supposed to work?

The back door was locked. "Radha? It's Ally. I know you're in there! Can we just talk?"

Nothing.

I peered through the lace curtains and thought I saw a flicker of movement. "Radha. I'm not mad at you. No one is. Not Sandy, not Micki. Let's just talk about things."

Nothing.

"How about I get Kylie here? Will you talk to her?"

The door opened a smidge. I saw one dark eye and the side of Radha's mouth. She was frowning.

"Don't get Kylie involved in this," Radha said. "It's my mess."

"Okay. Can I come in then?"

"No."

I tried to keep my tone light. "Why? What's going on?"

Radha paused. "I'm saying goodbye to the store. If they come to pick me up, they won't give me the chance."

"They?"

"Children's services. You know, the state people."

"Oh, honey." I tucked the tip of my boot into the sliver of the opening. "That's not going to happen."

"It always happens."

Her tone was so gloomy, I decided to change my tactic. "It's really freaking cold out here. Can I come inside for a minute to warm up? I won't stop you from what you're doing."

"You can't text anyone to tell them I'm here. I need a little time."

"Promise."

Slowly, reluctantly, Radha opened the door.

Her backpack, stuffed to the gills and open at the top, lay on the floor. Radha had been folding a bright pink sari.

"It's mine," she said quickly. "Micki already gave it to me. I didn't want to leave it behind."

"It's beautiful." I restrained myself from saying more, instinct telling me the triple reverse psychology trick to employ was . . . waiting. I pretended to study Micki's stash of fine fabrics.

"Bernie doesn't have anything," Radha said defensively. "She doesn't even have a fiancé. Did you know that? She likes to pretend she's getting married. To dream. She likes trying on the dresses and running her hands over them. I was trying to help her!"

"Maybe you did help her," I said soothingly. "I know your heart was in the right place."

"I put the dresses she liked in my backpack and brought them to her house. In case you were wondering. That was bad. I know it."

"Did you ever see the inside of her house?"

Radha nodded. "It made me feel worse about her. Where she lives is . . . not nice. I've had to stay in a lot of places like it. It doesn't make you feel good, all that emptiness. It made me want to help her more."

"Sweetie, Micki would have understood. You could have told her."

"I'm not stupid. I know the shop isn't doing well. Micki can't afford to give stuff away."

Radha wasn't anywhere near stupid, but I was. Why hadn't I been more observant? Why hadn't I questioned how Micki could write a check to me for seven thousand dollars? I made a mental note to ask her about it, and then shifted back to Radha.

She was pacing, her face a mask of worry and pain. I wondered how many times she'd been in a position of uncertainty, not knowing where she was going to sleep that night, not sure of who would be in charge of her life. My thoughts turned to the powerlessness of how I felt in the face of Kylie's illness. I felt the strain through my whole body, the worry infiltrated every thought, every response, every action.

"Come here," I said, and drew her into a tight hug. She melted into it, her cries tearing at my heart. "You meant to do something nice, but it was a mistake. It's okay. Everyone makes mistakes. I make them every day. The thing is, you have to own it. Say you're sorry to Micki and Sandeep."

"It's not going to help. They hate me," Radha said. "They'll want me to go away."

"That's not true at all. You should have seen their faces when they realized you were gone. They're so worried. Sandy is out looking for you, and Micki is pacing the apartment, waiting for you to come home."

Radha went still for a moment. "Ally," she said, "how do you know when something is real? When it's the truth? It's so hard for me to tell."

"I wish I could tell you there's a secret, but there isn't. You'll never know for sure. The only thing you can fully trust is your own judgment." I took a breath, and thought of my mother. "Consider this—if you are fairly certain someone trusts you, then it makes sense to trust them, right?"

"I guess," she said, but didn't sound very convinced.

"Think for a moment. Sandy trusted you with his culture. He taught you about the food, the clothes, the social rules. And you lived up to his trust. You honored it."

Radha started to sniffle again. "I loved it! All of it."

"Micki trusted you with the store. She trusted you to emcee the fashion show, and to pay special care and attention to clients."

"And I totally messed it up. God. I'm so, so sorry."

"You didn't mess everything up. You messed *one* thing up. I hope you can see that. I know Micki can. She loves you, sweetie, and when you love someone, you want to forgive them, especially if they're sorry and have an explanation. You have both."

"I'm still afraid to face them. I'm so embarrassed."

"Well, finding the courage to face someone we've wronged is part of learning to be a grown-up. You're almost there, Radha."

She swiped at her eyes. "Okay, I'm ready. Will you walk back with me?"

"I'm going to text Micki and tell her we're on our way."

~

I used to hate when people said, *I have no words.* There are always words. Sometimes they aren't the right ones, but they're there. When Radha ran to Micki, arms out, heart open and so, so sorry, my breath caught in my throat until she was welcomed, fully and with love, into Micki's arms. Then Sandy wrapped himself around the two of them. There they were. A family.

And when they opened their arms to include me, I rushed in.

And there *weren't* any words I could find to describe how I felt. I just knew that I never wanted to not feel that again.

CHAPTER 19

District 168 Parents: New Post

Vera Pastorelli: Hello! On November 1, the school will host a meet and greet for the school board candidates. Light appetizers and wine will be served. 7pm at the VFW hall on Hildy Street. All are welcome!

Cassie Flores: I'll set up an FB events page so we can get a good idea of how many people are interested. I can provide sandwiches, with vegetarian options, and I'll design a craft cocktail appropriate for the event. Looking forward to seeing everyone! I predict a stellar night!

Cole Flounders: What about us vegans? Will there be an option for us?

Cassie Flores: Done, Cole. Absolutely. Sorry for the oversight.

Cole Flounders: Apology accepted.

Bree Nguyen: Cassie, you make everything better. Seriously.

Jane Sturgeon: Will there be mocktails?

Cassie Flores: I will make sure to have virgin options available.

Jane Sturgeon: "Virgin"? Is that really appropriate? Must we stigmatize everyone?

Cassie Flores: You are absolutely right, Jane. My sincerest apologies.

Sawyer McMurphy: I work on my friend's farm in Michigan on the weekends I don't have my daughter. I've got homemade farmhouse gouda, apples we picked a few weeks ago, and some nice sausage I cured myself. If I can get down to the hives, I'll get some honey. I can make a charcuterie platter. (61 "Likes")

"These people are insane. Truly. Are you sure you want to be a part of this thing? I mean, homemade farmhouse gouda?"

"I'm used to specialized diets, aren't I? I can out-menu-design any of them."

We were hanging out at the back of the salon; Heather's first client was a no-show, and mine, Jenn with two *n*'s, was early, having decided she wanted a pixie cut because she'd read that the style elongated the neck. Apparently, she felt CrossFit was going to cause a spontaneous neck lengthening any minute, and she wanted to be prepared. Teresa had a few days off, and without our boss around, we stylists were feeling a little loose. After the events of the past few days, I was content to give my morning a slow start.

"You're letting other people take control of the conversation," Jenn with two *n*'s said to me. "You've got to get in there and make your mark."

Heather smiled. Jenn with two *n*'s lived for drama. "She's right. You've got to say something. Be a presence."

I wanted to think of something spectacular, but my brain was tired. And that morning Kylie had woken up with swollen elbow joints again and a pesky sore throat. "What can I say at this point?" I said. "That I'll hand-carve a table out of wood from a tree I cut down myself? I can't compete."

"I guess you can't," Heather admitted. "But only in this situation. You are otherwise awesome."

Jenn with two *n*'s stood up, indignant. "That kind of attitude is unacceptable. Of course you can compete. You can *always* compete. It's a matter of finding a weapon when you think you don't have any."

I imagined Cassie, Sawyer, and me in a three-way duel. Cassie would toss her multiple advanced degrees at us, Sawyer would politely smother us with his perfectly worn-in flannel shirts and homemade shea butter lip balm, and what would I do? Give them a fresh haircut?

"You know what? She's right. You want this badly," Heather said. "Kylie needs you in her corner. That has to mean something. Why don't you just trust yourself? Write the first thing that comes to mind."

I started typing, not really sure where I was going to go with this.

Ally Anderson: I will bring a good attitude and a smiling face. And I'll clean up afterward without bitching about it. Even if someone pukes up the mocktails.

I checked my spelling and grammar before posting.

"Nice," Heather said.

"I don't know if that's exactly how I would have expressed myself, but I think it works," Jenn with two *n*'s said. "It's confident, I'll give you that."

Heather pointed at the laptop screen. "You've already got a response. Those people don't mess around."

Jane Sturgeon: Profanity has no place on this community page. I'm alerting the moderator.

Sawyer McMurphy: Never underestimate the value of a positive attitude. Thanks for the reminder, Ally!

I clicked on his post, and gave it a big old "Like."

~

Halloween is more than terrifying for a nut allergy family—it's life-threatening. Trick-or-treating becomes a run through an active mine-field in a war-torn nation—one false move and you're done.

Every year, Matt and I had to psychologically prep Kylie for dis-appointment. She would not be able to accept most of what she was offered. She couldn't share candy or eat any on the move. Her bag must be fully inspected before she was allowed to keep anything. This year, after the incident with Bernie, we had to double down on our warnings while trying to not squeeze every bit of fun out of the one holiday that really is solely meant for kids.

"Grandma's got the teal pumpkin!" Kylie squealed. She zoomed around the house, dressed as a mildly scary zombie. My mom had just got home, having spent the day over at Bernie's. She was taken by that ninety-year-old vixen—her dry wit and opinionated persona matched my mother's perfectly. Neither of them suffered fools, and in their eyes, I'm sure the world was full of plenty of foolishness. Mom's disdain extended to me—we still hadn't discussed anything of import, our exchanges devolving to strained pleasantries in front of Kylie.

Mom lugged the teal pumpkin—a plastic version with a deep indentation on the top for nut-free candy—onto the front porch. A few years ago, she'd brought it home when she found out that teal pumpkins alerted the community that a house was safe for food allergy sufferers. We filled it with care, and were shocked at how many people thanked us because they were in a similar situation.

"I'll take her trick-or-treating tonight," Mom said. "Right after dinner."

I'd gotten a text from Micki, asking us if we'd like to come to the haunted house to see Sandy in all of his vampire glory. Surprisingly, Kylie seemed fine with going, and I was going to ask my mother to come. I thought there was a chance she'd say yes after all the time she'd spent with Bernie. I was fairly certain Bernie told her stories of Micki and Sandeep—maybe she'd be open to another meeting? I didn't expect her to build a relationship with them—why would she? What I needed was for her to know why *I* would want to give them a place in my life.

"Absolutely not," my mom said when I asked her. "Let's take Kylie trick-or-treating like we always do. We can get her to bed early. It'll be good for her."

"We don't have to stay long," I begged. "Please?"

Mom gestured to the bench. "Sit."

She folded her arms over her chest, her eyes darting around the room. I knew my mom well enough to keep my mouth shut and sit tight. When she gave this much concentrated thought to something, it was usually worth waiting her out.

"I'm sorry you didn't have your dad around much when you were a kid," she began. "But otherwise, you felt safe and secure and loved, right?"

My throat suddenly felt clogged. I nodded.

"I promised myself when I adopted you that I would make you feel like you were 100 percent my daughter *every single day of your life.* That I would love you as much as my parents loved me. They put their hearts and minds to it like they did everything else. When they passed on, they left me the bar to carry on their name. That's what they had to give me. And that's what I had to give you. See, I could give you almost everything, but I can't give you a history. I thought, in some way, giving you the bar would make up for that."

Mom's eyes filled. I moved to touch her arm, and she waved me away. "I don't think you understand. When I had to sell the tavern, it didn't just break my heart, it sliced it. It cut away that history I had to give. And that hurt. Really bad."

"And Micki Patel makes it worse?"

"In a way. She's got what I can't give you. It's like she has a knife and can continue slicing away if she wants to. Do you know what I mean?"

"I do. But I also don't think it has to be that way. You're forgetting one thing. You are my mom, and I love you."

Mom stood and squeezed my shoulder. "We're different, Ally. Our struggles are different, and so are our needs. Let's just leave it at that."

~

"Grandma, are you going with us to the haunted house?"

We sat on the front stoop, greeting the first wave of trick-or-treaters. Kylie was practically vibrating with excitement.

"I thought you hated haunted houses," Mom said, expertly deflecting the question.

"I do hate haunted houses," Kylie explained. "But Dr. Indigo says we should face our fears. I'm learning to calm the dog."

Mom looked at me. "What? What dog?"

"I'll explain later."

"Grandma," Kylie said, growing serious. "If you're afraid of haunted houses, then you need to go. Dr. Indigo taught us to share fears. I could share mine with you, and you could share yours with me. That kind of makes sense, doesn't it?"

Mom didn't answer. After a moment, she got up and went into the house. Some kids came by, and we showered them with peanut-free goodies.

"If we're going to go, let's go." Mom stood behind us. She had her purse slung over her shoulder and car keys in hand. "But I'm driving. And I decide when we leave."

~

During the half-hour drive to the haunted house, Kylie chattered nonstop, a bundle of anticipatory nerves, while my mom drove with her hands at ten and two, her lips cemented together. The woman could contain emotion better than a maximum-security prison. Nothing was escaping without her permission.

A security guard directed us toward a far parking lot, and on the long walk to the haunted village, Kylie grew quieter and quieter. "Are they allowed to touch people?" she finally said. "They're not, right?"

"I don't think so, baby," I assured her. But then, I wasn't really sure.

"If someone touches you," Mom said, "kick them."

"Mom!"

"Well, no one should be touching anyone," she protested. "I mean, what kind of place is this?"

A very crowded place. We moved through the witches, Harry Potters, the ghosts, the Morphsuits, pirates, and vampires. It was the latter I was staring at—where were *my* vampires? I'd texted Micki when we arrived, but hadn't heard anything.

We reached the front of the haunted house. It was enormous—a faux Victorian wonder, dark and dramatic against the night sky. It had eaves and turrets and a widow's walk. Blood-curdling screams echoed from its interior.

Wide-eyed, Kylie strained her neck to take it all in. "Will you hold my hand, Grandma?"

My mom narrowed her eyes at the haunted house. "I won't let go." She turned to me. "So, is it just us, then? Let's get in line and get this over with."

She didn't bother to hide her relief. I didn't bother to hide my disappointment. Where were they?

My phone chimed.

Micki Patel: 911. Come to the back of the house. You'll see me standing by a red door. Hurry!

"For the love of God," my mom said when I showed her my phone. "This is ridiculous."

Ridiculous as it was, we got out of line and circled to the back, which was curiously desolate.

"This is just as scary as the front side," Kylie muttered.

We found the red door, which was really a black door covered in fake blood. I was just about to knock when it burst open, and a zombie bride catapulted outside.

"Oh, I'm so glad you're here," Micki said, staring at my mom. "We hired some high schoolers to work tonight, and they came in drunk off their bottoms. We don't have enough monsters! Sandy's boss is losing his mind. Do you think you can help?"

"What do you think?" I asked Kylie.

"I don't know." I watched her mentally calculate the pros and cons, her fears against her desire to help Micki.

"We could go home, honey," Mom said. "If you're tired."

Radha, dressed in a black sari with vampire teeth and two rivulets of blood leaking out of the sides of her mouth, popped her head outside. "Are you guys going to help us out? We need more monsters!"

"Okay," Kylie said. "We'll help."

My mom's sigh could be heard over the screams.

Micki ushered us into a darkened hallway, and then into a room that looked like a smaller version of the bridal shop. Dark-colored costumes were strewn everywhere, and a table crammed full of makeup and wigs stood in the middle of the room.

Micki pointed at me. "You're a zombie. We need you in the cemetery set. Just get something suitable on. Quick."

"I'm already a zombie," Kylie said.

Radha started smearing some makeup on Kylie's cheek. "I'm going to make you even more zombie-riffic."

My mom picked up a tattered black dress and just as quickly tossed it to the side. "I'll wait outside until you're done. Meet me at the front entrance."

"Grandma, they need help," Kylie said. "Don't you want to help?"

Reluctantly, Mom retrieved the black dress. "What should I do with this?"

Micki nearly fell apart with excitement. "How about a witch?"

Mom smirked. "Sounds about right."

I felt a surge of something in the neighborhood of hope, kind of a restrained optimism. Mom was talking to Micki, or at least in her direction. She had agreed to dress up. This was a start, and starts could be good even if they didn't lead to a perfect finish.

"Oh, that looks great, Sophie!" Micki exclaimed when Mom was done. "Grab a broom and stick next to Sandy. He'll show you how it's done."

Mom looked less than pleased, but she grabbed the broom and let Radha give her caterpillar eyebrows and black lips. Radha then sprayed her hair with something that made it stick straight up in the air. "It's really easy to scare people in there," Radha said. "All you need to do is creep around and jump in front them. Say something like, 'I'll get you, my pretty!'"

"Easy enough," Mom said. She drew a black mole on the point of her chin. I couldn't believe it—my mom was getting into it!

I threw on a dress made of rags, donned a gray wig, ringed my eyes in black, and smeared some whitish-gray stuff on my face. "Ready," I said when I looked sufficiently scary.

Sandy appeared, drooling blood and smiling from ear to ear. "Oh, good! We need you out there!" After a second of surprise at seeing my mother, Sandy took her with him, and Kylie and I followed Micki and Radha.

"Ally, stand by the headstones with your arms outstretched. If you can manage a bloodcurdling scream, that would be great," Micki directed.

I laughed. "I thought zombies couldn't talk."

"They can scream," Micki said. "And it sounds awful."

"I think I can manage that."

"What about me?" Kylie said.

Micki stopped short. "How brave are you feeling? I need to know right now."

I watched Kylie work through her thoughts. *You are so strong*, I wanted to tell her, but she needed to come to the conclusion herself.

"Pretty brave," she said with determination.

Micki stretched out her hand. "Then you will command the hounds of hell."

Kylie almost yanked her hand back. "I'll what?"

"When people first come into the haunted house, there are two mechanical wolves. You'll stand between them. There's a remote control with a button that you'll push to make them howl and snap at the air. While they're doing that, you can scream and laugh like you're deranged. You can handle that, right?"

"I guess," Kylie said, but she looked skeptical.

She didn't have time to back out because Radha opened the door to the main part of the house, and we were inside, taking our places, and getting ready to howl at the moon.

~

Inciting terror was a whole lot of fun. I screamed and screamed, so much that I lost my voice completely by the end of the night. I spotted my mom, running through the cemetery set on her broom, screeching and cackling with abandon. She stuck close to Sandy at first, but then went off on her own. There was no denying it—Mom was having fun.

I watched Kylie command the hounds. Oversized and quite realistic, they sent some people running before even making it inside the haunted house. She had them snapping fiercely at the air, throwing their mechanized heads back, and howling at the full moon hanging ominously above our heads. By the end of the night, Kylie threw her head back, too, and let loose.

It was the best Halloween we'd had since she was a toddler.

CHAPTER 20

"We need to make a decision regarding Kylie's treatment," Dr. Indigo said. She sat behind her desk, regarding Matt, Kylie, and me with large, kohl-rimmed eyes. She wore a silvery tunic over purple paisley leggings. A large onyx pendant hung trapped between her boobs.

"I think the answer's apparent," Matt said, his tone abrupt. I had the feeling he was missing something to make this meeting. He'd driven himself, declining my offer of a carpool. Possibly a date with Cassie?

"I think we should continue," I said. "As long as it's safe. And it is, right?"

Dr. Indigo pursed her lips. "There is always risk. Kylie could have another reaction—that's true."

Matt snorted. "Well, then, why in the world would we risk it?"

"Because it could transform her life," Dr. Indigo responded calmly. "That hasn't changed simply because she had a reaction."

"Would you use the same protocol?" I asked, somewhat impressed with myself for knowing the lingo.

"I would start her again, this time with a lower dosage," Dr. Indigo said. "The desensitization process would take longer, but we wouldn't have to abandon it. These kinds of adjustments are not uncommon."

I understood Matt's reservations, but giving up was . . . giving up. When in doubt I always went with action, because inaction felt too much like death. I wanted Kylie to be able to really live her life in total freedom. And I trusted Dr. Indigo. I didn't fail to see that there were three people in this decision-making circle, so I put my arm around my daughter and said, "What do you think?"

"I don't know," she said, glancing at Matt. "Can we think about it?"

"Of course we can," Matt said.

Dr. Indigo nodded, smart enough to not push.

"I found out something," I said. "About my family's health history."

"Really?" Matt said. His tone changed, from anger to something more gentle. "From that DNA thing?"

"I found a relative through the DNA test. My mother . . ." I said, surprised by my upsurge of emotion. "My *biological* mother had rheumatoid arthritis. Her mother did too. I know it's not always a disease that gets passed down in families, but it helps to know that, right?"

"Knowledge always helps," Dr. Indigo said. She smiled wryly. "I know some people think otherwise."

"Am I going to get that disease?" Kylie asked.

"None of us know the future," Dr. Indigo said. "You might or you might not. But now you have something to look out for as you get older. Early treatment equals better outcomes. And there are effective treatments, and they'll continue to get better."

Kylie looked at the doctor straight on. "Are you making me better?"

"I'm helping you make yourself better."

That comment hung so heavy it almost knocked us off our chairs. How could Matt say no to that?

"I scheduled you for a full appointment," Dr. Indigo said, after our silence became uncomfortable, "so if you're all willing to stay, I'd like to do a group-guided meditation."

I could feel Matt's desire to leave. The tips of his shoes pointed to the side, toward the door. His brain had likely already made a run for it, heading to the freedom of the street, where he didn't have to think about his little girl swelling up and dying.

"We can stay," Kylie said. "Right, Mom and Dad?"

"Right," I said. "As long as we're done by five. I have to be somewhere at seven."

Matt flashed me a look. "I think we're going to the same place."

"So you can stay until five too," I said, my smile brittle.

"That would be . . . fine," Matt said. He took out his phone. "I just have to send a quick text."

While Matt texted, Kylie and I helped Dr. Indigo light candles and move chairs. We knew the metaphysical drill.

She had us sit cross-legged, knee to knee, in a tight circle.

"Are we going to try to calm the dog?" Kylie whispered.

"Close," Dr. Indigo said. "We're going to learn to visualize worry."

"I have no problem with seeing all there is to worry about," Matt said.

Dr. Indigo laughed. "Once we can imagine our worries as tangible entities, we can better manage them. Thinking of worry as something you can hold in your hands means thinking of it as something you can toss out the window or shove in a trash can."

"Can't worry be beneficial?" Matt asked. He didn't seem hostile, only curious. I had to admit, I thought the same thing. Doesn't worry sometimes mean you're thinking about the bad things that could happen so you can prepare yourself if any of them do?

"The question is, how much energy does worrying require?" Dr. Indigo said. "Your body requires energy for every process, from digesting food to blinking to fighting illness. Couldn't energy spent worrying be used for other, more productive, pursuits?"

Matt fidgeted. "I guess."

"Humor me," Dr. Indigo said. "Give this exercise a try. Now, all of you—close your eyes."

Matt didn't say anything, but he settled into stillness. We were going to do this.

"Matt, Kylie and Ally have already voiced fears in this office, but you have not, so we'll start with you. Tell us about one of your worries."

Silence. At first, I thought he was being resistant again, but then I thought back to the Matt I knew—his main worry was Kylie's health, but he didn't want Kylie to know that fear for her well-being occupied many of his daily thoughts. I'd felt the same way the last time I was here.

"I'm worried . . . ," he began. "I'm . . ."

"Go on," Dr. Indigo encouraged.

"I'm worried for Kylie. I don't like to put her at risk. I want my daughter to live a happy, healthy life, but I don't want to threaten her future by trying something that might turn out to hurt her."

I opened my mouth to say something and closed it just as quickly. It wasn't the time. Matt was allowed to have his fear. I resisted my impulse to pick it apart and analyze it. To my surprise, my hand found his knee and patted it.

"What does this worry look like?" Dr. Indigo asked.

"What do you mean?" Matt said. "Look like?"

"Describe it," she said. "What color is the fear? Does it have a texture, or is it smooth and round? Does it have a face?"

"I'm sorry, but this is ridiculous," Matt said. "Worry is an emotion. I can't describe that."

"Try," Dr. Indigo said.

"Fine," Matt said, shocking the heck out of me by responding to her authoritative manner. "It's red. Bright red."

"And?"

"Well . . . it's rough and bumpy, like it's covered in gravel." He paused for a moment. "It's got sharp spots. You'd have to be careful when you touched it."

He stopped, and so did Dr. Indigo. She knew the oldest mom trick in the book—stop talking and wait.

"It has slashes through it," Matt continued, "like someone attacked it with a knife. The slashes ooze something blackish. I . . . that's it, I think."

"That's good," Dr. Indigo encouraged. "Okay, visualize yourself picking it up gently, so it doesn't hurt you. Walk around for a bit, carrying it. Feel its weight, watch the slime ooze from it, this worry about Kylie's future. Where are you walking with it?"

"On a beach," Matt said. "I don't know why. I'm just there. The sand is hot. The sun . . . it's very bright."

"And the sky is very blue," Dr. Indigo said, her voice more hushed. "There aren't any people on the beach, but there's a pier. Can you see it?"

"I can," Matt said. "It's painted white, and it's long, reaching far into the ocean."

"I want you to walk down it. Slowly. You don't want to drop this ball of worry yet. Keep your strides even and your pace steady. Got it?"

"Yes. I'm doing it. I'm walking. The ocean is all around me."

"The waves are gently lapping at the pier. The sound is soothing and peaceful. Are you to the end of the pier yet?"

"Yes. The water is all around me. The beach seems far away."

"And you're still holding this worry. This bright-red ball, painful to touch, releasing black negative energy. This ball that only provides misery and terror. What do you want to do with it?"

"I don't know."

"You don't? Are you sure?"

"I want to get rid of it. I don't want it anymore. I want to toss it into the ocean."

"So do it," Dr. Indigo said forcefully. "Use all your might. The ocean is big and powerful and can swallow up a worry, no problem. Go ahead. Toss it."

"It's heavy," Matt said. "I don't know how far it's going to go."

"Even if it just goes a few feet, it will sink. Let it go, Matt. Give it to the ocean."

"I want to, but—"

"But what?"

"What if I need it?" His voice broke.

"It causes pain and misery. Why would you need it? Toss it, Matt. Let it go."

Matt let out a cry, a heartbreaking, nerve-rattling shriek. My eyes flew open. His were screwed shut, his face a mask of anguish.

"I did it," he said, heaving a sob. "I threw it, and the ocean swallowed it up. It's gone. It's gone. I can't even see it."

Dr. Indigo put a hand on his shoulder. "Good."

Tears streamed from Matt's eyes. I reached for him again. "Are you okay?"

He stood abruptly. "I have to go. I'm sorry."

"Dad?" Kylie sounded fearful. "I can go with you."

"No, baby. I'll see you later. I just need to be alone for a while."

He left, and Dr. Indigo turned the lights on. She extinguished the candles methodically.

"Was he hypnotized?" I asked. "Is he really okay?"

"I think he's more than okay," Dr. Indigo said. "He just has to get used to being that way."

"Could I be that way?" I asked. "More than okay?"

Dr. Indigo smiled at me, a rare, genuine, completely warm smile. "You already are. You've been coming to me all this time and you don't realize that? Come on, Ally."

"What about me?" Kylie said. "Am I okay too?"

Dr. Indigo turned this new and almost disturbingly intense high-wattage smile toward my daughter. "Of course you are."

Kylie smiled back. "Then why are we here?"

"Because I don't want anything to mess with your okayness, smart girl."

"So that's why you're teaching me to calm the dog," Kylie said. "I get it."

"I think you do."

Kylie took a breath and stood up. "I decided I want to try again."

Dr. Indigo glanced at me.

"I'll talk to Matt," I said, wondering if what had just transpired in this office had any effect on his opinion. "It's got to be a family decision."

CHAPTER 21

Kylie—Your Past Is a Present!
Report 30: Based on your DNA makeup, you are five times more likely to be tone deaf! Your ancestors weren't exactly members of the choir—think twice before trying out for American Idol!

We pulled into the VFW parking lot at 7:10 p.m. and sprinted for the door. Cassie had probably gotten there at six, with fancy food and craft cocktails worthy of a spread in *Gourmet* magazine. I brought nothing but a slightly sweaty body and a ten-year-old who should have been home doing her homework.

"Ally, we were waiting for you!" Bree Nguyen shouted, ruining my shot at slipping in unnoticed and pretending I'd been there for hours. She shoved a tray of food under my nose. "You've got to try some of these Manchego cheese bites Cassie made. They've got serrano ham inside and honey on the outside. Isn't that brilliant?"

I stuffed one in my mouth and nearly groaned with pleasure. I had to admit, they were amazing.

"Hey, Ally." Sawyer had somehow snuck up next to me. "How's it hanging?"

Seriously? Who said that? "I'm almost forty," I said through a mouthful of expensive Spanish cheese. "Everything's hanging."

"Sorry," he said, flushing. "I should spend my time around animals, not people. I don't always know how to act."

"I don't either," I said. "So don't worry about it."

"Want a cocktail?" he asked. "I sure do." He crouched down to Kylie's height. "There's organic apple cider, if you want some. I pressed it myself."

Kylie was too young to barf at that statement. "Cool," she said. "As long as it wasn't done on a press that came into contact with nuts, I'm good with it."

"Nope," he said. "No nuts. Promise. I'll be right back."

"We're going to ask the candidates to say a little something in five," Bree said, excited. "Sorry we didn't give advance warning, but you can speak off the cuff, right?"

"Right!" I said, a little too forcefully. Bree flinched.

"Okay, then," she said. "I'm going to go see if Cassie needs anything."

She walked off in the direction of Cassie, who wore a well-cut suit in Hillary Clinton blue.

I was wearing an army-green sweater with jeans. It was a nice sweater, and the jeans were skinny-style and flattering, but still.

Don't let it bother you, I told myself. *You're fine.*

Matt stood on one side of her, his features blank. On the other side, Riker lounged on his belly, Cassie's son sprawled next to him. I didn't let Riker's relaxed state fool me—he could strike at any time. The canine version of a rattlesnake.

The internal debate in my head—*Should I go say hi? Leave Matt alone?*—raged until it was too late to do anything at all. Sawyer had come back, carrying a plastic cup full of cider for Kylie and a bright pinkish-red cocktail for me.

I eyed it suspiciously. "What is this?"

"Hibiscus with organic, American distilled bourbon."

I took the glass and sniffed it. "It smells good."

Sawyer grinned. "I know something that will make it even better." He held his closed fist over my drink. "Count to three, Kylie."

She did. When she got to three, he opened his hand, and something dropped into my drink. It sunk to the bottom and began to uncurl.

"It's a dried hibiscus flower," he said. "You can eat it, if you want."

"You can?" Kylie said, incredulous.

"*You* can," he said with a grin. "No nuts. Just flower."

"Can you put one in apple cider?"

"I can't see why not," he said, and plunked one in her drink.

"Do you carry those around with you, just to impress women?"

"Did it work?"

"Yeah," I said, laughing. "It did."

"Then I'll keep stuffing my pockets with them," he said, and ambled off like a cowboy.

"He's nice," Kylie announced.

"I guess."

"Two minutes to start," Bree yelled.

I caught Vera Pastorelli rolling her eyes. Cassie's head bent upward, locked in an intense discussion with Matt. He said something to her, and his mouth brushed her ear. Memory brushed my own earlobe, and I felt a shiver of recognition.

I downed my cocktail in two gulps. It had been a while since I drank bourbon, but the familiar warmth traveled through my bloodstream, giving my frazzled nerves a hug.

Kylie tugged at my sleeve. "What are you going to say, Mom?"

That was a good question. And one I couldn't answer. "I don't know."

"How could you not know?" Kylie frowned. "Come up with something."

I glanced around. The crowd had really filled out, and the room was packed. Maybe I needed to flag down Sawyer McMurphy for another cocktail. Instead, I popped the hibiscus flower in my mouth and started chewing. The flavor was unfamiliar, but sweet and interesting.

Some delusional person handed Bree a microphone. I wondered if she'd ever give it back.

"Welcome! Welcome!" Feedback shrieked through the room. Bree held the mic away from her body. "Will the candidates please come forward?"

The three of us came from different points in the room, gladiators entering the ring. Cassie left her beast with Matt, thankfully.

Vera stepped forward, grabbing the mic from a flabbergasted Bree. "Each of you has three minutes to address the audience. No Q and A this time—you all had your chance at the debate. Right now the candidates have the floor, people. Got it?"

We three nodded like bobbleheads, though her comments weren't directed toward us. *Please don't pick me to go first*, I thought. Then, just as quickly, *Please let me go first to get it over with.*

"I think one of the ladies went first last time," Vera said, letting her gaze wander over Sawyer's flannel-and-jeans-covered body. "How about starting us off, Sawyer?"

"Yes, ma'am," Sawyer said, and the inevitable feminine sigh echoed through the space, however slightly muted. Maybe Sawyer was losing his luster?

"Well," he said, "I want to start by saying I'm very happy to be here, and honored to be standing next to such qualified candidates . . ."

Let's face it, I wasn't qualified to do anything more than cut hair. Which meant Sawyer was tap-dancing through his own bullshit—he had no idea what to say. I'd like to say this filled me with compassion, but honestly, I felt something close to relief.

"Being on the school board would mean a lot to me, because I would make decisions that would impact . . . the whole school . . . and I . . . take those decisions seriously because they are . . . serious decisions. Thank you."

Silence. I could hear the hibiscus flowers wilting in glasses throughout the room. Sawyer's hotness was finally not enough to cover up his awkwardness and ineptitude. My awkwardness and ineptitude had been on full display the entire campaign, so at least I would meet expectations.

"Ohhhkaay," Vera said. She pushed up her baseball hat (hot pink and patterned with flamingos) and turned her attention to me. "District 168 parents, I give you Ally . . . Anderson."

I got a tepid smattering of applause.

"Sometimes things need to change," I began. "People don't always like change—actually, people usually don't. But I think we've all learned as a—um—society that in order to include everyone, to make everyone feel a part of things, we have to change. To move forward into a future where most people can feel they are at least heard, one in which we will work together to try to help everyone get used to a new way, a better way."

The crowd perked up a bit, leaning in to hear more. My confidence didn't exactly soar, but it roused from its slumber.

"I became a candidate for school board because I saw some simple things that could be changed that would make my daughter's life easier. I know now that goal is a little narrow in scope. But the basic desire to seek better ways of doing things is something I can apply to so many areas of our students' lives. We need to stop fearing change. Change is difficult, but accepting it is what keeps us resilient and competitive."

I had them. They were nodding, smiling, mouthing the word *yes*. I needed a big finish.

"Change is the key to a thriving future for District 168," I said, trying to imbue my voice with a James Earl Jones level of authority. "To borrow from David Bowie . . ." I cleared my throat. "Ch-ch-ch-changes," I sang. "District 168 needs to face the strain. Ch-ch-changes . . ."

The nodding stopped. So did the smiling and all manner of positive commentary. Even Kylie looked pained. Matt cringed. Cassie gasped in horror.

Okay, so my voice wasn't all that great. Fine, it sounded like a screeching owl with a raging head cold.

Only Sawyer grinned at me like a lunatic. I'd just made him look better.

"Well," Vera said. "That was . . . interesting. Cassie? How about you take a shot at this?"

Cassie smiled broadly. "I'd love to."

She killed. Slayed. Demolished her weary opponents.

Cassie was on flipping point. She was convincing. She was informative. Charming. She managed to tell a lunch-lady joke without being offensive and without messing it up. She finished with: "I can't promise you your kids will get the best. That's not always in our budget or our grasp. What I can promise is that if you vote for me, your kids will get my very best effort, my dedicated heart, and persistent spirit. There is a creative solution for every problem. Just as there is something special about each and every child in this district. I give you my absolute word I will celebrate that."

The crowd of hard-to-impress District 168 parents actually went wild. They rushed Cassie as though she were a rock star, throwing compliments instead of underwear, and I found myself edged out until my back was literally almost against the door. I spotted Kylie with Matt and Cassie's son. She was warily petting Riker, who seemed somewhat docile in response to her attention. I knew Matt would keep an eye on her.

The whole scene felt like a movie I was watching while I folded laundry. I knew what was going on, but didn't have a firm grasp on the particulars. I couldn't shake the feeling that I didn't belong.

So I ducked out.

~

Outdoors, the night was still and quiet, and unseasonably warm. I sat on a bench facing a playground, the swings and monkey bars ghostly in the moonlight.

"Can I sit with you?"

It was Matt.

I sat up straight, mom-nerves jumping into action. "Where's Kylie?"

"She's with Cassie," Matt said. "And she's fine."

"With Cassie? Are you sure?"

"She's not that bad."

"I didn't mean to imply that she was," I said, though I totally was. "I just thought Cassie would be distracted by all the sycophants."

"They like her," Matt said, and I detected a note of pride in his voice. "She's very organized and dynamic."

"In other words, she'd be better at the job than I would."

"Maybe," Matt admitted, "but that doesn't make her a better person than you. I thought you did a good job too. You're new to this. She isn't. The race isn't exactly fair."

"Maybe this kind of thing just isn't in my genes."

"I don't know about that," he said, "but I do know singing isn't."

I laughed. "It was pretty bad, wasn't it?"

"My ears are still bleeding. You know, when you used to sing in the shower, I'd put a pillow over my head to block the sound."

At the reference to our marriage, we both went quiet.

"Do you miss being married?" I asked, though all the possible answers made the hibiscus flower in my stomach feel like it had tentacles.

"I don't know how to answer that. I miss you, Ally, for sure. I don't miss the fights, though. Being together started to amplify all the negatives—the anger, the worry, the frustration."

"That's true," I said quietly. "I have to admit it."

"And we'd be dishonest if we claimed Kylie's challenges caused all those things. The problems were always there, even when we were sincerely happy with each other. We just thought if we ignored them they'd go away."

"Also true."

"I'll always love you," Matt said.

"But . . ."

He put his arm over my shoulder. "No buts. I'll always love you. It's not the same kind of love as when we were happily married. It's more of an appreciation for that time, for what we once had."

"Does the other stuff—the fighting and anger and tears—does that stuff make you hate me a little?"

"I hate what we became. That bickering, sniping couple that made other people become uncomfortable in their presence."

I took a breath. "So we need to get a divorce, don't we?"

"We do."

"I want to make it easy on you," I said, and meant it, because I still loved him too. I always would. And it would always hurt, missing what we once were and mourning what we never allowed ourselves to become.

"I feel the same way," he said.

"I have a feeling that's easier said than done."

Matt sighed. "I have a feeling you're right. I guess we're just going to have to get the ball rolling and see how this plays out."

"I have an idea to help us keep on track, if you're willing."

"I'm open to anything."

"That exercise you did at Dr. Indigo's today. Why did you take off? Did it bother you?"

"Yes and no," Matt said. "I had to leave because it worked. The feelings were so intense. I had to be alone for a little while."

"What if we did something like that together? Got rid of our bad feelings toward each other. If we do, we'll be less likely to bicker over stuff like who gets the Chicago-skyline paperweight we both like or the framed *Pulp Fiction* poster."

"Do you think we'll be less likely to fight about Kylie?" Matt's voice was solemn.

"I don't know," I said. "But it's worth a try."

"Let's close our eyes, then," he said, taking my hand. "Gather up your bad feelings about us. The bitterness, the anger, the hopelessness. What does it look like?"

I thought for a moment, plucking the bad memories from my brain. "It's blue," I said. "Which sounds cliché, but it's true. Stormy blue, almost gray. It feels gritty, like sandpaper."

"I can see it," Matt said. "It has rings around it, like Saturn, but they're dark."

"It's heavy," I continued. "Really heavy. We have to figure out a way to hold it together. I can't lift it myself."

"Where are we?" Matt said. "I mean we're walking somewhere, right?"

"I think we're on a beach, like you were, only it's nighttime. There's a bonfire."

"We burn it," he said. "Incinerate it."

"Uh-huh. Exactly."

Matt held me close. "We do this together, Ally. One . . . two . . ."

"Three!" I said, and we both lurched forward.

"It's burning to nothing," I said, realizing tears were streaming down my face. "All those bad thoughts, those terrible moments."

"What's left is the good stuff. We fell in love. We put a beautiful girl in the world. We aren't throwing those things onto the fire."

"Those memories will always have a place in my heart, Matt. But it's time for me to move forward from that place."

"It is," he said. "I've been trying to do that."

We sat there, looking up at the stars, a romantic moment in that we were sharing something both of us needed, a little bit of peace. It felt different being next to Matt. He was solid and warm, but I'd lost the sense of oneness I'd always felt when he held me. I'd grieve that at some point, but at that moment, it was a relief. I could live without it. And I'd be okay.

"I'm going to head back inside," Matt said after a bit. "Want to come with?"

"I should go in and make sure that crazy dog hasn't eaten Kylie," I said. "But I need one more minute."

"Cassie needs a safety blanket. Like all of us, I guess. Hers is just . . . alive."

"I knew it! Riker *is* a therapy dog."

"Of sorts." Matt smiled. "When I figured it out, it made me like Cassie more."

"You know, it makes me like her more too. Even if she's going to beat my ass in the election."

Matt squeezed my shoulder. Before leaving, he said, "I can't pretend that the desensitization treatment doesn't still worry me, but I'll agree to resuming it. I reserve the right to stop treatment if Kylie reacts again, okay?"

"I can agree to that. See? We're getting along. Maybe Dr. Indigo does have all the answers."

"She definitely has all the patchouli," he joked, "I'll give her that."

~

"That was fantastically weird," Sawyer said, stepping out from behind a thick hedge. "I would have assumed you guys were on acid if I didn't know you."

"Maybe we are."

He grinned. "Can we get married, just so we can divorce with such grace?"

Sawyer was joking, but I wasn't when I said, "I don't ever want to get divorced again. At least I'm going to try not to. I think it'd be hard to survive it twice. Like with allergies—the first time you're exposed you get a reaction, the second time is when that reaction can turn anaphy-lactic, and you can die."

"Could be," Sawyer said. "But something tells me you wouldn't."

"So, you heard the whole thing? That's . . . kind of creepy. Why didn't you walk away and give us a little privacy?"

He shrugged. "I wanted to, but it was too interesting."

"You should be thankful you're blessed with good looks. You need them."

Sawyer folded his arms over his impressive chest and rocked back and forth on his heels. "This is probably the exact wrong time to do this, but do you want to go out sometime?"

I laughed. It felt . . . light. "So social awkwardness is your Achilles' heel. I like that."

"You do? It hasn't worked out so well for me."

"A lot of things haven't worked out for me," I said. "But . . . what-ever. I'll keep trying."

"I need you to translate. Does that mean yes?"

"It does."

"Is it okay if my daughter might come with?" he asked.

"Yep. As long as it's okay if my daughter comes too."

Sawyer laughed. "Our date might consist of making slime and friendship bracelets."

"I am so in. My favorite things to do."

Sawyer reached out and pulled me up from the bench. "Well, we've already got that in common. It can only get better."

CHAPTER 22

Love must have still been in the air when Heather, Kylie, and I showed up for work at The Not-So-Blushing-Bride shop the following Sunday.

"You have a gift, Heather," Radha said as soon as we walked in the door. "It got delivered ten minutes ago! Look!"

Sitting in the middle of one of the coffee tables was a gorgeous late-fall bouquet, artfully arranged in a square glass container.

Heather approached it as though the plants might reach out and strangle her. "This is weird, right? I mean, it's really weird. Who does this?"

"Classy people," Bernie said from the couch. "Flowers pave the way for love."

"I need to write that down," Micki said. "I can use that. It's catchy."

"Who would know you were here besides us?" Radha asked. "That's what's weird."

"I might have been . . . messaging someone," Heather said, her cheeks glowing with embarrassment. "I sort of told him I was hanging out here today."

I was glad to be in the shop. Micki had set up appointments with three clients for full hair and makeup consultation. Apparently, Christmas weddings were popular for the over-forty set. They valued the celebratory atmosphere and weren't bothered by the thought that everyone's attention might be a little scattered.

"Read the card," I said.

Heather flopped on the couch. "You read it. I just can't."

Enclosed in a heavy cream-colored envelope, the card only said, "It's just dinner. Bring a friend if you want."

"What does that mean?" Kylie said.

"I don't know," Heather said.

I flopped down right next to her. "Yes, you do. Spill."

"I ended up meeting that Melvin guy for coffee. We kind of hit it off. He wants to meet for dinner, you know, take it to the next level."

"You have to!" Radha shrieked. "Seriously, Heather!"

Heather drew her knees to her chest. "I don't know if that's a good idea."

"You don't have to do anything you don't want to," Micki said. "But it's just a meal, right? If you don't like him, you've only given away an hour of your time. Bring one of us with you."

"I'll go," Kylie offered.

I slipped my laptop out of my bag. "Here. We are all going to leave you alone for ten minutes. You decide either way, but don't leave the poor guy hanging."

We each busied ourselves in other corners of the store, but the place wasn't so big that we couldn't at least try to spy on what Heather was doing. She opened the laptop and stared at it for a moment. *Just go*, I thought. *What do you have to lose?*

After about five excruciating minutes, she quickly typed a message and then snapped the laptop shut. I was dying to know, and from the looks on everyone else's faces, they were also struggling to hold on to their need to ask. Heather didn't reveal a thing, and started organizing a hosiery display.

"When can we ask her?" Radha whispered to me. "I, like, *need* to know. Or I'm going to explode."

"I've never been very good at being patient," I told her. "But we have to try. I know Heather. She'll tell us when she's ready."

~

I'd just finished helping my second bride when I spotted Micki slip into her office. I took my moment, following her in. I had lots of things on my shopping list, but only one absolute goal. It was the reason I justified coming back to the shop.

"You're taking this back," I said, handing her a check. "I spent a thousand of it on Dr. Indigo, which I shouldn't have done. I'll work for free on Sundays until I pay you back."

Micki stared at the check as though it were a pit stain on a silk dress. "Nope," she said.

"I'm not spending this," I said. "Where did you get it anyway?"

I watched her face closely as she struggled for an answer. "It doesn't matter."

"Yes, it does. Did this come from sacrifice? I don't want you giving up anything for me."

"It's not for you," she said, growing angrier, "it's for Kylie."

"I love my daughter, and I'd do anything for her, but neither of us wants you to go without because you're paying our bills."

"We're family," Micki said. "That means something to me."

I've got to admit, as complicated as her answer was to me, it still sent a shiver of satisfaction up my spine. But still, I knew for a fact the Patels didn't have this kind of money to spare. "Where did you get it?" I repeated. "I need to know."

Micki sat at her sewing table. She unspooled a length of ribbon and wrapped it around her fingers. "I took out a small business loan."

"You what? Oh, Micki."

She shook her head. "People do it all the time, and for lesser reasons. Sandy and I made the decision together."

My bullshit meter started spinning. "Sandy agreed to give this money to me, a stranger? I have a hard time believing that."

She tugged hard on her hot-pink sweatshirt. "I think I'm getting a hot flash."

"You are not. Tell me the truth."

"Fine. Sandy only agreed to it if I promised to use half of the money to fund our adoption of Radha."

That felt like a swift punch to my midsection. "*All* of your money should be used toward making that happen."

"Two good causes. You can't argue with that."

I needed to argue with it, but I couldn't find the words.

It turned out I'd have a while to come up with something.

~

"Mommy, help!"

Kylie's voice reached me through the closed door. I grabbed my purse with the EpiPen.

"Mommy!"

My heart stalled, but my feet didn't. I could feel Micki at my heels.

But it wasn't Kylie who needed my help, it was Bernie.

She lay on the floor, a tiny, fallen bird. A large man was bent over her, carefully administering CPR. Heather was screaming into the phone, pacing. Radha was curled up into a little ball.

I knelt at Bernie's head. "I can take over if you need," I told the man. "I'm trained."

He nodded, red-faced. "She's so fragile. I'm afraid I'm hurting her."

I quickly took his place, shutting down my emotions as best I could. I tilted Bernie's small head back, gave her what I hoped were breaths her body would accept, and then began my compressions.

"I called 911," Heather yelled, though she was right next to me. "Oh my God."

I kept going, focusing on the task. I could hear Kylie crying, but I didn't let anything register. Breath, breath, compressions. Breath, breath, compressions. I didn't know if it was working. I didn't stop.

I couldn't tell how much time passed before the EMTs took over. I fell back against the coffee table, disoriented and panting. The paramedics were already getting Bernie into the back of the ambulance before it struck me that I should follow.

"Can I come with?" I asked.

I heard someone say, "Are you family?"

"No."

"I am," Micki said, pushing past everyone and climbing in. "I'm her daughter."

The EMT gave her a look but didn't protest.

"Call us!" I shouted. And then the doors slammed, and the sirens blared, and somehow I found my way back inside.

~

"So, what happened?"

Heather made coffee for me and the helpful stranger, and hot cocoa for Kylie and Radha. We sat huddled in the middle of the store, numb with both shock and worry, and tried not to stare at Bernie's abandoned purse and sweater on the floor in front of us.

"She wanted to try on a veil. Radha grabbed it while I was chatting with Melvin here, who just walked in to say hi."

"It's Mel," said the man. He smiled at me, and I saw kindness in his eyes. "I came to see Heather. I manage O'Malley's Pub on the weekends, right next door."

I knew I should say it was nice to meet him, or some kind of pleasantry, but I could only bob my head a little.

"I didn't get the veil she wanted," Radha said miserably. "She was crabbing at me, and I said to hold up, I'd find the right one. When I turned around, I heard a loud noise." Radha started to cry. "Bernie fell over. She was on the carpet, and she wasn't moving."

"Then, Mel said he knew CPR, and I called 911," Heather said. Her hand was shaking so much she put down her mug. "She looked so pale and lifeless. Did it seem like the CPR was working?"

"I'm not sure," Mel said. "I don't even know if I was doing it right. I've only practiced on mannequins. It's a lot harder in real life."

"She's so fragile," I said. "Her tiny bones. I didn't want to hurt her. I hope I didn't break any of her ribs."

"You had her life in your hands," Heather said. "I don't think Bernie's going to mind a broken rib."

I thought about that. I'd had Kylie's life in my hands when I administered the EpiPen that kept her throat from closing up. I'd felt in control then. With Bernie, it felt like trying to grasp sand as it slipped through your fingers—her spirit flittered in and out of this world. Was I supposed to keep pulling it back? Regardless, I had to try. I sent a quick message out into the universe. *Please let her make it. I don't think she's done here.*

We waited. Radha closed up the shop, and Mel had food sent over from the pub, though none of us could eat. I had a few nut-free snacks for Kylie, and she picked at them.

I should take her home, I thought. *She's exhausted, and she has school tomorrow.* Her face was flushed, and red shot through the whites of her eyes. I shifted closer to her and pulled her skinny body onto my lap. "You tired, baby? Do you want to go home?"

Kylie sat upright. "No. No way. We have to wait until we hear Bernie is okay."

A cold thought, a shard of ice piercing my frontal lobe, nearly stole my breath. We all wanted Bernie to be okay, but I knew too well how little that could mean sometimes. "Let's hope," I told Kylie. "That's all we can do."

Sometimes hope is not enough. Three hours later Micki came back, supported by a devastated Sandy. "She's gone," she said as we rushed her. "Oh my God, she's gone."

CHAPTER 23

It felt wrong, being in Bernie's house, going through her meager belongings, trying to pretend we had a right. Micki actually did have every reason to be there—we'd found Bernie's important papers neatly stacked in an old metal file cabinet, and Micki was both sole beneficiary and executor.

"Well, that's pretty convenient," my mom said, not bothering to lower her voice.

"Shut it," I scolded her. "I mean it."

"It's fine," Micki said, though her forehead scrunched like she was trying not to cry.

My mom took the news hard. It had been years since her parents had died, but Bernie's passing resurrected the angriest part of her grief. She'd insisted on coming along, and her mood was protective and suspicious.

Micki, Sandy, Radha, Mom, Kylie, Heather, and I—our strange sort of family moved through Bernie's house, searching for clues about how she lived her life, in the hopes it would tell us how she wanted us to honor her death.

"Bernadette Dunleavy. Was she Catholic?" Mom asked. "She'd want a church ceremony and a burial."

"We don't know," Sandy said. "She was around all the time, but she wasn't very forthcoming about her life."

Kylie and I went through her closet, an irony that wasn't lost on me. Without the wedding dresses, the space was nearly empty. Bernie had been mortified when Micki gently explained what Radha had been doing, and she'd returned the wedding dresses immediately. Though giving them back had been the right thing for her to do, I almost wished she'd died with them in her closet, a strange sort of legacy. "Find a nice outfit for Bernie," I said to Kylie. "One she'd really like."

Timid about going through someone else's things, Kylie hesitated. "Why?"

"Because we need something to bury her in," I said, deciding to be honest. "We need to bring it to the funeral home."

"She liked wedding dresses," Kylie said. "Let's ask Micki if we could have one."

Was that macabre? Inappropriate? I wasn't certain, but I agreed to ask.

Kylie placed a palm on the closet door. "When Grandma's mom died, we made those posters with all the old photos, remember?"

"I sure do." Gathering up the photos of my grandmother had been traumatic, but taping them to the poster board was the first step toward healing—my grandmother had lived a full life, a happy life. It was there for all to see, and as people made their way to pay their final respects, they smiled with satisfaction, remembering Gloria Stefancyk exactly as they should have, a happy, grounded, community pillar of a woman.

"We need to do that for Bernie," Kylie insisted. "So everyone who comes can see who she was."

"That is a fantastic idea, my little warrior." I glanced around. "Finding photos might be a little tricky, but everyone has some, right? Let's look."

We looked. And looked. Bernie could confound a CIA operative—Kylie and I could not find a single shred of evidence that she had a past. After a while, Kylie gave up and dashed off to help my mom, who had insisted on finishing up the projects she'd promised Bernie.

I sat on Bernie's stiff mattress, scanning the room one more time. *Where would I keep my valuables if I was an intensely private ninety-year-old woman?*

I stood up quickly and lifted the mattress. It was the oldest hiding place in the book. But then, Bernie probably was around when the book was written.

Jackpot. There were some assorted papers and manila folders, and a clear sleeve envelope that held a few photographs.

Selfishly, I wanted to sift through them by myself first. The envelope was stiff with age. I reached inside and pulled out a photograph. The colors got me first, the saturated Kodak colors of postwar America, the colors that made everything look cleaner and more vibrant. I recognized Bernie immediately. Her cropped silver hair was a rich chestnut, and she wore a full-skirted dress in peacock blue. With her head thrown back in laughter, she looked exactly as she did during the fashion show, when her dress revealed more than we'd intended.

Another woman, taller and rounder than Bernie, sat next to her. Her cheeks were rosy and cherubic, and her honey-toned hair hung loose to her shoulders. Her laugh was more reserved, but the glee in her eyes told me that she was just as amused. It was a lovely photograph. We could definitely use it.

I turned it over, eager to see if she'd written the year or any other information on the back.

Me and Regina, 1956.

My heart went still.

Regina.

Reggie.

Oh, Bernie, I thought. *Oh, you sweet woman. This was your love.*

There were four more. Bernie and Regina standing in front of Marshall Field's in the '60s, older but still laughing. Bernie and Regina sitting in front of a Christmas tree in some nondescript house, pointing at an older man wearing a Beatles mop top wig. Bernie and Regina sitting in the front row of what looked like an in-store fashion show, in the '50s.

But it was the last one that took my shattered heart and pounded it some more.

Regina, gray-haired and stout, stood next to some guards in front of Buckingham Palace. *Wish You Were Here!* was printed across the bottom.

That was it. Did Bernie ever join her?

I'd never know what really happened, but I could say with certainty that it was a sad story.

Because Bernie had never gotten her wedding.

She never got to wear her perfect dress.

I needed to talk to Micki about giving Bernie her chance.

~

"I'm not taking a damn thing!" My mom slammed her hand on the kitchen counter. "I promised her I'd help out, and I intend to keep that promise."

"It doesn't matter anymore," Micki said flatly. "If you're going to do this work, it's going to be for the new owners. You should get paid."

"Not taking a dime," Mom said. "Final word."

I watched them bicker, amazed at how even the most different people could be similar in certain ways. My mind flashed to Micki refusing to take my check. Mom and Micki shared a stubbornness that would have made me smile if they weren't snarling at each other.

Micki took out her checkbook and started writing, pressing too hard with her pen. "If you could admit we're family, then I wouldn't be writing this, because family takes care of their own. But you've gone

out of your way to stress how much we are not connected! So . . . here!"
She ripped the check from her checkbook and shoved it in Mom's hand.

"We don't share one drop of blood. You might share some random
genetic material with my daughter, but I don't remember ever seeing
you around while *I* was raising her. It looks like you have a perfectly
nice family already. Don't try to take mine." And with one withering
look, my mother crumpled up the check, dropped it on the floor, and
walked out.

~

"You need to give her time. She's grieving," Sandy said, pouring us all
tea. We'd gone back to the Patels' apartment after being at Bernie's had
wrung our hearts dry. I'd texted my mom to check in, but she hadn't
responded.

"Grandma sometimes needs to be alone to cool down," Kylie said,
with a wisdom that almost made me smile. "She's not mean, she just
really believes in her feelings sometimes."

"I shouldn't have done that," Micki said. "I just got so mad."

Radha, perhaps sensing things were about to get deep, nudged
Kylie in the shoulder. "Hey, your mom taught me how to do updos. I
want to practice on you. Want to go to my room?"

Kylie broke into a grin. "Yeah!"

"She's a good kid," Sandy said wistfully.

"They both are," Micki said. "They're so much alike that way."

"My mom is a good person too," I said. "I sprung this all on her.
She didn't deserve that."

"I deserved what she said," Micki said. "I didn't come looking for
you. Ever."

"It wasn't an open adoption," I said. "You weren't supposed to."

"When have I ever followed rules?" she said. "I guess I was ashamed of my sister, and ashamed of myself for not stepping up and taking you."

I put my hand on her arm so she'd know what I said next wasn't a condemnation. "Why didn't you take me?"

Micki frowned. "The man I was living with didn't want to. He was strong and I was weak. I've learned a lot since then, about myself and relationships."

"I like my life," I said, realizing I meant it. "Things worked out the way they were supposed to."

"Even if that's true," Micki said, "I'm still furious with myself."

"We honor the people we love by making good choices," Sandy said. "And it's never too late to make those. Leave Sophie be. She might accept our friendship, or she might not. We need to respect her choice. It's not our place to force anything. You need to make the choice to let her decide how all of this will play out. In doing that you honor Ally as well."

"You make it sound so easy," Micki muttered, but she smiled at her husband.

As we sipped our tea, I brought out the photos of Bernie and Regina, and explained what I'd found.

"I wish she would have told us," Micki said sadly after studying the photographs. "My heart is just breaking for her."

"I have no idea what the full story is, but I doubt they told many people," I said. "This was over fifty years ago. Different times."

"She'll get her wedding dress," Micki said. "I mean, why not? Men get buried in Blackhawks jerseys and Cubs T-shirts. Why can't a ninety-year-old woman get sent to her final rest in a gown?"

"The mermaid dress," I suggested. "The one that showed off her bum."

Sandy laughed. "She would like that."

"No," Micki said solemnly. "The magical one. Remember the day you did her makeup? She couldn't stop gazing at herself in the mirror."

I told them about Kylie's idea of a photo display, and Sandy found a three-fold poster board left over from one of Radha's science projects. We laid it on the floor and placed the photos of Bernie and Regina in a small, artful rectangle.

"Looks a little sparse," Sandy said. "Two full panels are empty."

Micki got up and disappeared into her bedroom. When she returned, she held her family photo albums in her hands. "Bernie was family. So her family is my family. Those old biddies who work at the library will never know the difference."

I loved the idea. We ransacked the albums, pulling photographs and carefully taping them to the panels. I had some photos of the fashion show on my phone, and we found one of Bernie in her mermaid dress, her face beaming in laughter. I also found the one I took of her on the day she had her hair and makeup done, in which she positively glowed, stunning in the dress she would be buried in. Sandy printed everything out, and we placed that last beautiful photo at the top of the display.

It was late by the time we finished. Kylie had fallen asleep on Radha's bed, her updo half-undone.

"Kylie has to go to school tomorrow," I told Micki as I lifted my daughter. "But I'll be at the funeral home early. I took off work."

"I'll bring the lipstick," she said, wiping a tear from under her eye. "She looked so pretty in it."

CHAPTER 24

I thought it would be spooky, sitting in a back room of a funeral parlor, applying makeup to a dead woman's skin, but it was oddly peaceful. Bernie's pixie face didn't need much enhancement in life, and it still retained its beauty in death. I brushed her silver cap of hair and applied the lipstick Radha had chosen for her, what suddenly seemed like a very long time ago. The white satin dress Micki had given her wrapped around her body like an embrace.

"You're beautiful," I whispered to Bernie, and then kissed her forehead. "Reggie would absolutely agree. I hope you're together now, happy and toasting each other at the greatest wedding ever."

"She's a vision," Micki said when she joined me. "Let's sit with her a moment. We've got a little time."

She took my hand. "You know, Bernie didn't have much. There was a reverse mortgage on that house."

"That doesn't surprise me," I said, still saddened by the evidence of the financial instability of Bernie's final years.

"What she did have, she left to me, to use as I see fit," Micki continued. "I'm not going to cash that check you gave me. Use the money. I can pay myself back now and tackle that loan."

"I don't know," I said. "It feels weird to say yes."

"It shouldn't," she continued. "You know, Bernie was heartsick about accidentally giving Kylie that candy. This is absolutely what she would want done with her money. If we could make Kylie better, we are all for the better. Consider it a public service."

"Thank you," I said, and kissed her cheek. "And thank you too," I said to Bernie.

~

The wake was not well attended, but those who showed up had enough goodwill for a roomful of people. The library ladies oohed and aahed over the photo display, commenting on how much Bernie hadn't changed over the years. A few customers from The Not-So-Blushing-Bride came by to pay their respects, all of them shedding a tear. Heather showed up with Melvin.

"I'm just so sorry," he said. "I wish I could have done a better job."

"You did just fine," I said. "You can honestly say you tried your best. I don't know if I believe everyone has a time to go, but she had ninety years on this planet. We have to be grateful for that, right?"

He gave me a hug and moved on to Micki.

Heather clung to me, sniffling. "I'm really going to miss her. I hope she haunts the shop."

"You know she will," I said. "She's probably already totally nosy about what's going on with you and Melvin."

Heather pulled back and grinned sheepishly. "Not much yet. We're taking it slow. But he's really nice, and really, truly bald, and I don't even mind!"

As Heather moved down the row, I noticed my mom walk in, holding Kylie's hand until Kylie broke free, running for Radha, who wore a black sari. Mom stopped at the photo display and studied it.

"Where did you find all of these?" she asked when I approached. "I didn't see anything more personal than a hairbrush in that house."

"I only found four. The rest of these are Micki's personal photos."

Mom moved a little closer to the poster board. "Her family then."

"Yes," I said, swallowing the lump that had suddenly formed in my throat, "and mine, in a way."

She nodded, scrutinizing each photo, a grim look on her face. "Are you up here?"

I pointed to the photo of Micki holding me. Mom looked at it for a very long time.

"That baby there"—my mom's voice had grown hoarse—"that's . . . you before you were mine?"

"It is me. Can you see the look on my face? I'm waiting for something. I was waiting for you."

She stood there, still and immovable as a redwood tree. Some other people got in line, waited a moment, then moved around us when they saw we weren't going anywhere. Tears ran down Mom's cheeks, and she swiped at them.

"I just love you so much," she finally said. "It's in me to fight anything that gets in the way of that love."

"I know, Mom." I hugged her for a moment, fiercely and tightly. "But you don't have to fight that battle because nothing ever will."

Then, with shaking hands, my mom peeled the photo of me from the board, and strode over to Micki.

"This is you," she demanded. "This woman holding my girl?"

"Yes," she said. "That's me. Holding Ally. Loving her. It broke my heart when Cissy gave her away, and it never mended. It's still broken. I'll be grateful for the rest of my life that she ended up with a mother who loves her as much as you do. My sister would feel the same."

Mom studied the photo one more time. She looked from it to Micki. "I can see Ally in you. She was a pistol when she was little, so full of energy. When she gave hugs, she held me like a vice with her chubby little arms. She had so much love to give. Still does."

"We'll take the extra love," Micki said quickly. "When there's too much."

Mom's smile had some warmth in it. "Micki Patel, I would like to get to know you and your husband and daughter, if that's still all right. Maybe we can have dinner occasionally or—"

"Oh, Sophie!" Micki said, throwing her arms around her. "It's more than all right! It's the way things should be."

When we got home that night, Mom and I tucked Kylie in. She had a headache, so I put a cool washcloth on her forehead and held her until she fell asleep. When I grabbed my laptop and headed for the reading bench, I noticed Mom sitting in the kitchen, sipping coffee, even though it would probably keep her up.

"I didn't know Bernie for all that long, but sometimes that doesn't matter," she said. "You know when someone is good people. I think Micki is good people too. I knew it, but I needed to sort things out in my head. You have to give people time to do that, Ally, okay? Life is not always on your timetable."

She was right, and I told her so. I just didn't know if, at this point, it could change my need for instant gratification.

"Don't give me that look, honey. You take action, and sometimes that's good. But you've got to let other people catch up, or even stand back if they want to."

I kissed my mom on her cheek, and she reached up and grabbed my shoulder. My mom's hugs were awkward, but they were hers, and they meant something. "You're pretty smart," I said. "I'll give you that."

After she turned in, I opened my laptop, eager to search the forums for parents whose kids had any kind of reaction while in the middle of desensitization treatment. I came up with very little, so I decided to check Facebook. The first post in my feed was from the District 168 parents group:

> Vera Pastorelli: Polls close in an hour! Get your vote in! Who will it be? Cassie Flores? Sawyer McMurphy? Ally Anderson?

Shit! With my mind so focused on Bernie, I'd forgotten the school board election was today. The post was from three hours ago. Not only hadn't I voted for myself, I hadn't voted at all.

> Bree Nguyen: Go, Cassie, go!!! Get out there, people, and vote for the best candidate—Cassie!! If you can have the best, you can forget the rest!

> Jane Sturgeon: Are we even allowed to do that, moderator? Campaigning in this thread seems a little unfair. This is an informational thread, is it not?

> Sawyer McMurphy: I'd just like to say that, informationally, it's an honor my name is on the ballot.

> Cole Flounders: There are paper ballots, correct? Should we be concerned about hacking?

> Vera Pastorelli: Rest easy, Cole. Rest easy.

I went directly to the District 168 page and refreshed.

> Vera Pastorelli: We have a winner! Cassie Flores is the newest school board member for District 168. Congratulations, Cassie. There will be a potluck reception tomorrow in the school gym

at 6:30 p.m. Please note what you will bring in this thread.

Cole Flounders: Vegan mock beef stew.

Shannon Washington: Brownies. And not the fun kind. Sorry!

Elliot Grossman: I don't cook, so I'll bring plates and napkins. They're biodegradable.

Jane Sturgeon: Why does every event have to center around eating and drinking? If you stop and think about it for a moment, this is almost a group psychosis.

Bree Nguyen: I'll bring red, white, and blue cupcakes displayed like an American flag. If I would have thought of it, I would have ordered cookie cutters in the shape of Cassie's face. I saw them on Pinterest, and it occurred to me to buy them because—let's face it, we all knew Cassie was our gal—but I forgot. So stupid, right?

Vera Pastorelli: Cupcakes are fine, Bree.

Sawyer McMurphy: Not gonna lie—I'm bummed. But kudos to you, Cassie. In your honor, I'll bring some homemade hard wheat crackers and a nice aged cheddar.

Bree Nguyen: Is that some kind of a dig, Sawyer? Because if it is, I think it's immature and ungracious.

Sawyer McMurphy: You don't like aged cheddar cheese?

Bree Nguyen: Unbelievable.

Cassie Flores: I humbly accept this position of responsibility! My heartfelt thanks for everyone who voted for me. I look forward to celebrating the bright future of District 168 tomorrow evening. I will bring the sparkling grape juice!

Paul Matthewson: If you're bringing nonalcoholic juice, I vote Shannon makes the fun kind of brownies.

Cole Flounders: Drug jokes are never funny, Paul. Ever. Moderator?

I had to respond. My disappointment didn't belong in this thread—that was for me to grapple with. Cassie won fairly.

Ally Anderson: Congrads, Casie.

Oh, for the love of—

Ally Anderson: I meant, "Congrats, Cassie." And I'll bring a treat for Riker.

CHAPTER 25

"I voted for Riker," Sawyer said.

We sat together on folding chairs, balancing plates of food on our laps and sipping the mouth-numbingly sweet sparkling grape juice. Cassie had brought a case.

"I didn't vote for anyone," I said. I tried to come across as flippant, but I still felt bad about flaking out on my civic duty. Deep down, I thought there might be a chance I'd cause an upset and win the election. I still felt I had something to offer, even if I wasn't the best and the brightest. I had energy and passion for my cause, and that meant something.

"I thought we could go to Paint a Pot for our first date," Sawyer said through a mouthful of cheese. "The girls would probably like that."

"Perfect," I said. Actually, it sounded really nice, and he was right—Kylie would love it.

"Speech!" Bree yelled. "Speech!"

Vera Pastorelli stood up. She wore a teal baseball hat bedazzled with *Dist. 168* on the brim. "Everyone, I'd like to introduce the newest member of our esteemed school board, Cassie Flores!"

Cassie, wearing a bright-red suit, shook hands with the current board members, all seated in the front row. Matt hovered nearby with

Riker, one hand firmly on his leash. He looked on proudly as Cassie moved through the crowd.

Was he falling in love with her? Strangely, the thought didn't send my insides roiling. Instead, I sent a wish into the universe that if he chose Cassie, they'd be happy together, for their sake and for Kylie's.

"Thank you," Cassie said when the applause quieted down. "I feel it's important for me to reiterate that I am a servant to the community. My goal is to improve the lives for all of the district's children. If anyone has suggestions or ideas, I'm always open to them. My email address is on the district website."

I could hear the sincerity in her voice. Cassie meant what she said. Everything else aside, she'd clearly expressed her desire to serve the families of our district. Sawyer and I had the same instincts, but they were muddled by a lack of preparation. I might not like Cassie, but I was inspired by her—she took action (like me), but she also thought through the implications of her actions (not so much like me, but it could be).

I thought for a moment. Really thought. Then, I quickly wrote a mental shopping list. *Remember, you have something valuable to offer! Think this through!*

I passed my plate to Sawyer and stood up. "I'd like to make a suggestion."

"Seriously?" Bree said. "Already?"

Cassie turned her laser-like focus to me. "Yes?"

"I wanted to be a member of the school board because I wanted to make some positive changes for kids with allergies," I said, feeling my palms begin to sweat. "Your goal was to make improvements for all kids, which tells me you're the right person to be standing there, not me. However, I'd like to submit my application for the role of allergy liaison. We need someone who understands the unique needs of kids whose allergies put them at varying levels of risk. I've given a lot of thought about how we can mitigate that risk. Will you give me a chance?"

Cole Flounders stood up. "There is no position of allergy liaison. How can you apply for something that doesn't exist?"

Cassie ignored him. "Would you call yourself an expert?"

"I'd call myself an obsessed mother of a kid who suffers from anaphylaxis. So . . . same difference. When you're that worried, you become an expert."

Vera took over. "Cassie, as an official board member, you can call an emergency meeting. We could vote on this issue tonight."

The other board members glanced nervously at each other. They were probably worried they wouldn't make it home to watch Jimmy Kimmel.

"Then I call an emergency meeting," Cassie said. "Let's vote on establishing this new position."

The board members filed out, one by one. We all helped ourselves to second helpings. I was stuffing my face with some fine aged cheddar when Matt approached, Riker eyeing my plate.

"Did you just think of that right now," Matt said, "or did you plan that before you came?"

"I had some vague stirrings before I walked in the door, but sitting there . . . I thought it through. I did. I know it sounds kind of crazy, but I don't think it is."

Matt said, "I don't think it is either."

"Thanks."

"By the way, I'm starting to gain more confidence about resuming Kylie's treatment," he continued. "I've done my own research, and though I'm not entirely convinced, I think her chances might be good. I'd like to be there for the next few trips to Dr. Indigo's. It'll help me feel like I have some kind of control over the situation."

"You won't run out of the office this time?"

He smiled. "I won't."

Riker nuzzled his head against my leg. "Well, look at that," I said. "I calmed the dog."

The board members filed back in after about fifteen minutes, settling back in their seats. Cassie remained standing.

"In my first vote as a member of the school board," she began, drawing it out a little to increase the anticipation, "I voted to establish the position of allergy liaison. This person will inform the school board of concerns related to safety and quality of life issues related to allergy sufferers."

"Will it be an elected position?" Cole asked.

Cassie shook her head. "It's appointed. We've decided Ms. Anderson is perfect for the job."

"Who's Ms. Anderson?" I heard someone say.

"I am," I said.

"Don't sit down right away," Sawyer said. "Just revel in being awesome for a moment."

I did allow myself to feel awesome. The feeling was both foreign and oddly familiar, and it was coming from deep inside. It was part of *me*.

And I didn't need a DNA test to tell me that.

Which type of person are you?

Personality Test results for ALLY!

ALLY, you are 68% FEARLESS WARRIOR!

Things might not always go your way, but you take on every challenge with courage and ingenuity. You don't just live on the edge, you thrive on it! You are a FEARLESS WARRIOR, Personality Type 1. Remember to use your powers for good—take action when your heart demands it, but keep in mind that your brain is your most effective weapon! For more information on how to make the most of your personality type, ALLY, click on the link below.

CHAPTER 26

One Year Later

I kicked at the door to Dr. Indigo's. The patchouli scent was comforting today, enveloping us in the familiar. And we needed familiar, because the territory we were entering was anything but. It was a new life.

Dr. Indigo appeared, a vision in a gold sari, made to her measurements by Aunt Micki. "Welcome," she said, sweeping her arms in a dramatic fashion. "Please file into my office and form a circle. Kylie, please stand in the center."

We filed in—Kylie, Matt, Mom, Aunt Micki, Uncle Sandeep, Radha, Heather. My family. Cassie, Sawyer, and Melvin rounded out the group.

The office glowed with lit candles.

"Today is a very special day," Dr. Indigo intoned. "One we've been waiting for. Are you ready to calm the dog, Kylie?"

Kylie nodded. She stood bravely, back straight, taking deep breaths. She wore her own sari, white with a rainbow-striped sash. "I can do it," she said. "I can calm the dog."

Dr. Indigo took a small blue box from her desk. Inside, nestled in a velvet lining, was a single peanut. With great fanfare she held out the box and stood in front of Kylie, who had her palm outstretched. "Everyone standing in this room loves you, no matter what happens today. There is no failure, only more steps to take if this doesn't work." Dr. Indigo considered everyone in the circle. "Taking turns, I want everyone to say something supportive to Kylie. It will send the positive vibrational energy through the roof. Let's start with you"—she pointed at Radha—"and work our way around."

Radha fidgeted, tugging at her hair. "Um, Kylie, you've totally got this. And I know it 'cause I *know* you."

"Peanuts don't even grow on trees," Sawyer said. "They hide in the ground. You don't hide at all, so you're better than them."

"You can do it, sweetheart," Melvin contributed.

"I have full faith in the process," Cassie said. "And you've completed every step. I'm extremely proud of you."

"No doubt," Heather said. "You are all over it, Miss Kylie."

"I love you, sweetie," Aunt Micki said. "You show that crazy nut who's boss."

"We are all right here, only for you," Sandy said.

"You're my girl," my mom said. "I know you can do this. Perseverance is in your genes."

"I've never known anyone stronger," Matt said. "I love you, Kylie."

Everyone looked at me.

I swallowed, unsure if I could do this. How in the world could I fit a lifetime of love into a few words?

"You're my hero," I said, "before you even begin chewing. I look at you right now, ready to take this risk, and you've already won, baby. You're the bravest person I've ever met. I love you for a million reasons, but right now because you are taking this on with a smile on your face."

"Thanks, everyone," Kylie said. She reached into the box, pinched the peanut between her index finger and thumb, tossed it up in the air . . .

. . . and caught it in her mouth.

ACKNOWLEDGMENTS

Autoimmune disorders are frustrating, sneaky, tricky, difficult to diagnose, and unfortunately, more and more common. I wrote this book because I saw suffering all around me—family, friends, coworkers—it seems everyone has been touched in some way by autoimmune troubles. I felt helpless in the face of all that suffering. I'm no doctor, but I am a writer, so I wrote this story in the hopes that it might spark some understanding and compassion from those who are not physically affected, and some validation and hope for those who are. Again, I'm not a medical professional, and this is fiction—it's not meant to promote an agenda. Dr. Indigo's methods are not the norm. My intent was simply to point out that kindness and positivity should not be absent from the medical arena—on the contrary. In facing illnesses that are difficult to treat, we need to remember that there is a person attached to each symptom, a person deserving of dignity, respect, and understanding.

I spoke with many people while conducting research for this book, but I'd like to point out two in particular who were exceedingly gracious with their time. Both are moms of kids who have experienced desensitization therapy—Joyce Georgi and Julie Tippett Simon. I can't thank you both enough for your honesty and openness. I wish I could name all the other folks who helped, particularly those who reached out to me on Facebook, but I'd need pages and pages. Please know that I am grateful to all.

I'd also like to give a special shout-out to Lynn Prindes and her daughter Emily, who never fail to put a smile on my face.

I'm incredibly thankful for my editor, Jodi Warshaw, who is open to all my crazy ideas, but also knows how to rein me in. She's smart, gracious, and kind. This book also greatly benefitted from the sharp eye and lively mind of Jenna Free, developmental editor extraordinaire. The team at Lake Union continues to impress me with their commitment to giving writers the best possible shot at success. I feel very lucky that LU has my back. Thanks also to my agent and cheerleader, Patricia Nelson of Marsal Lyon.

Special thanks and love to my family, particularly my two sweet boys, Dan and Jack, and my lovely stepdaughters, Hannah and Sophia.

My husband, Gus Richter, is my touchstone for unconditional love, patience, acceptance, and commitment. Without his steadying presence I would not be able to do what I do. I'm forever grateful.

BOOK CLUB QUESTIONS

1. Ally waited thirty-eight years to seek out the truth about her birth family. Why is this? Do you think she's being honest about her reasons, or does her avoidance stem from deeper issues?

2. Dr. Indigo offers alternative therapies to Kylie. What are some of the benefits of her unusual methods? What are some of the negatives? Would you submit to Dr. Indigo's exercises? Would you continue to take your child to see her?

3. Why does the thought of Ally seeking information about her biological family make Sophie uncomfortable? Can you sympathize with her thought process?

4. What does Bernie need from Micki and Radha at The Not-So-Blushing-Bride? Why does she keep returning to the store? How does the discovery of Reggie's identity change your perception of Bernie's experience?

5. How do Ally's insecurities get in her way? How does she overcome them? Does her perception of herself match your understanding of her character?

6. What is the root of Ally and Matt's dysfunction as a couple? Do you understand Matt's need to date? Do you understand Ally's difficulty accepting his choice?

7. How does the information Micki gives Ally about her birth mother affect Ally's perception of herself? Of other people, particularly Sophie and Kylie?

8. How would the characters in the book define "family" at the start of the story? At the end?

ABOUT THE AUTHOR

Loretta Nyhan is the bestselling author of *Digging In*, *All the Good Parts*, and the teen paranormal thrillers *The Witch Collector Part I* and *The Witch Collector Part II*. With Suzanne Hayes, she coauthored the historical novels *Empire Girls* and *Home Front Girls*. Loretta was a reader before she was a writer, devouring everything she could get her hands on, including the backs of cereal boxes and the instruction booklet for building the Barbie Dreamhouse. Later, her obsession with reading evolved into an absolute need to write. After college, she wrote for national trade magazines, taught writing to college freshmen, and eventually found the guts to try fiction. When she's not writing, Nyhan is knitting, baking, and doing all kinds of things her high school self would have found hilarious. Find her online at www.lorettanyhan.com.